TOMORROW
and ALWAYS

OTHER BOOKS BY RACHEL ANN NUNES

Ariana: The Making of a Queen

Ariana: A Gift Most Precious

Ariana: A New Beginning

Ariana: A Glimpse of Eternity

Love to the Highest Bidder

Framed for Love

Love on the Run

To Love and to Promise

TOMORROW
and ALWAYS

a novel

RACHEL ANN NUNES

Covenant Communications, Inc.

Digital Imagery © copyright 2000 PhotoDisc, Inc

Cover and book design © 2000 by Covenant Communications, Inc.

Published by Covenant Communications, Inc.
American Fork, Utah

Printed in the United States of America
First Printing: September 2000

07 06 05 04 03 02 01 00   10 9 8 7 6 5 4 3 2 1

ISBN 1-57734-718-8

Library of Congress Cataloging-in-Publication Data

Nunes, Rachel Ann, 1966-
   Tomorrow and always / Rachel Ann Nunes.
      p.   cm.
   ISBN 1-57734-718-8
   1. Married women--Fiction 2. Childlessness--Fiction. 3. Mormon women--Fiction 4.
Abortion--Fiction. 5. Alaska--Fiction. I. Title.

PS3564.U468 T65 2000
813'.54--dc21   00-043049

To my sister Rebecca
for her invaluable help with this novel, particularly the medical scenarios
in the latter half of the book. Her real-life courage and endurance in the
face of her daughter's illness gave our family an example we will never
forget.

And to my niece Stephanie, who is an inspiration to us all.

ACKNOWLEDGMENTS

A special thank-you to Stacy Keith for her memories of Kodiak Island. As she shared her experiences and her pictures of Kodiak, I saw the island through her eyes—and fell in love with this unique slice of Alaska. Thank you, Stacy, for answering my endless questions and for sharing your memories so vividly and with such enthusiasm that I could see it for myself as though I were there.

Thanks also to the editors and readers at Covenant who gave valuable insights that helped me add the final polish. You're great!

CHAPTER 1

Karissa Mathees sat at her desk, staring at the computer screen. Her eyes were sore and begged for relief, but she had work to finish. Despite the tiredness, a part of her relished the fact that she felt needed and vital—for the first time in a very long time.

Her right hand reached for the mouse as she forced her eyes to focus. It had never been this difficult to concentrate. In the old days in Los Angeles, she had always reveled in the challenge of meeting deadlines and doing her work well. But that had been before moving to this small, confining Alaskan island. And certainly before Jesse and Brionney Hergarter had arrived on Kodiak with their three beautiful little girls. Since then, the last vestiges of Karissa's contentment had vanished, replaced by the secret ache she had hidden for so long.

With her left hand, she pushed back her dark hair that curled in gentle, shiny waves, reaching nearly to her waist. Cut to one length, it often fell to block her vision. She was tall for a woman, and slender, with long, cultured-looking hands and trimmed fingernails. She wore faded jeans, and the shirt was an old one from her husband's drawer— her weekend working clothes. Her narrow feet were clad only in socks, her hiking boots flung carelessly under the huge oak desk.

She tried to concentrate on the screen, but it seemed to reflect back not the new accounts-receivable program Jesse Hergarter had written, but the tiny cherubic faces of his daughters. It was difficult— no, painful was perhaps a better word—seeing Brionney and Jesse with their children. And now Brionney was expecting again. She became pregnant so easily. How could it be so difficult for Karissa?

Her mind refused to stay focused. She glanced above the computer at a framed picture of the Savior with a dark-haired little girl. The picture had been a gift, and the giver had gone through such an effort to visit her at work and to hang it there that she hadn't the heart to object, though the picture almost always gave her a pang of sadness and resentment. She often took it down and stored it in one of the desk drawers, hanging it again hurriedly when the secretary warned her of a visit from the donor. She had been tempted to throw it away. But even an inactive Mormon couldn't just throw away a picture of the Savior.

And the little girl, with her dark eyelashes and bright eyes . . .

No, better not to think in that direction.

A wall clock fashioned out of a slice of tree trunk polished and lacquered to a brilliant shine hung next to the picture. Malcolm had made it for her when they had married nine years before. It was his hobby, something he did so little of these days. Now he was as absorbed by his work as she had once been with hers.

Why did I ever agree to come to Kodiak? she thought. Sometimes she wanted to scream at how enclosed she felt, how isolated. Most people dreamed of living on a remote island; she dreamed of leaving one.

Last year, Malcolm had insisted they move here, back to the place where he had been born. "Our children will have room to roam, Karissa," he had said. He had always wanted a big family, and the words gave her renewed hope. "The property my grandfather left me is way out in the middle of nowhere," he had added, as if that were all-important. "We'll build our dream house, anything you want. It'll be a great place for filming my commercials. And you'll love the pace there. We'll have time to be together."

What he hadn't said aloud was that their marriage was failing and that moving to Kodiak was a last-ditch effort to stem the leak that slowly drained their love.

His commercials mean more to him than I do, she thought. Sadly, she wasn't sure if she even cared.

The gold-colored hand on the clock read six A.M. It was Saturday morning. The night hours had fled and she still wasn't finished. She turned her head back to the screen, but her eyes wandered to the silver-framed picture of her husband next to the monitor. His younger self stared back at her: laughing gray eyes, straight dark hair, and chiseled features. He was good-looking, and even as she stared, a rush of emotion grew in her breast. She did love Malcolm. But did that feeling belong only to the days before, the days when they had been younger and had hope for the future? To the days when she could still give him a child?

Tears squeezed out the corners of her eyes as she shut them against the pain that seemed to encompass her entire body. Why hadn't she been given a child? Of course she already knew the answer. Guilt ate at her, but her terrible secret had been kept so long that she was unable to give voice to it. Not even to Malcolm. She knew she was being punished, and more importantly, that she deserved every bit of agony the sentence gave her.

The doctors had assured her they could find no reason for the infertility, except for a slightly lower sperm count on Malcolm's part. "Just relax and forget about it," they had told her years ago. "It'll probably happen when you least expect it."

She had immersed herself in her career as assistant administrator of a medium-sized hospital outside of L.A. and had pushed thoughts of a family aside. She and Malcolm had drifted further apart each day.

"Come on, you work too hard." The words Malcolm had said more than a year earlier sounded in her ears, almost as if he were in front of her saying them again. "Let's move to Kodiak. I've seen their ad for a hospital administrator there, and you'd be perfect for the job. That's what gave me the idea, in fact. You'd be your own boss. And since they only have one big hospital on the island, plus a few clinics, it's a pretty important job, too."

The idea had excited her. She knew she could make a hospital run very well under her own authority. And she had done even better than she had hoped. In the face of her new responsibilities, she had succeeded in forgetting her deepest longing. She had even stopped wanting a baby—almost. The only problem was that Kodiak wasn't L.A., and life, even as top administrator of the Providence Kodiak Island Medical Center, wasn't very exciting. There were no surprises, nothing to challenge or excite her soul, and she soon became dissatisfied.

Her problems intensified when Jesse Hergarter, an old acquaintance of Malcolm's, contracted with the hospital to upgrade their computers and programs. Last month, his small programming team, his wife Brionney, and their three little girls had arrived on Kodiak. Since Malcolm had been the missionary who had first taught Jesse the gospel twelve years ago in Arizona, Karissa had been forced to spend time with the family. Malcolm had even invited the Hergarters to stay with them for two days while they searched for a place to rent. For once, their house had come alive with the laughter of children. But the laughter made Karissa realize how empty her life really was, and how she and Malcolm seemed like strangers.

At least she had comfort in knowing the Hergarters wouldn't be on Kodiak forever. Jesse would finish the work at the hospital in a few months, and then take care of the other contracts he'd picked up in Anchorage. With any luck, they would be gone from Alaska by the end of the year. Until then, she could simply stay away from them and their rented house near the hospital.

"You almost done, Kar?"

Karissa looked up to see Damon Wolfe standing in the open door. She forced a smile. He was on the board of directors, and had flown in only yesterday from Anchorage to see how her new hospital programs were coming along. On Monday, the rest of the hospital board would be here to examine the progress they had made.

Damon looked as beat as she felt. His blonde hair was nearly white under the stark fluorescent lighting, and his dark amber eyes were bloodshot. His face was haggard, and the ends of his short moustache twisted slightly as they always did when any serious changes were made at the hospital. Twisting them helped him think, he'd say. The sharp curves of his face reminded her of a falcon—slightly hooked nose, angular cheeks and jaw, yellow-brown eyes, thick feathery eyebrows. He was tall and strong looking, and had the magnetism of a man who knew his direction in life. In that respect alone, he reminded her of Malcolm.

"Almost. I've about an hour left," she said.

"Why don't you knock off then? You need a break—and, by the looks of you, some sleep. You can finish Monday morning."

Karissa's smile became real. It said something that Damon, who was part owner of the hospital and essentially her boss, trusted her to finish the work before the Monday afternoon appointment with the board. "Thanks. I think I will." She certainly wasn't accomplishing anything by thinking about the Hergarters.

Damon nodded, then tossed her something from his shirt pocket. Karissa caught it in mid-air. A pack of Camels.

"Thanks," she said wryly, looking at the full ashtray on the desk. "I'm out."

"I figured you would be. I wanted you to have something to keep you awake on your drive home."

Karissa laughed. "I didn't know you cared."

"Of course I do. With all the money I'm paying you, I can't afford to have you laid up in an accident."

Karissa laughed again, and with a few deft strokes shut down the computer. She slipped on her boots, not bothering with the laces, and snatched her bag from the bottom drawer of the desk. Shrugging on her fur-lined leather jacket, she crossed to the door and reached for the light switch, plunging the room into darkness.

"Maybe I'll come in tomorrow," she murmured, "just to be sure." There wasn't much else she would be doing on a Sunday.

"You can't," Damon said. "You have some homecoming or something, don't you? You mentioned it weeks ago."

Karissa had been opening the pack of Camels when he spoke. A wave of guilt fell over her, and she thrust the cigarettes, still unopened, into her purse. "That's right. I'd almost forgotten." Malcolm's brother had invited them to his son's missionary homecoming, with the traditional family party afterwards. "We usually get out of these things, but this time Malcolm ran out of excuses."

"Don't you like your family? I thought you Mormons were a close bunch."

"We're not supposed to smoke, either," Karissa retorted, her voice taking on a sharp edge.

Damon grimaced. "Sorry. None of my business, I guess."

She sighed. "No, I'm sorry, Damon. I'm just tired."

"Let's get you home." Damon took her arm and propelled her down the wallpapered hallway. Her feet dragged over the smooth tile, feeling heavy, and her eyes burned. It took much longer than she remembered to arrive at the employee entrance.

"I'm not going to be here tomorrow anyway," Damon said. "I'm flying home today to be with the kids. But I'll be back Monday morning, bright and early." The "kids" were Damon's two children, a fourteen-year-old son and a four-year-old daughter. His wife had died the previous year after a long bout with cancer, and though he had a live-in housekeeper and nanny, he didn't like to leave his children for long stretches.

Damon walked with her to her new four-wheel-drive Nissan truck. It gleamed a dark, shiny green against the melting snow in the parking lot. The early morning April air was brisk and fresh, and Karissa zipped up her jacket and rummaged in her purse for her matching brown leather gloves.

"Ciao," Damon said, shutting her door. "See ya Monday. Don't be late." He smiled, knowing that she, more likely than not, would be there long before he arrived.

"Ciao," she repeated. She turned the key, and the engine flared to life. Automatically, she checked the gasoline guage. Since the station closest to her house was a forty-minute drive, it didn't pay to run out of gas.

The sun had just begun to lighten the sky above the ocean, turning it to a pale shimmer of orange and gold. The small city of Kodiak, Alaska, was mostly still sleeping, except for the fishing boats that already dotted the water. She drove through the town, her thoughts wandering.

When she had first moved to Kodiak Island with Malcolm, she had hated the idea of Alaska's cold and barren landscape. But he had been born here, and most of his family lived in Anchorage. He wouldn't give up his dream.

"Alaska means The Great Land," he had said. "And Kodiak is the best part of Alaska."

"What kind of a name is Kodiak?" she asked. "It sounds like film."

"It's a native name. Aleut. They live on the island too. I promise you, once there you'll never want to leave."

Karissa hadn't been sure, but excitement about her new position as administrator at the hospital diminished the unease in her heart.

Kodiak had been a surprise. Due to the Japan Current, its weather was surprisingly mild. The island still became cold in the winter and the snow was very wet, but it wasn't any worse than northern Washington, where her grandparents lived. The snow-capped mountains had a certain austere beauty. In the summer, everything was green, almost to the tips of the mountains. Last fall, Malcolm had taken her to Pillar Mountain to pick lingan berries, small cranberry-like berries that mixed tart and sweet as only nature could. Though everyone on the island called them cranberries, they were so much better than the cranberries she was used to. Her mouth watered as she remembered.

It had all been so strange to her—the boat harbor and canneries on one side of town next to the ocean; the city of Kodiak, with its quaint, nearly all-wood structures nestled against Pillar Mountain; the many breathtaking bays and unique small villages; the ocean going on forever until it curved out of sight over the horizon.

And she hated all of it. Every single bit.

The quiet, fertile beauty emphasized the barrenness of her womb. It was much easier to forget her dark secret in the bustling city life. In L.A., she had always been too caught up in her work; here she had time to think—and to mourn.

The medical center was situated in the Northern outskirts of Kodiak. She lived forty-five minutes away to the south, which meant she had to drive through the small city to reach what she laughingly called their "estate." The land had been given to Malcolm by his grandfather, who was Aleut. Malcolm and his six older siblings each inherited land on Kodiak when the old man died, yet only Malcolm had built on it; the others lived in Anchorage on the mainland.

Their house had gone up quickly, despite the island's remoteness, and for a brief time she and Malcolm had been close like in the old days, when they had first met at the University. Back then they had been so much in love.

Karissa turned the wheel slightly as she hugged the curve of the road. They had been so young in college, and there had still been hope for the forgiveness she craved. Now it was too late, and there was no one to blame but herself.

"Pay attention!" she said aloud, struggling to keep her eyes open as the truck passed the airport and the Coast Guard base.

Thirty minutes outside of Kodiak, she pushed harder on the gas to climb the small hill at Dell Flats where several houses studded the landscape. Here the paved road became dirt. Almost home. Just ten minutes more.

Her neck ached and her body felt sluggish as she drew up to the two-story house they had designed with an architect in the first year of their marriage, long before coming to Kodiak. The gray-painted wood house with the wide double-pane windows nestled among lofty spruce and cottonwood trees. A vast greenhouse stood off the back of the house. The kitchen and family room on the main floor had huge windows facing inside to the greenhouse. On the second floor, Karissa's office had a wall of glass that also faced the greenhouse and its year-round greenery. Originally, she had meant the greenhouse for a play-room, a place where her children could build in the sand and romp among the plants when snow covered the ground outside, or when the rain drizzled for weeks, as it so often did on Kodiak. But now she doubted that her child's laughter would ever echo in the stillness.

Karissa parked in the garage next to Malcolm's black Jeep. She dragged one foot after the other until she climbed the steps from the garage to the kitchen. She inserted her key, but the door was already open. Malcolm almost always forgot to lock up after arriving home. At least the unlocked door meant he had finished his shoot early and had come home.

The kitchen was eerily silent, and though her stomach grumbled, her tired eyes could hardly focus on the rows of white-varnished oak cupboards. She clumsily removed her wet boots near the door. A painting of Jesus caught her eye, one with Him sitting on a rock teaching the people—another gift she felt compelled to keep on her wall. His face seemed to follow her movements. Purposely averting her gaze, she skirted around the eating bar in the middle of the room and headed for the hall that led to their master bedroom.

Malcolm was asleep. In the light of the thin rays peeking through the blinds, she could see his lithe body flung out in abandon over the bed. He didn't wake as she moved quietly to her side of the bed and slumped onto it, sighing and at last shutting her eyes.

Exhaustion plagued her, but though she had slept less than four hours in the last forty-eight, her body would not surrender to sleep.

The approaching missionary homecoming reminded her of her own family, most of whom were still in California. She was the fourth of six sisters and two brothers. Months had passed since she had talked to any of her family, and a part of her missed them. She opened her eyes and stared at the dark ceiling. Oh, to be young again and able to make new choices! The right choices.

When she did talk with her siblings or parents, it was hard to abide their preaching, especially the stern disapproval of her father. Of all her parents' eight children, she alone had married out of the temple. She was also the only one in her family who had left the Church completely, and now she felt separated from those she loved by an impassable gulf.

At first she had planned to seal her marriage in the temple, but by the time her education was finished, she was thoroughly addicted to smoking and couldn't give it up. At least that was what she told herself. But inside, she knew the real reason she could never marry in the temple, why she wouldn't go to heaven, and why she couldn't have children.

Karissa squeezed her eyes shut. They still burned, but gradually were soothed by the tears that escaped her tight control. Her thoughts continued wildly, with no hope of suspension until they reached their loathsome end.

God would never allow her to have a child after what she had done. Karissa had committed a murder of the most despicable kind, and for that there was no forgiveness or salvation.

"Karissa?" Malcolm whispered. He sat up, clumsy with sleep, squinting his eyes at the increasing light. His stiff, dark hair was slightly gray-peppered at the temples. The effect usually gave him a distinguished look, but now his hair stood on end as if he had run his hands through it repeatedly, giving him the appearance of a small child rather than that of a grown thirty-three-year-old man.

"Uh-huh," she grunted.

"What time is it?" He squinted at the clock. "Almost seven? Did you work all night?"

"Mm-hum."

"That's not good for your health."

She opened her eyes. "You're a fine one to talk."

He snorted. "Well, yeah, I guess. So did you get the accounts done?"

"Not yet. I'm going to finish Monday morning."

"That's cutting it short."

"I'll manage." She wished he would talk to her about something other than work; that was all they ever talked about anymore. She didn't know how much longer they could go on living as strangers and clinging to the dream of real togetherness. Then he spoke again, and she immediately regretted her wish.

"You do remember the doctor's appointment Monday, don't you?"

How could she have forgotten? It was only the single most important thing on her mind. The only excuse was her gross lack of sleep, but she couldn't credit it to that. No, the truth was she had *wanted* to forget. The new fertility specialist was coming in from Anchorage specifically to visit them, but surely he could only tell them what the others before him had already determined: there was no physical reason why they shouldn't be able to have children. Yet only she would know the real reason.

"Sure, I remember," she lied. "I'll go in to work early, or back today after I sleep a little. That way I'll be free."

"Maybe this guy'll know what he's talking about." Malcolm's mouth curved in a hopeful smile. "We've let this ride for long enough, don't you think?"

Karissa nodded numbly. How could she tell him the truth? She wouldn't even know where to begin. What would he think of her? Would their marriage be over if he knew? Did she even care?

For the quadrillionth time she wished that she could go back and change the past. Her guilt was heavy and too repulsive a thing to bear. Yet she deserved it, and never could she forgive herself. Nor would God or her family. No matter how much time passed and no matter how she looked at it, abortion was still murder.

Finally Karissa slept, but it wasn't peaceful. The dream came again as it had every so often since coming to the island. *She walked onto the balcony, holding the baby. She tripped and watched helplessly as the infant fell over the railing. She tried desparately to cling to the baby's dress, but it slipped out of her hands.*

"Why?" asked the baby as she fell.

CHAPTER 2

When Malcolm awoke the second time, it was nearly noon. He stretched and yawned noisily before remembering that Karissa still slept soundly. The room was awash with light peeking through the blinds, splattering an odd pattern on the light green walls and on his wife's tousled brown hair. Unlike him, she always slept in a fetal position: feet tucked, back curled, one arm under and the other drawn up to her head as if to clap the hand over her ear.

The blanket had fallen back to reveal her worn jeans and oversized shirt. Obviously, she had been too tired to change. But she was beautiful to him. He stifled the desire to wake her with kisses and hugs, knowing she wouldn't appreciate it after the long hours of work. Once, she wouldn't have minded, and he wouldn't have hesitated, but that was long ago.

He remembered the first time he had seen her at a friend's apartment. It was just after midterms, and they were celebrating. She had mesmerized him with her emerald-green eyes and the long, dark-brown hair that looked as soft as silk. But the feature that impressed him the most were the hollows beneath the soft curve of her high cheekbones. The shadows there gave her an illusion of mystery and hinted at fragility. When she left the party early, he had followed her out the door, hoping for an excuse to talk with her. She stopped in the dark to tie her shoes, and he had stumbled over her. Amidst the ensuing laughter, he asked her out. They dated nearly a year before he was sure he wanted to spend the rest of his life with her.

"Okay," she had said when he finally proposed during a hike in Provo Canyon.

"Yes!" he whooped, jumping up from his knees to hug her.

There had been no question of marrying in the temple, since neither of them attended church and Karissa smoked. At first this vice had surprised him, because she looked like all the other Mormon girls he had dated—untouched, innocent, and religious. Instead of objecting, however, he felt relieved that she wouldn't hold him to all the things his parents had always expected. He had served a mission, had even enjoyed it, but he didn't believe in everything his parents did. Drifting away from their religion hadn't been difficult. And later, his passion for Karissa had blotted out all else.

Both of their families had been disappointed at their decision to marry out of the temple, but Malcolm had plunged ahead, counting himself lucky to have found Karissa. There would be time enough for religion when they were old—after they had lived a little. He, too, began to smoke and drink socially. Nine years later, not having a religion didn't seem to have made any difference in their lives.

Or had it?

He sighed and left the warm bed. Pausing, he tucked the covers gently around his wife, then shoved his legs into the cold confines of his Levis and headed toward the kitchen. In his thin T-shirt he felt chilly, and he stopped in the hallway to check the heat guage, but it read the moderate seventy-two degrees that he and Karissa had agreed upon. Even so, the heat bills were outrageous. Yet to him it was a fair exchange for the higher wages, unsullied landscapes, and fresh island air. There really was truth to the Alaskan motto "North to the Future." Alaska had been in his blood since the day he took his first step on her dirt; it was his future.

Only the future hadn't gone exactly as planned. The gulf between him and Karissa increased daily, and he didn't understand why. It wasn't only the lack of children, though that certainly tore at them. The rift was rooted in something more serious, something he couldn't put a name to. He tried repeatedly to talk to Karissa about the situation, but when he did, she withdrew even more, and he had stopped his questions for fear of losing her altogether.

In the kitchen, Malcolm checked the cupboards for cigarettes. There were none, and precious little to eat. Neither of them had time for shopping. Digging deeper, he found some coffee. While it was heating, he slumped on a bar stool and studied the black and white ceramic tiled floor. It reminded him of a checker board and the games he and his father had played when he was younger. He frowned and raised his eyes.

Karissa's purse was on the counter, and he rummaged through it, searching for a cigarette. He found a pack of Camels with three missing. Camels had always been her favorite brand.

The phone rang, and he scooped it up quickly before the one in the bedroom could wake Karissa. "Hello?"

"Hi, Uncle Malcolm. It's me, Curtis. I'm just calling to make sure you'll be at the church tomorrow for my talk."

"Uh, sure. I remember. We'll be there."

"Great. It'll be good to see you." The boy paused. "Hey, would you mind saying the opening prayer? My friend who was going to say it can't come."

There was an awkward silence. "No, I don't think so," Malcolm mumbled. "I haven't been to church since your little brother was blessed. I'm not the one to ask." He didn't add that he was far from worthy. He had thought the boy had understood his lifestyle. Probably his asking was a missionary tactic, something similar to what Malcolm himself had used on his mission in Arizona. It wouldn't work on him.

"Oh." Curtis sounded disappointed. "I don't suppose Aunt Karissa can do it."

"No. But we'll be there."

"Okay, well, thanks. I'd better hang up and find someone. Bye."

"See you tomorrow." Malcolm set down the receiver. His family never gave up on him, it seemed. They were determined if nothing else, and their fervor was topped only by that of Karissa's family, who all seemed to be on the fast track to the celestial kingdom, if there were such a thing.

He didn't know why he was even going to the homecoming. He just hadn't been able to make up excuses to Curtis, whom he'd used to baby-sit as a child. Maybe he was even curious to see how the boy had changed in the last two years.

Malcolm's own mission had been the best two years of his life, though he didn't like to admit it. "It was because I was young, that's all," he muttered. He poured the coffee, but the bitter taste didn't appeal to him as it normally did. He gulped it down, burning his tongue. He cursed and dumped the rest into the sink. Checking his coat for his wallet, he walked to the kitchen door and shoved his stockinged feet into the hiking boots he had been too tired to store in their shoe closet earlier. Karissa's boots were there too, still wet after her trek from the hospital to the truck.

He stopped and wrote a note for Karissa: *Gone to Kodiak to pick up some stuff at Safeway.*

He left the house, shutting the kitchen door softly behind him. He should have done the shopping yesterday, but the commercial he was shooting in the Aleutian village Karluk had taken longer than he had expected. He had run into several of his grandfather's friends, and couldn't resist taking the time to find out more about the weathered old man he barely remembered from his youth. Because Malcolm's skin and bone structure resembled his father's side of the family, who had more Russian and Norwegian in them than anything else, it had taken some time to convince the men that his mother was native Aleut, making Malcolm a half-breed and indeed his grandfather's descendant. The only parts of Malcolm that looked native were his straight black hair and dark eyes.

When the men had finally opened up to him, they were full of information. "Once I saw Katmai wrestle a brown bear," a shriveled man told him.

"Really? Here on Kodiak?" This was a story Malcolm had never heard about his grandfather.

The grizzled head nodded regally. "We was out fishing on the mountain and the bear went after our load of fish. Katmai wasn't going to let 'im git away with it. He growled right back at that bear, and the bear went for 'im."

"How'd he get away?"

A slight smile came over wrinkled lips. "I shot the bear, that's what. I still have the hide." He led Malcolm into his small wooden house to prove it.

Most of what he had learned about his grandfather convinced Malcolm that he was strong, agile, and clever. He liked to think they were a lot alike.

Shaking off the memories, Malcolm backed out of the garage and started down the dirt road. The air was cool enough to require the top on his Jeep, but the sky was a blue so clear it made his gut ache with an odd longing. The sky always looked this way, especially in the spring after a week-long bout of drizzle—like a rainbow, only all made out of blue, a promise of the warmth soon to come. Yet he knew Karissa wanted to leave the island, and he wondered if he would go with her when she did.

Once in town, Malcolm's stomach demanded that he stop at Subway for something to eat. Inside, he sauntered to the counter.

"Malcolm?"

He turned and recognized his home teacher. Too late to make a getaway. "Uh, hi, Jud. How's it going?"

"Busy. You know, getting the halibut taken care of." Jud managed one of the canneries on the southern part of Kodiak near the river. "I'm sorry I haven't been able to see you lately."

"Well, I've not been home that much." The truth was that Jud Kennedy tried to make appointments each month, but Malcolm continually shrugged him off. He knew Jud from the time when he had been active in the Church, before his family had moved to Anchorage. As children they had played together at ward activities. Since Jud had become his home teacher, Malcolm had made it a rule not to return his phone calls. Several times Jud had dropped by without warning, and Malcolm had just happened to be home. Other than that, they had no contact.

"The ward's really growing," Jud said. His sandy-blonde hair was cut neatly above his ears, and a round balding spot showed on his crown as he ducked his head nervously. An anxious expression covered his fleshy face, and the muscles beneath his left eye twitched.

Malcolm didn't have to ask which ward; there was only one on Kodiak. "Good, good." They stared at each other awkwardly. *Ask me,* Malcolm thought. *Let's get this over with.*

"How about tomorrow? Can I come by?" Again the muscles twitched.

"No. Sorry."

Jud's large face didn't show surprise, though the twitch below his eye worked furiously.

Malcolm felt the strange need to explain himself. "I'm going to the mainland for a mission homecoming."

"Oh, who came home?" Jud adjusted his belt on his wide girth.

"Charles's oldest boy, Curtis."

"Yeah, I remember Charles. I saw him a few years back in Anchorage at a conference. I didn't realize he had a son that old. How the years pass. How is Charles, anyway?"

"Doing well." Malcolm really didn't know, but he wasn't going to admit it. He noticed with relief that his order was ready. "Well, nice to see ya, Jud. I've got to get going now. I have a ton of things to do. See ya around."

Jud opened his mouth to say something more, but Malcolm turned on his heel, pretending not to see. At the door he paused, lit one of Karissa's Camels, and breathed in before going out into the crisp air. Out of the corner of his eye, he saw Jud watching him with a frown on his meaty lips, and he smiled. *That'll teach him.* Had it been one of his commercials, he would have yelled, "Cut! That's a wrap, folks!"

Chuckling, Malcolm, strode out the door and to his Jeep, his hiking boots sloshing through the mounds of melting snow. He wolfed down the sandwich on his way through town, wishing he had bought two. He would have to remember to buy more sandwich makings at Safeway.

The grocery store was bustling with activity when he arrived. Saturday was the worst time to shop, and it seemed as if every house-wife in Kodiak was there. Still, amidst the bustle, the store was oddly quiet, and it took Malcolm time to realize what was missing. The children! Yes, there weren't nearly as many children as there were on the mainland. Or especially in Utah. It had been one of the things that had fascinated him when he attended school. How could the women get anything done with all those children? He smiled. It had been years since he had remembered what it was like in Utah. If he ever had a child, he would bring him here to Safeway and let him make some noise.

In this tender frame of mind, Malcolm bought all of Karissa's favorite foods. Maybe this afternoon they could spend some time together by the fireplace. They could watch a video or go to a restaurant. It would be just the two of them, with no interruptions, like in the old days.

He drove more quickly than usual to the house, for the first time wishing they didn't live so far out. A soft, steady rain began, the kind that often lasted for a week on Kodiak. The already slushy snow would soon become a muddy gray carpet, and eventually sink out of sight altogether into the fertile soil. Then the rush of green would begin. New life. A happy tune ran through his mind, a song from his childhood, something about popcorn on an apricot tree. His lips pursed to whistle aloud.

His smile died when he arrived home. Karissa's Nissan wasn't in the garage. In the kitchen, he let the big bags of groceries slide to the counter top as he grabbed at the note by the phone.

Gone in to work, it read. *See you tonight. Karissa.*

That meant he would be lucky to see her before midnight. He crumpled the note and threw it into the garbage. Then he sat on one of the bar stools and put his elbows on the counter-top, his head in his hands. He felt like crying. With slow movements he brought out a bottle of wine and uncorked it, drinking straight from the bottle. No use saving it now. He wouldn't get to see Karissa laugh as the bubbles tickled her nose.

CHAPTER 3

Jesse Hergarter's eyes blinked open in the late Saturday-morning light. He didn't feel like getting up. He loved his job, but the past week had been long and tiresome. At least he and his two partners had the programs at the hospital finished enough to pass through the board's initial review on Monday. Then there would be the months of follow-up and additions until everything was perfectly tuned to the hospital. The work wouldn't be too demanding, and they would have time to work on the additional contracts they had picked up on Kodiak and in Anchorage.

"I love working for myself," he said, stretching luxuriously on the double bed. "And Kodiak is a wonderful place for a vacation. You know, the best thing that ever happened to me besides meeting you was getting laid off last year. Otherwise, I would never have gone on my own."

Beside him, Brionney groaned.

"What's wrong?" he asked, raising himself up on his elbow. His wife's vibrant blue eyes peered out from her round face. The skin on her forehead drew together, making it look like a wrinkled blanket, and her shoulder-length hair was matted as if from a long, sleepless night.

"Another headache?" he asked. Her headaches had been getting worse.

"There's something wrong with this house," she said. "I can't explain it, but something's wrong."

Jesse yawned and tried to pull her close. "It's nothing. You're pregnant, that's all. I'll rub your neck; maybe that will help."

"It's not because I'm pregnant!" she snapped. Then she sighed and laid her head on his chest. "I'm sorry, honey. But I'm only just over two months along. I've never had headaches this early. It all started when we moved in here. I was fine for the days we stayed at Malcolm's."

"Could it be the stress?" he asked, smoothing her near-white hair until the strands fanned out over his pajama top.

"I guess."

Jesse glanced around the bedroom. Like the rest of the house, the room was small and in poor repair. The building was old, maybe a hundred years, and looked every hour of its age, despite an obvious attempt to fix it up for renters. New wallpaper had been placed over peeling paint, and in most places he could see the unevenness underneath. The blue carpet was new, too, but it couldn't change the smell of the ancient boards hidden below.

The owners had rented the house furnished, but the furniture was mostly old and mismatched. The battered nightstand held an odd green-colored lamp. The small bookshelf sagged, and the wood on the right side bowed outward. A sturdy wood dresser in the corner was the only piece worth anything. It was ancient but well built, and had somehow survived the neglect.

His eyes focused on something strange. "Brionney, do you see anything near the door?" His hand stopped massaging her neck, but was still tangled in her long tresses.

She tilted her head as if it hurt her to do so. "The cloud! I told you I'd seen it!"

"So you did," Jesse murmured. Near the doorway, a white miasma hung suspended, like a steam of water vapor. A tremor of fear passed through him, but he forced it down.

"What is it?" Brionney asked.

"I don't know."

He eased out of bed and approached the mass, sniffing. Goose bumps erupted over his skin. "I think it smells like gas."

"I know what natural gas smells like. It can't be that."

"But we should call the company, just to make sure. Why don't we take the children out to breakfast while we wait to see what they say?"

Brionney's blue eyes lost their frightened look as she concentrated on what to do next. When they awoke their three young daughters, it seemed to Jesse that they were sleepier than usual. That worried him further. Brionney dressed the girls while he called the gas company.

Before they left the house, Jesse returned to their room, but the white cloud had vanished. Had it been in his imagination?

Out in the crisp air, Brionney's headache seemed to abate. "I knew there was something odd about that house," she said.

* * * *

Malcolm had nearly drained the bottle of wine in the quiet of the kitchen, broken only faintly by the rain hitting the roof. The phone rang and he picked it up wearily, settling on the stool, his back hunched.

"Hello?"

"Malcolm? This is Jesse."

"Hi, Jesse. How's it going?" He and Karissa had helped the younger couple and their children settle into their rented house in Kodiak. They had also shown them around the island a few times. Lately, though, Brionney's morning sickness was getting worse, and she hadn't cared to explore.

"Well, we've got a little problem and wondered if you would be willing to help."

Malcolm straightened. He was good at solving other people's problems. "If I can. What's up?"

"We've had a gas leak here. Evidently, it's been leaking for some time. I think that's what's been causing Brionney's headaches. They've fixed it, but Brionney's frantic to leave. She's afraid it'll happen again and the children will get hurt. She wants to find another place—today. But that's impossible. I can't really blame her for wanting to leave; the place is a dive anyway. We could stay at a hotel for a few days, but the budget's really tight right now. We wondered if we could stay with you for a couple of nights until I have a chance to find a better place. Some of the ward members offered their houses, but five of us are a lot to squeeze into one room, and I don't like to deprive the members of the little space they do have. I know it's a spur-of-the-moment thing, but would it be too much of an inconvenience?"

"Of course not," Malcolm said without hesitating. "The whole upstairs is still empty except for our offices. The rooms you stayed in before are just like you left them." Jesse and Brionney had stayed two nights with them when they had first come to Kodiak a month earlier. It had been the least Malcolm could do for someone he had introduced to the Church on his mission to Arizona. Besides, Malcolm was partly responsible for Jesse's being in Kodiak in the first place. They had kept in touch on a yearly basis since Malcolm had left Arizona, and when the contract with the hospital opened up a few months after Jesse lost his job, Malcolm had suggested that Jesse submit a bid.

"You're welcome to use the rooms," Malcolm continued. "They're just going to waste. Meanwhile, I'll put out the word about a new apartment or house. It shouldn't take longer than a week or so to find something more liveable."

"Thanks, Malcolm." Jesse sounded relieved. "I didn't know what to do."

"Hey, we're friends. I know you'd do the same for us. So, what time should I expect you?"

"Is around seven okay? It'll take us that long to get our things together."

"Great. See ya then." Malcolm hung up the phone, feeling better. He put away the groceries, glad that he had bought some cookies. Little girls loved cookies.

* * * *

The front doorbell rang shortly before seven. Malcolm stubbed out his cigarette and walked to the entryway. The hardwood floor was polished to a bright shine. Maggie, the lady who came in three times weekly to clean, had done her usual immaculate job.

The Hergarter family stood outside, slightly wet but now protected from the rain by the wide overhang covering the porch. "Come on in," Malcolm said, reaching for one of the suitcases in Jesse's hand.

Jesse had dark hair and eyes, and his stocky figure was a good six inches shorter than Malcolm's. He seemed solid and ready to face any challenge. He hadn't changed since the day Malcolm had met him on the street in Arizona. Malcolm had been twenty-one then, and at the end of his mission; Jesse had been just eighteen. It had frustrated

Malcolm that Jesse had refused to be baptized, though he knew the Church was true. But it had taken Jesse three years to gather courage to oppose his parents' wishes and take the plunge. Yet since his baptism and subsequent mission to England, he had been stronger in the Church than Malcolm had ever been.

"Thanks so much for this, Malcolm," Brionney said, bringing him back to the present. She was short and somewhat rounded, but exceptionally pretty. Her eyes were a bright blue, like the color of the sky on a warm, cloudless day, and her long hair an unusual white-blonde. "I don't know what we would have done otherwise."

"It's nothing, really," Malcolm told her.

"I like staying with you, Uncle Malcolm," Savannah said. The seven-and-a-half-year-old was a miniature of her mother, all white hair and blue eyes.

Malcolm smiled. "I like it too. We're gonna have fun."

On the sidewalk, Camille, who was nearly five, and little three-year-old Rosalie investigated a small pile of mushy snow. They looked up, their brown eyes studying him. Camille's hair was dark like her father's, and little Rosalie's was a darker version of her mother's blonde hair. Malcolm smiled at them, but they glanced away shyly.

"Come on in," he repeated, backing into the entryway. He showed them to the front staircase, which led up to the second floor. There was another staircase leading to the second floor from the kitchen, but with the luggage it would be easier to use the wider main staircase. "You can have the same two bedrooms as before, and the long front room as a toy room for the girls."

Savannah clapped her hands. "You mean the one with all the windows looking into the greenhouse?"

"That's the one." Malcolm was continually amazed at the girls' enthusiasm over small things.

"And will Aunt Karissa let us play in the greenhouse this time, do ya think?" Savannah asked.

"You'll have to talk to her," Malcolm said. Karissa was funny about the greenhouse. The last time the Hergarters had stayed she had managed to avoid the issue, but they might be here longer this time.

"Don't you dare go in there until she says so," Brionney warned.

Savannah looked up at her. "Of course, Mom."

"I've put some clean sheets at the foot of the bed, and some extra blankets." Malcolm set the suitcase he carried on the floor inside the room the little girls would be sharing. "Is there more luggage in the car?"

It didn't take long to settle the Hergarters' belongings in their new accommodations, but unpacking the groceries Jesse and Brionney had brought took much longer. The unending paper sacks made Malcolm's earlier attempt at food buying pale in comparison.

"Why don't I make some dinner while you guys watch TV?" Brionney asked when they put away the last bag of groceries.

Jesse looked at her in concern. "Are you sure you're feeling up to it?"

"I'm fine. And actually, it'd be nice to hear myself think for a change." Brionney inclined her head pointedly toward their daughters.

"Come on then, girls." Jesse motioned for them to follow.

"Wait," Brionney said. "I don't see the ice cream. Did we leave it in the car?"

"Yikes! It'll be melted by now." Jesse hurried for the door.

Malcolm led the children down the hall and into the family room. He flipped on the TV, turning the channel to *The Pretender,* one of his favorite shows. He didn't waste much time watching television, but when he did, it had to be good. With a sigh, he settled back in his easy chair and took out a cigarette, forgetting that he had promised himself not to smoke around the girls.

"Smoking's bad," Camille said suddenly, standing in front of him.

Malcolm nearly choked as he tried to light up. Smoke rushed out of his nose, stinging as it went. All three girls stared at him, but it was Camille who continued, "It's against the Wisdom Word." Malcolm noticed her eyes were a lighter brown than little Rosalie's, as if her mother's blue color had softened them. They seemed to see into his soul.

"The Word of Wisdom," he corrected mechanically.

"I told you a hundred times it was the Word of Wisdom," Savannah added.

Camille didn't seem to hear her, but continued to regard Malcolm gravely. "Mommy said it hurts your throat and makes you die. Do you want to die, Uncle Malcolm?"

Malcolm glanced up to see Brionney standing in the doorway, but she didn't speak; she seemed to be waiting for him. Savannah and Camille waited too. Even little Rosalie stared at him intently. Behind them the Pretender was flying a plane in the frame of Malcolm's large-screened TV. He wished he could watch it.

"Are you going to die?" Camille asked.

"Everyone dies." He saw Brionney's frown and added hastily, "Eventually. I mean everybody eventually dies. But don't worry, Camille. I'm not going to die."

"But smoking's bad."

"Yes. It is. I wouldn't want you ever to do such a thing."

"Then why do you?"

He glanced again at Brionney, but her lips clamped shut. She wasn't helping him out of this one. "It's because I can't stop," he admitted. "That's why you should never start. Cigarettes are addicting."

"What's that?"

"Addicting?" he asked. The child nodded. "Addicting means there's a drug inside it that makes you have to smoke once you start. It is very hard to stop."

"Oh." Camille glanced curiously at the cigarette, still smoldering in his hand.

"Do you want to sit on my lap and watch *The Pretender?*" Malcolm asked, attempting to change the subject.

The little head shook vigorously. "No. That's smells bad." She pointed at the cigarette.

"Stinks," agreed Rosalie.

Self-consciously, Malcolm stabbed out the cigarette, not daring to look up at Brionney. Undoubtedly, she'd be laughing. When he finally did glance at the door, she had already disappeared into the hall.

"Come on." He patted his knees. "I have room for two little girls. And no stinking cigarettes. I know my clothes still smell a bit, but you'll get used to it." Giggling shyly, Camille and Rosalie climbed onto his lap.

* * * *

Malcolm was in bed before Karissa arrived home. Her steps dragged sluggishly as she came down the hall and sank to the bed. She smelled damp and brought with her a chill from outside.

"Finished?" he asked.

She sighed. "Yes." She seemed very pale and almost wraithlike in the dark.

"You hungry?"

"No, I stopped at McDonalds. I'm just tired." She began to undress.

"Just in case, there are leftovers from dinner. Brionney made a very tasty casserole."

"Brionney?"

"They had a gas leak. I told them they could stay here till they found a new place." Malcolm could almost hear her frowning at his words. He strained his eyes in the dark, but couldn't see her expression. "Isn't that okay? They had nowhere else to go except a hotel, and those are so expensive, especially with so many children."

"That's fine," she said, her voice hurried and remote. "It's very nice of you." She tugged on her nightgown and pulled back the blankets, slipping her legs beneath them. With her right hand she pushed her hair back from her narrow face, a gesture Malcolm had always found alluring. He scooted close to her, hoping she would turn to him, but she yawned and lay back. Almost immediately, he heard her soft snores.

Moonlight filtered through the blinds. Malcolm reached out tentatively and stroked her arm. She turned over in her sleep, away from him. Strange that she could be so close, yet so far away.

It was a long time before he slept.

CHAPTER 4

Music was playing as Malcolm and Karissa walked hurriedly into the chapel in Anchorage. On the stand, Curtis sat contentedly with his parents, Teresa and Charles, and the bishopric. Behind them, a lady with bright red hair led the congregation in a hymn. Karissa felt strangely comfortable, as if this unknown place was somehow familiar. Of course, it was a typical-looking ward, much like those back in California, and that could account for the feeling.

As they walked up the aisle toward a seat, someone tugged on the back of her jade-green dress. It was Lisa Mathees, one of Malcolm's sisters-in-law. "Sit with us. We have room." Beside her, Jeffrey, Malcolm's brother, was sliding over and pushing his five children along the padded bench.

Karissa sat gratefully, then scanned the congregation for other relatives. She saw only Malcolm's parents, Richard and Faith, and Kathleen, one of Malcolm's sisters, sitting with her husband, Troy. Karissa knew the others must be present, but hidden from her view. *Malcolm, Richard, Kathleen, Charles, Jeffrey—what stuffy, proper names,* she thought.

"Didn't anyone ever call your father Rick, your brother Chuck, or your sister Kathy?" she had asked once.

"No." Malcolm had replied matter-of-factly. "And Jeffrey, Carolyn, Philip, Gregory, and I never shortened our names either. Why should we?" That at least explained why Malcolm never called her Kar as other people did.

Along the bench, the children poked each other and giggled. Their father looked at them sharply and the noise stopped—until he glanced away. Karissa smiled, remembering her own time in church as a child. Her father had glared at her too many times to count.

Malcolm handed her the hymnal, but she shook her head. She didn't feel like singing. What she wished she could do was sleep. But if she slept, she might have to take medication so the dream wouldn't return to haunt her.

They had missed the opening prayer and announcements, and when the song ended the young boys passed the sacrament. Karissa felt as if all eyes were on her as she refused the bread and water. Why had she agreed to come? Painful memories stalked her conscience. *Maybe I should have just taken it.* But no; she and Malcolm both knew they weren't worthy, and she couldn't bring herself to mock God further.

Finally the torturous ordinance was complete, and Teresa and Charles took turns speaking, mostly about how proud they were of their son and how much they loved the gospel. Karissa felt increasingly uncomfortable. Then Curtis arose.

"It's good to be back," he said. "I have to admit, though, that I was pretty reluctant to come home. I've have just spent the two best years of my life—so far." He paused and searched the crowd with his eyes. "I know that's because my mission was so spiritual. But like all of you, I also know that I will go on to have even more spiritual experiences as I marry, have children, and fulfill church callings. I'm so grateful for the foundation the Lord gave me while serving a mission. I can never repay Him for that. I just hope I can go forward and not look back on these last two years as always being the best of my whole life, because I know from my parents' example that there is so much more in store. We should always progress."

Karissa glanced at Malcolm to see a strange look on his face. She wondered what he was thinking. Perhaps about his own mission to Arizona all those years ago? Did he think of them as the two best years of his life? The thought brought a sadness to her heart, one she had thought she was beyond feeling.

"Let me introduce you to a few of the people I met while in Canada," Curtis continued. He began to describe a family and their challenges in accepting the gospel.

Karissa's mind wandered. It sounded like every other missionary talk she had ever heard. She began counting the children, comparing their ratio with the adults—about three to one. When she was finished, she thought about how long it had taken to work her way up to her first administration job at a hospital, and how she was now the top person, except for the board. She couldn't ask for a better job, though she missed the challenges a bigger hospital might provide. If only she could forget her appalling secret, she might consider herself happy. *No, I won't think about that now. Better to listen to Curtis.*

"And our mission president told us that if we were willing to give up our greatest sin, the thing we wanted most would be granted to us," Curtis was saying. He paused to wipe his eyes with sturdy fingertips. Now Karissa's attention was riveted on the boy. The thing he wanted most would be granted to him? What was he saying?

"I tell you it's true. We tried it, and the family was able to come to terms with their problems and be baptized. If ever you want something, ask yourself what you are willing to give up to get it. Which of your sins will you sacrifice to receive your greatest desire? Like He did with me, I know Heavenly Father will bless you."

Karissa didn't hear much after that. The impact of Curtis' statement burrowed into her heart, and she couldn't get it out. What could it mean to her? She had abandoned her God so long ago that He probably didn't remember her, even if she was willing to give up any of her sins—which she wasn't. She liked her life the way it was.

Didn't she?

After the service, they drove to Charles' house, where the family room seemed a mass of darting youngsters. Malcolm's six siblings each had a host of children. Only he had none.

Karissa sat off to the side, watching the family and not feeling part of it. Malcolm was talking with several of his brothers, apparently enjoying himself. He did stay away from his father, she noticed, and was glad. The last time they had been together they had fought about his smoking and his lifestyle. Not that she and Malcolm flaunted their beliefs. It was just difficult to cover up the smell of tobacco. She wished she could go out in the yard and have a cigarette now, but she didn't want to cause problems; things were awkward enough. Maybe after dinner she and Malcolm could escape for a walk and a little freedom before their flight back to Kodiak.

"You know, I believe the body can heal itself," a voice said at her shoulder.

Karissa looked over to see Faith, Malcolm's mother. She had straight black hair reaching nearly to her waist, dark eyes, and full lips. Because of her Aleutian blood, she reminded Karissa of an Eskimo. The Aleuts and Eskimos had always seemed similar to her, though Malcolm claimed they looked nothing alike. Yet, in Karissa's opinion, Faith could have appeared at home in an igloo. Only the round glasses on her face were out of place.

"If you eat right, and don't take things into your body that can harm it, your body will be able to heal itself," Faith repeated.

Karissa blinked, trying to figure out what the woman was saying. "I'm healthy," she ventured. From her taller height, she could see the top of Faith's black head.

"You don't have a child," the other woman said softly.

Karissa stared at her, feeling her face darken as rage, embarrassment, and shame vied for preeminence in her emotions. "What does that have to with anything?" she managed to say, her voice tense, but still polite.

"Good foods are for the body, to help it. Smoking is particularly bad."

"The Word of Wisdom." Karissa seethed inwardly.

The older woman smiled. "Not just that. My people have always believed in taking care of the body. It is a way of life."

"Oh, it's *native* folklore," Karissa answered somewhat condescendingly. Though people of many races were born on Kodiak Island, only those of Aleutian blood were called natives.

Faith seemed unperturbed at her outburst. "You and Malcolm need to stop smoking and eat right if you want to have a baby."

"Malcolm too?" That seemed to be stretching credibility.

"Of course. It takes two to have a baby." Her voice was matter-of-fact.

"Of course," Karissa repeated dryly. Only because Faith was Malcolm's mother did she restrain herself from rolling her eyes in disbelief.

"Having fun?" a grinning Malcolm asked, appearing beside her.

Karissa flipped back the ends of her hair. "Well, your mother here thinks that if we stopped smoking, we could have a baby."

"And eat right," Faith added.

"Oh, yes, and eat right. No more fast food, especially those McDonald's french fries." Karissa's voice was light, but she felt Malcolm glance at her sharply. He knew her too well.

"Smoking?" Malcolm asked innocently.

Faith's black eyes narrowed. "I can smell it on you, Malcolm. I always can, no matter how you wash before you visit."

"The Word of Wisdom," he said. "Do we have to go through this again?"

"Native," Karissa corrected him. "This time it's native." For some reason, that bothered her even more. She had ignored Joseph Smith's revelation for a long time now, but she found it more difficult to disregard native beliefs. She had been on Kodiak long enough to see midwives deliver babies and treat illnesses with herbs as competently as any doctor. She had always respected them.

Malcolm steered her away from his mother. "I want to go home," she whispered. "Now. I can't stand this."

"She's harmless, Karissa. Don't listen to her. She's just an old woman who wants grandchildren."

"She has plenty of grandchildren."

"Not from me."

Guilt assailed Karissa. Why wouldn't her body work? "It's not just her." She hesitated. It had been a long time since she had confided anything to Malcolm. "I'm nervous about tomorrow, seeing the new specialist and all. What if—" She broke off.

"What if he doesn't have anything new to tell us?" Malcolm finished. A bleak expression came over his face. "I don't know. I just don't know."

Karissa wanted to hug him, to say that everything would be all right, but she couldn't. She knew it would never be all right again. Her infertility was her cross to bear, a payment for her sin. She turned from him. "Let's go home—please." Without looking back, she walked out the door and down the walkway. He could follow or stay as he pleased, but she was going to take the first plane back to Kodiak.

Mounds of snow lined the freshly shoveled walk, but Karissa's boots crunched on a few stray clumps of ice and snow. Malcolm joined her before she reached their rented car. "What did you tell them?" she asked.

"That you weren't feeling well. They didn't seem to mind too much about our leaving. I think my mother felt bad, though. You know, sometimes I think it would be better if she had never left the Russian Orthodox Church. Such cute little buildings."

"Well their churches are interesting, to be sure, but that hardly seems a reason to change religions."

"Look, there's one now." He pointed to a white building in the distance, trimmed with green and topped with a dome. "Even Karluk has one, you know." Karissa knew that Karluk was one of the small native villages on Kodiak near where Malcolm was filming.

"Do you really wish she hadn't joined the Mormons?" Karissa asked. Years had passed since they had discussed religion. For some reason it bothered her that Malcolm could consider any other faith than The Church of Jesus Christ of Latter-day Saints.

His brow furrowed thoughtfully. "It's just that Mormons take things so seriously." He opened the car door for her.

She waited until he was settled in the seat beside her before continuing. "Mormons take things too seriously? Or do *we* take things too lightheartedly?" Before Malcolm could answer, she asked, "Do you consider yourself a Mormon?"

"I guess so. I don't think about it much."

His statement seemed significant somehow. For herself, she knew the Church was true; but knowing made her guilt even more grievous.

They didn't talk much on the hour-long plane ride back to Kodiak Island. Nor did they talk as Malcolm drove his Jeep to the house through the incessant rain. Before Karissa knew it, she had drifted off to sleep in her seat.

And the dream came. *She walked through the house, a baby girl in her arms. As she passed through a doorway, she walked too close and the baby's head hit the door. A simple mistake. The baby cried, and Karissa tried to comfort her.*

The baby looked at her and said, "Why did you kill me? I would have loved you." Then the baby lay still in her arms and did not move again.

Karissa awoke with a start.

"I'm sorry," Malcolm said. "I knew I took that corner a little sharp. Did I wake you?"

"No. It was a dream." She was still groggy enough to tell him the truth.

"Oh? What about?"

"Nothing. I don't remember now." But as always, when having the dream or a variation of the dream, Karissa felt shaken to her core.

She breathed a sigh of relief when they finally arrived at their house. Now she could take some medication to help her sleep and go right to bed. She would forget this whole miserable day.

But a delicious aroma came from the kitchen, filling the garage. She sniffed appreciatively, her mouth watering. "Brionney must be cooking."

"I wonder if there's enough for us," Malcolm said. He looked hungry.

"I'll race you!" In seconds she threw open the kitchen door.

Brionney started. "Oh, you're home. You're just in time to eat—if you're hungry. I'm sorry I didn't see you this morning before you left. I've been spending a lot of time over the toilet, if you know what I mean. I don't remember ever being so sick." She grimaced. "Oh, that must make the food sound really appetizing. I'm sorry."

Malcolm grinned. "We skipped lunch, so I'd eat anything right now. Even if it didn't smell so wonderful."

Her face lit in a wide smile. "Then sit down." Both Karissa and Malcolm dived to the bar stools.

"How are your headaches?" Karissa asked, scooping a great forkful of cheese-covered casserole.

Two dimples brightened Brionney's face. "Gone completely since leaving that house. You can't believe what a relief that is."

"Natural gas can be dangerous," Malcolm said, stating the obvious.

Brionney nodded. "I feel the Lord protected us."

"Oh, well, maybe He did," Malcolm replied. "Where's Jesse?"

"He's home teaching, but he'll be back soon. We always read scriptures with the girls before putting them to bed. The girls are upstairs now, getting ready."

"This is delicious!" Malcolm reached for another forkful.

"It really is," Karissa agreed. She couldn't remember the last time she had cooked a meal from scratch. It hardly seemed worth the effort for just the two of them. But how easy Brionney made it seem! She must have been born to be a wife and mother. *I'll bet she's never had a serious problem in her whole life,* Karissa thought.

Malcolm finished his second helping while Karissa pulled out a cigarette. She sighed in contentment. Maybe it was time to hire someone to cook for them. It wasn't as if they couldn't afford it.

Her peace was shattered by a chorus of giggles and whispering as Savannah, Camille, and Rosalie burst into the room. "Is Dad home yet?" Savannah asked. She fell silent when she saw Karissa and Malcolm.

"There she is. Ask her," Camille whispered loud enough for everyone to hear. She elbowed her older sister.

Savannah returned the nudge. "No, you ask her," she whispered, equally loud.

"Ask me what?" Karissa took a puff of her cigarette.

The girls said nothing.

Karissa looked away, and the whispering began again. This time she could discern only a word or two. Finally, the girls grew silent. As Karissa glanced at them out of the corner of her eye, Savannah and Camille were trying to push Rosalie in her direction. Rosalie resisted until Savannah whispered, "I'll buy you a candy bar."

Little Rosalie set her jaw and walked timidly up to Karissa. "Can we, uh, play in the plants?" she mumbled. "I not break them. Promise."

"The plants?"

"There." Rosalie pointed over her shoulder to the far wall, where the huge window looked out on the greenhouse.

Only then did Karissa understand. The girls wanted to play in the greenhouse! She knew they had wanted to play in it the last time they had stayed, but she had managed to find their parents a house before the request had actually been voiced. Now she had no choice but to confront the question.

It wasn't as easy as it might have been. Originally, she had built it for the children who would have been hers, but now it had become a kind of monument to them. To have other children playing there would seem to desecrate her own children's imaginary presence.

"That's okay if you don't want us to," Savannah added, coming to stand beside her little sister. "You wouldn't want us to get the sand everywhere anyway." She stared sadly at Karissa. With her blonde hair and bright blue eyes, the girl looked like a small angel.

Suddenly, Karissa wanted to see all three girls in the greenhouse among the plants, cavorting and laughing to their hearts' content.

It was high time that sad, silent place heard the laughter of innocent children.

Karissa could feel Malcolm's eyes on her, and Brionney's too. She took a deep breath and stubbed out her cigarette. "Come with me," she said, taking Rosalie's hand.

She led the way to the laundry room, situated between the kitchen and the family room. "Now, I know you will be careful not to hurt the plants," she told them. "But when you come inside you must remember to clean up here before going into the rest of the house. We don't want sand everywhere. There are some towels you can use." She pointed to a rack between the sink and the washer. "Just get them a little wet, clean up, and put them in the washer when you're through."

The girls' eyes danced as she opened the door and led them into the greenhouse. A row of six- and eight-foot house trees circled the vast space, with plenty of room left to reach the ceiling. Cobblestones lined small pathways around of the trunks. Toward the middle of the greenhouse was a huge patch of sand encircled by a low concrete wall. To the far side, a small waterfall rushed down some rocks into an ankle-deep pond where goldfish swam in lazy circles. Hanging plants and creeping vines along the two-story ceiling nearly masked the double-layered plastic walls that were fogged from the outside rain, making it seem as if they were in another world completely.

"It's pretty!" Camille exclaimed. She went to stand next to several palm trees near the door, touching the leaves gently.

Karissa smiled. "That's a bamboo palm," she said, remembering how long it had taken her to find the tree in Anchorage. "And that one's a pygmy date palm. I have eleven varieties of palms. But come, I'll show you my favorite tree." She led the way to the ficus benjamina that now reached above her head. "This is a weeping fig. That's its common name." She ran her hands lightly through the small, bright-green leaves.

"I like this one the best," Camille said, pointing to a plant with large leaves. "What's it called?"

"Monstera deliciosa or split-leaf philodendron," Karissa replied. "All plants have at least two names, you know. Their Latin one and their common one."

"The air feels funny in here," Savannah said.

"It's the moisture in the air. But it's not nearly as high as these plants would like. I keep the temperature and the humidity just high enough so they can flourish, but not high enough to make it too uncomfortable for humans. I wanted it to be—" She stopped abruptly. These children didn't need to know about her desperate wish to have a child.

"Enough of this," she said. "Don't you want to play in the sand?"

All the children looked longingly at the huge circle of sand, and Rosalie took a step in that direction. Savannah stopped her. "We can't. It's Sunday, you know. And besides, we're in our pajamas."

Karissa was amazed at their strength and self-discipline. "We'll come back tomorrow, then," she promised.

"Oh, can't you tell us some more names of the plants?" begged Camille.

Karissa thought she might have just found a kindred soul. "Sure. Look, this one's an orange tree. And I have a grapefruit as well. I brought those with me from California."

"Do they give real fruit?"

"Yes, really small ones in October. But only if I remember to pollinate them."

"What?"

"Pollinate. It's what the bees usually do. But here I have to shake the blossoms to spread the pollen around. It's quite involved."

Karissa continued with her explanation as Camille listened in fascination and the others with tolerance. Then she moved on to the next plant. Before she realized it, she had named over half the plants in the greenhouse.

"Girls," Brionney called from the door, "your father's home. Time for scripture and prayer."

"Bye, Aunt Karissa," the girls chimed together. Savannah and Rosalie ran toward their mother, but Camille paused. "I really like the plants," she said. "Do you think I could help you water them tomorrow?"

"Sure, Camille."

The little girl ran off, padding on her bare feet along the pathway.

"Thank you, Karissa," Brionney said from the doorway. "I appreciate your letting the girls come in here, and for letting us stay at your house."

"You're welcome." Karissa found she meant it. "Besides, if you keep making food like that, I'm going to beg you to stay."

Brionney laughed. "Trial and error, you know. I wasn't always such a good cook. And now I'm afraid I eat too much. I was thin once—not like you, but thinner than now. Only I keep getting pregnant and never have the chance to get it off." She shrugged. "My only comfort is that Jesse has gained weight, too."

They laughed together. "Jesse really loves you," Karissa told her. "I don't think it matters to him what you weigh."

"You're right, it doesn't. But all men aren't that way." A curious shadow flitted over her face and was gone. Karissa wondered what it meant. For the first time, she felt something other than envy for the other woman. Perhaps it was the beginning of friendship.

After Brionney left, Karissa made the rounds to her favorite plants, checking for pests and watering problems. She had enjoyed being with the girls, and an idea was forming in her mind. Even though she couldn't have her own children, perhaps she could find a way to share in these three little girls' lives.

Or perhaps finally a specialist would be able to help her have a baby. Karissa couldn't help the new hope burgeoning inside. Fresh and painful though the feeling was, she didn't fight it. For once, she would allow herself to dream, however briefly, of a happier future.

She went to bed happily, curled up against Malcolm. But she had forgotten the medication, and the dream came again, relentlessly pushing its way into her subconscious. *She was looking out the window in an upper floor of her house, a baby cradled in her arms. The baby clapped her hands joyfully as Karissa showed her the outside world. Then the baby was falling from the window as Karissa clutched at the empty air after her, screaming in horror, "No! I didn't drop you! Come back!"*

The baby looked at her calmly as she plunged to the dark earth, seeming to ask, "Why did you do it?"

Karissa awoke, sweating in the cold of the night. At her side, Malcolm slept soundly. She felt at the nightstand beside her bed and grabbed a sleeping pill, swallowing it dry. There. Now there would be no more dreams.

CHAPTER 5

Malcolm awoke early on Monday morning. He showered and dressed before Karissa had even stirred. Finally, he woke her with a single kiss on her cheek. She opened her eyes groggily.

"Sorry to wake you," he said, "but the doctor's coming in especially for us. We wouldn't want to keep him waiting."

The hope flared in her emerald eyes before she could stop it. For a moment she looked so . . . so unprotected in her white nightgown with her tousled hair framing her face. As if reading his thoughts, she turned her head. When she next met his gaze, her feelings had been masked, leaving only the memory.

She should have hope, he thought. He did. He could never believe they wouldn't have children, even if they were to adopt. Having Jesse's daughters at the house had only increased his desire for a child. But would Karissa agree to adoption? The only time he had ever brought it up, she had reacted violently. "There's nothing wrong with me!" she had said. Her face flushed, and he sensed there was something she was not telling him.

"But maybe this is what we're supposed to do," he'd countered.

"If God wants us to have a baby, then He'll give us a reason why we can't have children. Or He'll send us a baby. Maybe we're not ready to be parents yet. Let's just give it more time!"

So he had backed off, thinking that maybe she wasn't ready. Now two more years had slipped away.

While Karissa showered, Malcolm made coffee and toast. She appeared a mere fifteen minutes later with her hair still hanging in wet tendrils. She was dressed in a sleek black and white plaid suit that hugged her slender figure and accentuated her womanliness. He had always appreciated her beauty. It was what had drawn him to her at the first, though he had found so much more beyond her physical appearance. Or at least he had once.

"Coffee?" he asked.

She shook her head. "Not today. Is there any orange juice?"

"Yes, but I think Brionney must have brought it. Have some, and we'll replace hers on the way back."

They ate their toast and jam in silence, occasionally glancing at each other. *Why don't we have anything to say?* Malcolm wondered.

A flurry of footsteps on the kitchen stairs broke the silence, and he looked up to see three curious faces peering in the door. Malcolm glanced at Karissa, whose features softened as she spied the children. Once again, he was reminded of the woman he had married.

Jesse appeared in the doorway behind the girls, rubbing his eyes. He looked at Malcolm. "Looks like I'm on breakfast detail for the next few months. Brionney can barely get out of bed in the morning. She still feels sick during the afternoon, but at least she can function somewhat then. I feel so bad for her."

"She's sick because we're going to have a baby," Savannah said.

"I wish Mom would have two so I could have one all to myself," Camille mumbled. Jesse gave a short, abrupt laugh, but for a brief moment his brown eyes looked strangely sad.

Malcolm smiled. "We'll leave you to it, then. Karissa and I have an appointment in Kodiak." He glanced at his watch. "You ready, hon?"

"Yes." She said good-bye to the girls and followed him out the door.

Since both needed to go to work after the appointment, they drove separately to Kodiak in the drizzling rain. As they approached the hospital, Malcolm's nervousness grew. So much seemed to be riding on this new doctor; he didn't know if their marriage could take one more failure.

The sky was streaked with different shades of gray, looking like a child's painting, but one with a certain something that demanded his attention. The clouds were not puffy like those from a storybook, but were long, irregular ones, random and erratic, yet striking a chord within him. Behind these odd clouds, the sun tried to poke through, sending shafts of frail light into the bold gray. Far beyond the clouds, out over the water, Malcolm could see a large blue stretch of sky, reaching as far as he could see. The end to the rain was on the way—if the direction of the wind held.

He stifled the urge to stop and get out the video camera he usually kept in the Jeep for opportunities like this. The clouds would make a great scene in his documentary.

Dr. Taylor had arrived at the hospital and was waiting for them in one of the examining rooms. He was an extremely thin, youngish man of average height who had pale hazel eyes. He was nearly bald, except for a scruffy fringe of white hair circling the back of his head. "Ah, Mr. and Mrs. Mathees? Come on in. How are you today?"

"Good, thanks. And yourself?" Malcolm asked, shaking the man's hand. Karissa shook his hand as well, but was strangely silent, her face drawn and white.

The doctor smiled as he picked up their file. Each of his motions exuded a sense of brisk confidence. "I've examined your records, and I must say, I feel the other doctors' assessments were correct. However, I'm willing to do all the tests again, if that's what you want."

"It is," Karissa said.

"Very well, let's do it. Maybe we'll find something the others missed." Dr. Taylor called in his assistant and went to work.

"I'll call you by the end of the week to let you know the results, and about any additional tests we might need," the doctor said when they were finished.

Malcolm stood up and proffered his hand. "Thank you."

"Uh, Dr. Taylor?" Karissa began hesitantly. "Do you think that the way a person eats could affect fertility? I mean, if we ate right and didn't smoke, could it have any effect?"

"Well, nutrition is vital in reproduction, and while I don't think it has actually been proven to affect conception, my feeling is this: if it helps during pregnancy, then why not before? Certainly stranger things have happened. If I can find nothing physically wrong with you, then it's as good a chance as anything that poor nutrition or smoking could be the cause. We're a long way from knowing everything about the human body.

"As to whether or not you should quit smoking in the overall picture, consider that if you don't quit smoking, any baby you do have will be at risk. In fact, I just recently read that over six thousand children die annually in the United States because their parents smoke. Many of the deaths are caused by low birth weight because their mothers smoked while they were pregnant, and another two thousand deaths that are labeled sudden infant death syndrome are actually ascribed to secondhand smoke. Then there are more than a thousand respiratory failures and hundreds of children who are burned to death in fires related to smoking. And children also die from smoking- related asthma attacks. Our country spends billions of dollars a year to treat asthma and ear infections that could be eliminated if the children's parents would quit smoking." The doctor shook his head. "Those are not pretty numbers, either in dollars or in deaths."

"I had never realized it was so serious," Karissa said, her green eyes open wider than Malcolm had ever seen them.

"Then there's the whole question of your own health," the doctor continued, "and the choices your child will make when he's older. Do you want your child to smoke? Do you want to die of lung cancer before you get to play with your grandchildren? These are some serious questions all smoking parents have to ask themselves. Me, I'd rather see those cancer-sticks banned completely. I've seen too much hurt and death because of them."

For a moment the doctor's professional manner had slipped, and Malcolm could see the inner man. He had the distinct impression that Dr. Taylor cared about them deeply, that he was the type who cared not only about his own patients, but even people he only read about. In Malcolm's opinion, there were not many men like him left in the world.

"Now, your last doctor prescribed fertility pills," Dr. Taylor continued in his former brisk manner. "I'd rather wait until all the tests come in before I do that again. I'm hopeful we'll find and resolve whatever it is that's holding you up."

"Thank you," Karissa said, then walked with him to the door. "I appreciate your coming in to see us."

"Anytime. But you're not my only patients on this island, only my first. I'm seeing four other couples today."

Malcolm nodded. When specialists did visit Kodiak, they usually had people lined up to see them. Dr. Taylor would probably have others coming in besides those with firm appointments.

As they left the room, Karissa looked at Malcolm, holding his eyes with her gaze. "What would you consider your greatest sin?"

Malcolm's eyebrows rose in surprise. "My greatest sin?"

"Yes. You do believe in sin, don't you?"

"Well, I've sinned in the past—"

"No, I don't mean those kinds of sins." She glanced briefly down at the shiny tile in the hospital corridor where the overhead lights reflected from above, then focused again intently on his face. "There's nothing you can do about those kinds of sins. You can't go back and change the past. I mean sins we do every day, like smoking."

"Is smoking a sin?" he asked, wishing he knew what she was driving at.

"The Church says it is, and so does the medical community. It hurts our bodies." She paused, as though waiting for him to say something.

"Yes, I guess it is a sin," he said. "I just haven't thought about it. But is it any worse than drinking and not going to church? I don't know how you can classify sins as being better or worse. They're all sins."

"Would you be willing to give up smoking and coffee and alcohol for a baby?" Her green eyes still refused to leave his, and he couldn't look away.

"Does this have anything to do with my mother?" He didn't bother to keep the aggravation from his voice.

Her lips pursed slightly. "Maybe. But your nephew said that if we wanting something, we should be willing to give up our greatest sin. Do you think that might work for us? Despite . . . despite . . ."

Whatever she had planned on saying, she obviously couldn't finish it. Malcolm felt a rush of tenderness toward his wife. She was usually so self-assured. "Are you asking me if God would help us?"

She looked away. "I—I guess so."

He wanted to reply, but didn't know the answer. It had been a long time since he had been sure about anything regarding religion. He took a step away, finally free of her eyes, but she put a hand on his arm.

"I'm willing to do it, Malcolm." She met his gaze once again. "Are you? I'll give up smoking and everything that's not healthy, if you will."

He made a quick decision, prompted by her desperate expression. "Let's give it a try."

She shook her head. "No. I can't just try. I have to do it. Trying makes it sounds like I might fail." She had never looked so vulnerable as she did at that moment, and Malcolm knew he still loved her.

"Okay, Karissa. We'll do it." He hugged her tightly. When he let her go, she had hold of his cigarettes, lifted from the front pocket of his button-down shirt. She tossed them into a garbage can, then rummaged through her purse to throw her Camels into the bin as well. She looked determined, and Malcolm felt guilty for the craving already rising in his gut.

"Are you going out to Karluk again?" she asked.

He nodded. "We finished the commercial, but I decided to work on my documentary while I'm there. It'll be another day or so before I have enough footage of the area, then I'll move to the other parts of Kodiak that I want to film. I especially want to get some good shots from the top of Pillar, and of course I'll need to go to the National Wildlife Refuge. Not everyone knows that three quarters of Kodiak is a wildlife preserve."

"Not many people outside of Alaska have even heard of Kodiak."

"They will when my documentary is aired." He still felt content-ment at having found ample backing for his pet project. He enjoyed the work much more than shooting commercials.

"Better not make it too good, or we'll have more tourists than we can handle," she teased.

He was glad to see her smile again. "But where else can you catch halibut over three hundred pounds?"

She laughed. "A lot of places in Alaska."

"Yeah, but none so pretty as Kodiak."

"I guess." Her voice lacked conviction, as it always did when they discussed Kodiak's wonders. Before he could think about it too deeply, she grimaced at her watch. "I've got to go. Good luck. I'll see you tonight." She kissed him quickly on the lips, then turned and disappeared in the direction of her office.

Malcolm watched after her for a moment. Then he glanced down and saw his full pack of cigarettes in the open wastebasket. With a quick check to make sure no one was looking, he scooped them out and put them back in his pocket. No use letting a full pack go to waste. He could give it to one of the guys working the cameras for him.

"Hey Malcolm!"

Guiltily he turned. "Hi, Jesse."

"Have you seen Karissa?" Jesse was out of breath, as though he had been hurrying. "She's not in her office, and I've got to go over some of these papers with her. I'm late getting here because of Brionney being sick and because Savannah took so long getting ready for school, and now I'm worried about having the presentation ready before this afternoon."

"She should be in her office now. We just finished our appointment."

"Oh, thanks." Jesse ran his hand through his hair. "For such a small place, Kodiak can get awfully hectic." He turned to go. "At least the rain seems to be letting up."

"Uh, Jesse," Malcolm said.

His friend paused. "Yes?"

"Well, I was just going to ask you about your mission. You went to England, right?"

"Yeah. It was great."

"The best two years of your life?" Malcolm tried to make his voice light, but the words his nephew had spoken at his homecoming had been bothering him.

"The best two years? I don't know about that. It was fun and hard and spiritual, but nothing compared to when Brionney and I were married in the Provo Temple. And then my daughters were born— that was really neat. And I've had some wonderful experiences blessing them or spending time with them. No, my mission definitely wasn't the best two years of my life, not at all. And I expect the future holds even better things in store." He watched Malcolm curiously. "What's this about, anyway?"

Malcolm shrugged. "Just wondering. Some men say their missions were the best two years of their entire lives. I wanted to know what you thought."

"Well, you could ask yourself. I mean, I'll bet you and Karissa have had some touching moments, experiences that keep you together. You know." He clapped Malcolm on the back. "We'll see you at your place. I really appreciate your letting us stay there." He snapped his fingers. "That reminds me, I'm supposed to pick up a treat for family night. Can't forget, or the girls'll never forgive me." Pulling out a thin note pad, he scribbled something as he walked down the hall.

The minute Jesse was out of sight, Malcolm's smile vanished. What *was* keeping him and Karissa together? They had no great moments together, no spiritual experiences worth mentioning. They had their work, their occasional trips, and their house. That was all. He thought he loved her, but sometimes she was more distant than a stranger.

As he left the hospital, Malcolm automatically felt for his cigarettes. He remembered at the last moment and shoved them back into his pocket. Already he could tell it was going to be a long day.

CHAPTER 6

Karissa eyed the members of the board surrounding the large table. Each seemed satisfied with her presentation of how the new programs were simplifying procedures at the hospital. Now she just had to sit back and let Jesse explain how he and his two partners would further customize his designs. As she listened, she was impressed with his attention to detail. Malcolm had been right; Jesse was a good choice for this job.

Weak beams of light beat at the pair of elongated windows on one side of the room, but not a hint of warmth penetrated the thick panes. Karissa felt cold. At least the rain had finally stopped its incessant patter. Malcolm would be glad for the blue sky and the opportunity to film without interruption—until the next deluge. The constant rain was one more irritating thing about Kodiak. She hated the continuous drizzle. Who cared if that was what made the summers so green? She wished she didn't have to be on Kodiak this summer—or at all, for that matter.

Her mind wandered back to Dr. Taylor's fertility tests and her decision to give up smoking. Stopping after so many years wouldn't be easy, but she *had* to succeed, if only to prove to herself that she was doing everything in her power to conceive a child. As though reading her mind, Damon Wolfe pulled a pack of cigarettes from his pocket. He flicked one out and put it between his lips, for a moment looking more falcon-like than usual. He proffered the pack to her.

Her mouth felt dry, and it was all she could do not to accept just one little cigarette. Several others on the board were also smoking, as the board room was one of the few places smoking was allowed in the hospital. No one would think anything about her joining in with the others.

But she would know. And if she really wanted to have a baby, she *had* to beat this habit.

She shook her head at Damon, and instead reached inside her jacket pocket for the Lifesavers she had bought from the vending machine in the hall. In front of her on the mahogany table, a cup of water had replaced the coffee she usually drank. She felt tired, and wished for the kick the caffeine normally gave her. Would just a swallow or two hurt? She bit the inside of her lower lip. *I won't give in.*

It was going to be a long day.

She didn't let herself think about the nights. Without sleeping pills would the dreams come more often? No matter, she would endure them. Her body would be free of all detrimental substances, one way or the other.

* * * *

When Karissa arrived home at six o'clock, dinner was in the oven and Brionney sat on a bar stool near the sink, washing vegetables for a salad. Her legs, clad in black stretch pants, twisted to one side so she could sit closer to the running water. A growing pile of washed lettuce made a large mound on the cutting board.

"Smells good." Karissa removed her high heels and slipped them into the closet near the door, exchanging them for her comfortable slippers. The hiking boots she had worn Saturday had finally dried, and she kicked them into the closet with the other shoes.

"It's roast. The first thing I ever learned to cook."

Karissa smiled. "Me too. Need a hand?"

"No. I'm just about finished. Why don't you sit and rest?"

"You're the one who should be resting."

Brionney flashed her a dimpled smile. "That's why I'm sitting on this chair. Besides, as long as I keep my stomach comfortably full and don't stand up too much, I can get by. I keep telling myself it'll only be for the first six months." Her laugh warmed Karissa's heart.

"I thought the magic number was three."

"Well, I guess no one heard that in my family. We always feel much better after about six."

"That's rotten."

"Yeah, tell me about it."

"So where are the girls?"

Brionney grimaced. "In the greenhouse. I hope you don't mind. They told me you said it was all right. They played outside in the snow, but it's so slushy and they got so wet and cold . . ."

"It's okay." The headache that pounded at Karissa's temples seemed to throb with more intensity. She shuffled to the large window and peered through the plants into the greenhouse. The girls were there, all right. Savannah and Rosalie played in the sand while Camille flitted from plant to plant, studying and occasionally reaching out to smooth a shiny leaf. "They look like they're having a good time."

Brionney hopped off the stool, drying her hands with her apron. "I warned them about hurting anything."

Karissa met Brionney's anxious stare and shrugged. "They can't hurt anything that can't be replaced." As she said it, the words became true. Her body felt almost tingly—a sensation she hadn't felt in years, though it seemed familiar. What could it be?

"Did you have a hard day?" asked Brionney. "You seem kind of tired."

"I quit smoking," Karissa said.

"You did? Why?"

"It was time."

Brionney seemed to understand that Karissa didn't want to be questioned further. "If there's anything I can do, I would love to help. You and Malcolm have really been great to us."

Karissa's headache had eased now. For some inexplicable reason, she felt drawn to Brionney. Why was she so easy to talk to? She could almost be one of Karissa's sisters. "There is something," she said impulsively. "But I wouldn't insist if it didn't appeal to you, especially since you're pregnant. I mean, you probably wouldn't want to, but in case you didn't mind—"

"What is it?" Brionney asked, a slight smile playing on her lips.

Karissa took a deep breath. It wasn't like her to be so indecisive. "Well, instead of finding some other place to rent, you could stay here. In return for your stay, you could make dinner. Just Monday through Friday. Something healthy. I've never been one for taking the time to do it, and I feel ready for a change."

The other woman looked thoughtful. "That seems too good to be true. I mean, when you're fixing a meal anyway, two extra people don't make much difference. But maybe we could pay you something in addition."

Karissa shook her head. "It won't cost us anything extra to have you here. Just water and heat and the like. And that will be in exchange for you making the dinners."

"Well, I really like that idea. Jesse could drive Savannah in to school, and I could pick her up in the afternoon. And I could make extra dinners on Saturdays and freeze them, just in case I'm not feeling well during the week. I admit, I've certainly slept better since coming here. But your home is so beautiful, so private. Are you sure we won't be too much of a bother?"

Karissa took a deep breath through her nose, enjoying the smell of the roast. "Not if you keep cooking like that."

Brionney seemed pleased. "Well, I'll have to talk to Jesse, but for me, I like the idea. We could try it, say, for a month, and see how we like it."

"Deal," Karissa agreed. "Now, do you think we have time to build a sandcastle before the men come home?"

Brionney laughed and untied her apron. "Why not?"

In the end, Brionney made a castle with Savannah and Rosalie, while Karissa showed Camille her array of plant books. Camille was fascinated, and Karissa relished the attention to her beloved plants.

All too soon the men arrived, and they gathered in the dining room for a proper dinner. The rectangular room was comfortably large without being ostentatious. The floor was carpeted in a dark gray, except for beneath the cherry table, where a large rectangle of ceramic tile had been inserted to catch spills. The walls were painted off-white up to the dark wood trim at their halfway point, and above this a ginger-colored wallpaper broke the monotony. An oversized mirror took up one of the longer walls, and under it stood a small wall table with knickknacks. On the opposite wall hung a large picture of Jesus, double-matted and framed in cherry wood. He had black hair and kind brown eyes. Over a loose white shirt he wore a red robe.

Karissa covered the long table with the hand-embroidered and crocheted cloth Malcolm's mother had given them for their wedding. It was the first time she had used it.

"What's the special occasion?" Malcolm asked.

"Our quitting smoking," she said lightly. Of course there was more news, but she and Brionney had agreed to talk to their husbands privately before opening her idea up for discussion.

Camille hugged Malcolm's leg. "Oh, thank you, Uncle Malcolm! I've been praying so hard that you wouldn't die."

Malcolm chuckled uneasily. He bent and picked Camille up, setting her gently on a chair.

"Now don't spill anything," Jesse warned, "or we'll be kicked out in the snow."

Karissa laughed. "The tablecloth can be washed."

The noise level in the room was high but comfortable. Karissa felt transported back in time to her own large family. Oh, how she missed them! Malcolm's face curved into a satisfied smile, and she knew he must also be remembering his own days as a child.

After dinner, the children insisted that Malcolm and Karissa have family night with them. Malcolm immediately gave in to Savannah's pleading blue eyes and Camille's trusting smile. Karissa felt more reluctant.

"Why don't we use the sitting room?" Malcolm suggested.

Brionney blanched. "I think it would be better to use the toy room upstairs. The girls have a hard time keeping still."

"But it's perfect for a family night," Malcolm said. "Come on, I'll show you."

The sitting room was off the main entrance where the polished oak staircase swept up to the second floor. Though they mostly used the kitchen stairway, Karissa had insisted on this more elaborate one when they were building the house. She had long envisioned her daughter sweeping down the stairs in an elegant prom dress, while her date stared in awe below.

They passed the staircase and went into the sitting room. A tall window graced the front wall, with a six-foot ficus tree on one side and a slightly smaller avocado on the other. All the furniture in the room was of light oak, handmade by Malcolm in his high school years. "I used to make things out of wood," he told the girls. "See this long couch? I made the wood part. The cushions I had buy 'cause I didn't have time for sewing, but see how comfortable it is?"

A clock like the one he had given Karissa for her office hung on the wall above the fireplace, and a handmade doily from his mother decorated the coffee table. A two-foot-high figure of a little girl with long hair sat on the marble hearth.

Savannah pointed to the little girl. "Did you make that?"

"Not me," Malcolm answered, reverently touching the wood. "Though I might try one some day. But my grandfather made this one. He was Aleut, you know."

"What's Al-ee-oot?" asked Rosalie.

"The Aleut are the native people who were here before the white folk," Malcolm said. "You've seen them around." The girls nodded. "I'm half Aleut myself," he continued. "My mother's family have been on the island for generations."

"Is that why you make good things out of wood?" asked Camille.

"Well, not really. I just learned by watching my grandfather when I was really little. He died, though, when I was about your age, and I learned the rest in school and from books." He settled on the couch next to Karissa, with Rosalie in his arms. "But that's enough about wood, don't you think? Let's get down to family night—and especially the treat. You did remember that, didn't you, Jesse?"

Jesse nodded, and the girls cheered.

To Karissa's embarrassment, the family night lesson was on the Word of Wisdom. She fumed inwardly. Why had she given in to her impulse and asked Brionney to stay? Now she would have to endure censorship in her own home. *I can eat or drink what I please,* she thought, before remembering that a scarce eleven hours before, it was she who had decided to change her habits—that in fact, her desire to eat right was the principal reason she had asked Brionney to stay.

"Maybe Aunt Karissa can tell us why she decided to quit smoking," Brionney said. Her eyes fell on Karissa, not demanding, but curious.

"It's not good for my body," Karissa replied. *And I want to have a baby.* But she didn't say the last words aloud. Those were too private. Only Malcolm knew her secret. She flashed him a look, warning without words; he nodded imperceptibly. To her relief, Brionney moved on to other aspects of the Word of Wisdom. The lesson was surprisingly brief.

"We keep it short to hold their attention," Jesse whispered to Karissa.

Karissa smiled, but inside she still fumed. There was no way she wanted them to stay now. Why hadn't she thought it through before opening her big mouth?

Much later, in the privacy of their room, Karissa told Malcolm about her invitation to the Hergarters. "I love the idea," Malcolm said. "Those kids are so cute. And we could stand having a few regular meals together, couldn't we? They'd be healthy meals, too." His arms encircled her waist, pulling her close. He kissed her lingeringly on the mouth.

Karissa could tell he was in a romantic mood, as he always was when they decided to try again for a baby, but she was too caught up in figuring out how to un-invite the Hergarters to respond to him. The only way she could think of going back on the deal was to have Malcolm refuse.

"Of course, that means more wear and tear on the house and furniture," she said. "I'd better tell them it's not a good idea."

His hand tangled in her long hair. "But we always meant to have a lot of children, like our parents. This will be good practice."

Karissa wanted to tell him that at thirty-one, it wasn't likely she would be having "a lot of children." She would be grateful for just one or two.

"But they'll interrupt our privacy and get in the way," Karissa ventured.

"I feel very private," he murmured in her ear. "This house could hold three families and we wouldn't run into each other. I think you made a good decision. Besides, since you've decided that I'm not smoking anymore, at least allow me some good food."

"Me! We're doing this for a baby!" she retorted before she saw his teasing smile.

"Come on. Forget them. Let's talk about what kind of baby crib I'm going to make. I ordered the wood today before going to Karluk. I've got the plans right here." He pointed to a book on the table next to the bed.

Karissa couldn't remember the last time had Malcolm built something, and the thought brought a lump to her throat. She smiled and kissed him. "I want one that rocks," she said softly.

That night the dream didn't come.

CHAPTER 7

Malcolm was on his way to Karluk long before the sun rose Tuesday morning. He had wanted to capture on film the way sunrise angled into the valley and the details of Aleutian morning life. He wanted to catch the men leaving to fish and the women cooking or hanging their laundry to dry. The black-haired, large-eyed children were his favorite. Their ready smiles stood out on their chubby cheeks whenever they caught sight of him.

Without taking his eyes from the road, he opened the glove compartment in his Jeep to check his supply of candy for the Aleutian children. The dim light revealed a whole package of taffy—the children's favorite—and also the pack of cigarettes Karissa had tried to throw away the day before.

He made a guttural noise. A whole day without cigarettes! Yesterday he had kept feeling his shirt pocket for a cigarette, and each time had felt relief that he had left them in the jeep. Of course, he had meant to give the pack to the camera crew—like him, they weren't partial to any brand—and he still didn't know why he hadn't remembered.

A sudden craving bit deep into him, penetrating his entire body. The Jeep slowed and came to a stop on the dirt road. The engine stalled. For a long moment, Malcolm sat staring at the pack of cigarettes nestled in the dash compartment. The only light came from the tiny bulb inside. He licked his lips and felt them grow cold in the freezing air. The windows began to fog from the heat of his breath.

No one would know, he thought.

He pictured Karissa's face, and knew how hurt she would be if she found out he hadn't upheld his part of the bargain, even though it

had been a bargain she had forced upon him. He found it difficult to
believe that quitting smoking would help them have a child—at least
not on his part. Karissa's quitting made sense, since her body carried a
limited supply of eggs, but a man's reproductive system was continually renewing itself. Smoking should make no difference.

But you said you would try, his conscience whispered.

He sighed. "I'll have a piece of candy instead. It worked
yesterday." He laughed, but the sound held no mirth. "At this rate,
I'm going to gain weight."

He pulled out the bag of taffy, but the cigarettes on top came
with it. His hand closed over them almost greedily.

Throw them out, he told himself. *Now, quick.*

But he couldn't litter. Besides, that would mean good money
going to waste. "I'll just finish this pack," he murmured.. Then no
more. I can do it. It's not like I'm really addicted or anything. I can
stop when I want to."

He felt relief at the decision and quickly started the Jeep. Not
until he was moving again did he light up. He breathed the smoke in
deeply, and gradually the jitters he had felt for the past day subsided.

Just this pack, he thought. *Then I'll quit. No one will ever have to know.*

* * * *

Early Tuesday morning Brionney sat on the edge of the tub,
facing in the direction of the toilet, just in case. Not for the first time
she wished the guest bathroom was smaller, instead of half the size of
their spacious bedroom. It took her three large steps to make it to the
toilet in the corner. She'd counted them. So far, she'd made it every
time. Her stomach moved uneasily, and she imagined she was on a
ship in a stormy sea. She felt terrible, but knew the feeling would
pass. Why couldn't she remember how awful pregnancy was until it
was upon her? If only she had remembered, she might have put it off
a bit longer.

Three children already, she thought. *How on earth can I handle
another?* When Rosalie turned three, Brionney had felt ready, but now
she was not so sure. The uncertainty triggered a mountain of guilt.
The picture of Jesus on the wall next to the sink seemed to look down
on her with knowing eyes. *Can you help me?* she pleaded silently.

She studied the picture. Jesus was siting on a rock, teaching a group of people. *What is this picture doing here in the bathroom?* Now that she thought about it, there were many pictures of Jesus in the house. In every room practically, except maybe the sitting room; she didn't remember seeing one there. Maybe Karissa and Malcolm weren't as far removed from religious matters as she had thought. How could she help them? She gave a long sigh.

"Are you sure you want to stay here?" Jesse asked sympathetically, standing in front of the sink across the room. He had been shaving when she barreled into the bathroom. Now he stood helplessly, the lather still covering most of his face, not knowing how to help her. "I mean, it might be too much work for you."

"I have to make dinner anyway. And with their cleaning lady, I won't have to clean much."

"But I thought you didn't like Karissa. You thought she was too cold."

She met his gaze. "I think I may have been wrong." She held up her hand. "I know, I know. You always say that I judge too quickly, but in my experience, the worst generally is true." Jesse frowned, but Brionney pretended not to notice. The wounds of her past were healed, but not completely forgotten, despite her husband's devotion. "I know it may seem strange," she continued, "but I feel we should stay. And I really am beginning to like Karissa. She's a nice person."

Jesse nodded and faced the mirror, but turned again when a sob escaped her. He tossed his razor into the sink and crossed the space between them. "What's wrong?"

"I keep thinking about the gas." She nearly choked on the words. "What if we lose this baby because of it?" She caressed her stomach. Already it seemed as if she could feel her child there, growing. Unbidden, the green plant container on her dresser came to mind. In it there was dirt, topped by two flat rocks—a remembrance she could not let go. Not yet.

He sat next to her on the edge of the tub. "We're not going to lose him."

"Him?" she asked.

"Hey, it's gotta happen sometime."

She smiled. "Maybe." But her smile vanished as suddenly as it had come. "Sometimes I think I can't handle any more children, that maybe it wouldn't be so bad to have a another miscarriage. But then I feel like I would die if that were to happen. I just can't face it! Already I love this baby!"

"It won't happen. We won't let it." He caressed her neck and kissed her cheek. The white cream on his face rubbed off onto hers. "If you're really worried, let's have the doctor do an ultrasound. I can make an appointment when I go to the hospital today."

"No, not yet. I'd rather wait until he suggests it. I don't want to be chasing ghosts because of . . . of the last time."

"Then trust me," he said. "I have a feeling about this one. In less than seven months, we'll be changing his diapers." He paused to let the words sink in. "And just to show you how much I appreciate my first son, I'll change all his diapers for two whole weeks. Except the six-wipe diapers. I can't take those."

Brionney chuckled, and this time she felt happy. Jesse had always made her laugh. It was one of the reasons she had married him. "I love you, Jesse Hergarter, but I'm holding you to that promise, *including* the six-wipe diapers."

He sighed. "You are so demanding."

"Get used to it," she returned with a smile.

He stood up to finish his shave. "Only seven more months to go."

CHAPTER 8

Karissa hummed as she arrived home from work on Friday evening. It was still light outside, and each day was getting lighter earlier as summer approached. The snow was nearly all melted now, and she could feel spring in the air. Of course, another snowstorm could delay spring, but not for long.

She parked in the garage, noticing that the door to Malcolm's studio was ajar. The spacious room in back of the house connected to the garage by a set of double doors that opened wide enough for his filming equipment. Karissa could hear giggles coming from the room.

Her good mood evaporated. *What were those girls up to now?* Malcolm hated people in his studio when he wasn't present. This could very well be the end to the Hergarters' stay. Karissa couldn't decide if she was disappointed or relieved. The week had passed smoothly without further awkward incident, and the meals had been spectacular. She found she enjoyed having the children greet her as she came home, and Brionney was fast becoming like a sister. But there was another side as well. The Hergarters' presence was a daily reminder of her barrenness.

"But that's going to change," she mumbled. Only today she had heard from the doctor.

The laughter sounded again, and Karissa quickened her pace. Maybe she could get them out before Malcolm returned home.

"Girls—" She broke off as she passed into the room. Malcolm was on the couch with Savannah and Rosalie beside him, their blonde heads pressed against his body. The dark-haired Camille sprawled on his lap. The group sat with stares fixed on the half-sized movie screen Malcolm used to view and edit his work.

"Oh, look at that!" Camille said. Her brown eyes twinkled, seeming to emphasize the blue wash that made their color unique. "I love bears. I wish I could see one in real life."

"Hi," Karissa said. She had the strange feeling that she was intruding.

Malcolm scooted over and patted the seat beside Rosalie. "Come and watch. I saw a bear yesterday, and I filmed it for the girls. He's a beauty."

"It looks so close." The sheer power of the animal made Karissa nervous. She knew Malcolm had lenses that were able to take these pictures from a distance, but the reality was overwhelming.

Rosalie snuggled up to her with wide eyes. "I'm scared." But she didn't act afraid.

"Well, that's it," Malcolm said as the footage ended.

"Can we see it again?" the girls chimed.

"Later," he agreed. "But go see if you can help your mother with dinner. We'll be right in." Obediently, the girls scampered away.

"I heard from the doctor," Karissa said when the noise from the children had faded.

He sat up straighter. "And?"

She focused on the collection of pistols and rifles Malcolm kept on the far wall. The light reflected off the shiny bluing of the barrels. What was it with men and guns?

"Well?" he pressed.

She sighed. "Same as before. No reason why we can't have children. He says we should keep track of my ovulation, and he recommended some new fertility pills."

Malcolm's gray eyes bore into hers. "Maybe we should think about adopting."

Karissa stared toward the door where the girls had disappeared. There was a tenseness in her husband that she had never noticed before. "Maybe," she said. "But I really feel optimistic. I know it may sound silly, but since we quit smoking and started eating so many fruits and vegetables, my body seems stronger. Maybe this is working."

"You don't find it hard not to smoke?"

"Oh, yeah. But I try to tell myself it's mostly psychological. That helps." She didn't add that for all the urges to smoke, she had even stronger feelings of relief. It wasn't until she had quit that she realized how guilty she had felt each time she lit up. Now the guilt was gone, and for the first time since she started smoking, she was free.

"I've talked to several of the doctors at work about it, too," she added. "They've told me all about the psychological part. They're very supportive."

"Sort of your own built-in set of shrinks, eh?"

Karissa smiled. "Something like that. But the worst for me is the coffee. I've discovered that I'm not a morning person."

"I could have told you that." He leaned over and kissed her cheek.

Karissa laid her head on his shoulder. How long had it been since she had felt so close to him? "I think it's going to be okay," she murmured. He smoothed her hair, sending a delicious chill down her spine.

"Dinner!" Savannah's high voice called from the door. "Daddy's home and everything's on the table."

Karissa bounced up from the couch. "Good, I'm starved."

"It goes with not smoking," Malcolm said. "We'll probably get fat." An odd, sullen note in his voice made Karissa glance back at him. But he smiled. "I'll be right there. I just have to put away my film."

* * * *

Dinner was scarcely over when the doorbell rang. Karissa looked over the dish-covered table and met Malcolm's eyes. He shrugged, indicating that he wasn't expecting anyone. Their house was secluded, and visitors rarely popped in for a visit; if they weren't home, it would be a waste of a long drive. She pushed back her chair, hearing it scrape against the ceramic tile, and went to the door.

Delinda Goodrich smiled up at her from the porch. With her was her oldest daughter, whose name Karissa had forgotten. The young girl clutched a brown-wrapped package in her hand. Karissa already knew what was inside.

"Hi, Karissa," Delinda chirped brightly. She tossed her short red-brown hair as she spoke, and her heavy gold earrings sparkled in the evening light. In her fur coat, she reminded Karissa of the bear Malcolm had filmed. "We're so glad to have caught you at home. May we come in for a minute? I promise we won't stay long."

Karissa sighed and opened the door wider to allow her visiting teachers to come in. She didn't lead the way to the sitting room, but stood back in the entryway, wondering how quickly she could get rid of them. Delinda and her daughter were nice, but Karissa wished they would stop interrupting her life.

If Delinda noticed the lukewarm reception, she didn't let on. She removed her heavy fur coat amidst a tinkling of gold bracelets and quickly hung it in the closet. Underneath the coat, the woman looked much less like a bear, though her hips in the tight skirt were still large with many years of childbearing.

"May we sit?" Delinda asked. Her brown eyes met Karissa's without blinking or embarrassment.

"Sure. Come on."

Delinda followed Karissa into the sitting room, practically dragging her daughter along. The girl's hand clung to the lapels of her jacket as if to save herself from drowning, her pale, watery blue eyes avoiding Karissa's.

Do I look that scary? Karissa thought, feeling sorry for her.

Delinda plopped onto one end of the sofa Malcolm had made. She looked around the room appreciatively. "I love this room, ya know?" She reached out and grabbed hold of a wood bust on the table which depicted an old Aleut man. "I should start collecting stuff like this."

"I bought it for Malcolm," Karissa said. "It's made locally. You could probably find one."

"Maybe I will," Delinda said. She smiled. "The truth is, the instant I have any extra money, I spend it on jewelry." She held up her arm and shook it dramatically. A small array of thin gold bands tinkled.

Karissa had always been too busy trying to get rid of Delinda to find out much about her. In truth, the woman never stopped asking questions long enough for Karissa to do much but answer. It didn't seem right that Delinda should be so concerned with Karissa's life when Karissa didn't really care about Delinda's.

"Why do you like jewelry so much?" she found herself asking.

Delinda tugged on the thick gold rope around her neck. "Oh, I don't know. I think it has something to do with how I was raised. My mother is a very pretty woman, but she never cared much for jewelry or makeup. She's kind of like granola, ya know. Wholesome but not very head-turning like those elegant woman ya sometimes see. I wanted to be like that, and jewelry makes me feel that way."

"It becomes you," Karissa said. Delinda did look more glamorous for the jewelry.

"I like Grandma," Delinda's daughter said suddenly, darting a timid look at Karissa. She sat on the edge of the sofa gingerly, her body tucked in on itself. A nervous hand poked her long bright red hair behind her small ear, and her nose twitched as if the myriad of freckles on her face itched all at once.

"Why, landsakes, June, so do I! We're different, that's all."

Karissa suspected that June was more like her granola grandmother than her gold-dripping mother.

"Well, we just came to see what you was doing," Delinda babbled on. "I talked to Sister Hergarter, and she said she thought you'd be home tonight."

Brionney! So that was why they were here. *How dare she interfere!* Maybe this would be a good excuse to terminate their arrangement. Of course, that would mean no more good meals.

"Not that I told her I was coming," Delinda added. "I just wanted to know if I could call tonight. But when she said she thought you'd be home, I decided to drive up and see ya personally."

And get a hundred percent on your visiting teaching this month. Karissa bit her tongue to keep the words inside.

"We brought ya this," June said. Uncurling slightly, she leaned forward and shoved the package into Karissa's unwilling hand.

"How nice of you," Karissa murmured, not meaning it. She already knew what was inside. Every month they somehow managed to catch her at home or at the office, and each time they brought her another picture.

"I framed it myself," Delinda said. That, too, Karissa already knew. Delinda and seven of her nine children ran a picture framing business from their home in Kodiak, while Delinda's husband worked at one of the canneries.

"Open it," Delinda urged. Both visitors watched Karissa intently as she tore off the paper.

This time the picture of Jesus had been sketched in black and white. The Savior had tears coming from His eyes, and blood oozed from His forehead where a crown of plaited thorns encircled His head. Karissa felt His sad eyes beckon to her. She knew her sin had caused part of His pain, and to her His eyes held not only sadness but reproach. She looked away quickly.

"I love it." To her chagrin, a tear escaped the corner of her eye and her voice felt scratchy.

"I thought you could hang it in here," Delinda said. "I framed it in that light oak so it would match." The woman's sharp eyes hadn't misled her. The picture would go perfectly in the sitting room, as all the others hadn't.

"It will go great in here," Karissa said. "Which is good, since I don't have anyplace else to put it. The other pictures you've given me are hung in just about every room in the house, and of course there's that one you put up in my office." Her voice couldn't hide the irony. In fact, the only place that didn't sport one of Delinda's pictures was their bedroom and the connecting bathroom. She had drawn the line at that. Malcolm's studio had two pictures.

Delinda shrugged. "Never enough pictures of our Savior," she said. "But I chose this one because it goes with our lesson. The Savior died for our sins because He loves us so much. There is no sin His atonement can't cover."

But Karissa knew Delinda was wrong. She knew there were some things that were too serious, too horrifying for even the Savior to fix. Sighing inwardly, she steeled herself for the rest of the lesson.

* * * *

The next morning, Malcolm immersed himself in his studio. Karissa was in the greenhouse with the children, seeming happier than he had seen her for a long time. Maybe she was already expecting. Maybe now they would fill their house with love.

Was that what was missing? He couldn't understand how that could be the answer; he and Karissa loved each other. A baby would only cement their love.

He smiled. Pregnancy was supposed to make women beautiful, and Karissa was certainly that, though he had noticed that she did seem to be thinner than usual. Her collarbone stuck out more and the curves of her nose, chin, and cheeks were sharper. The shadowed hollows beneath her cheekbones had grown deeper, and her lithe figure had little of Brionney's attractive womanly roundness. Not that he was comparing the two women. Karissa was his, and he liked her just the way she was. But he did worry about her health. Had stress caused her to lose weight?

Habit drew him to the bottom drawer of the editing desk. In the back, behind a few rolls of blank film, he fingered the pack of unopened cigarettes. He had stretched out the other pack, having only a few each day, but yesterday he had used the last one. When he had gone to pick up the Friday paper, somehow this new pack had come with it. He couldn't remember buying it, though he knew he had.

He put the cigarettes back into the drawer, shut it, and tried to focus on his work.

Then he pulled open the drawer and took the pack out again.

And put it back without shutting the drawer. He stared at it for a long time, feeling a craving so large it filled his entire being.

Finally he reached in, removed the cellophane from the cigarettes, and took out just one.

CHAPTER 9

Saturday morning in late June came early. Warm sunlight reflected through the oversized windows and washed over the bedroom. Brionney stifled a yawn as she exchanged her bathrobe for a teal and white plaid top and matching solid teal stretch pants. "I don't think I'll ever get so used to it being light so much of the time."

Jessed grinned. "It is hard to sleep. But in the winter it'll be the opposite—too much dark."

"At least there's no snow now. And it's quiet. Sometimes I just lie in bed listening to the silence." She laughed and smoothed her top over her stomach. "Wow, if I'm this big before I'm even five months, what am I going to look like at nine?" In the ten weeks they had been at the Mathees', she had gained twenty pounds.

"You say that every time," Jesse said. "And you look cute."

"Thanks."

"I mean it."

"Remember, you get the diapers for two weeks."

"Not the six-wipe ones."

"Oh, yeah. Those too."

He sighed. "I think I'm gaining weight right along with you. These pants are too small." He tugged at the dark denim.

"We forgot your maternity clothes in Utah," Brionney said, batting her eyes at him innocently.

Jesse joined in her laughter. Every time she had been pregnant, he had gained nearly as much weight as she did. After the births, they would lose it together—or at least some of it.

"So what are you going to do while Malcolm and I go fishing?" he asked.

"Karissa and I are taking the kids to the park, and then going grocery shopping."

"Then get some lemons. We're going to need them to cook all the fish we're gonna catch."

Brionney kissed Jesse good-bye and headed toward the girls' room to see if they were dressed and ready to go. In the hall, the familiar queasiness bubbled up inside her, and she stopped and shut her eyes until the discomfort eased. *I hate being pregnant!*

"Are you all right?" Karissa asked, coming from her upstairs office.

Brionney opened her eyes. "Yeah. It'll pass."

"I can do the shopping alone," Karissa said. "And I can take the girls, too. You could stay home and rest."

Brionney fought the temptation to accept. She had come to know Karissa better during the past weeks, and she knew she could trust the other woman with her children. "No, I want to go. I need to get out. I really do." She rubbed a hand over her stomach and watched Karissa's eyes follow the motion.

"Do you feel it moving?" Karissa asked.

Brionney nodded.

"What does it feel like?"

Brionney thought for a moment. "Well, at first it feels like butter-flies, with their wings barely fluttering against my insides. Then it gradually gets harder as the baby grows. I knew one woman who claimed that her baby actually kicked her husband out of bed!"

Karissa smiled, her eyes going back to Brionney's stomach. "I wish I knew what it felt like." The overt longing in her voice brought a lump to Brionney's throat, and her guilt at not feeling ready for another child came to the surface. It didn't seem fair for her to be reluctantly blessed with a child when Karissa wanted one so badly.

"I wish you did too," she said. "I think you'd make a good mother."

"It's all I ever think about," Karissa admitted.

Brionney was surprised at the admission. Karissa usually avoided the topic of having children. She knew the Mathees were seeing a fertility specialist, but that was as much as she had learned.

"I just want a baby," Karissa continued, "but each month the test is negative." Tears came to her green eyes, reminding Brionney of emeralds in a pool of clear water. She reached out tentatively to the other woman, and felt relieved when Karissa didn't pull away.

"I thought quitting smoking would be more difficult," Karissa continued. "I thought I would suffer withdrawal and have to use those nicotine patches or something, but all I have to do is imagine my baby or watch your daughters play, and the desire leaves. That's got to mean something, doesn't it?"

"I think so," Brionney said. "Just give it a little more time."

Karissa nodded. "I appreciate you, Brionney, I really do. Thank you so much for sharing your family with me."

Brionney hugged her. "And thank you for sharing your house," she replied, not knowing what else to say.

Karissa drew away, slowly but deliberately. Brionney recognized the motion as a physical sign of the imaginary wall Karissa would now build around herself, a wall to hide from her pain. "Maybe it's all for the best," Karissa muttered.

Brionney grabbed her arm before it was out of reach. "No, I can't believe that. But I do believe the Lord knows what He's doing."

It was the wrong thing to say. A shadow flitted over Karissa's face like a dark convulsion. In that instant, Brionney saw a hint of the inner torture that was Karissa's, something that told of much more than her longing for a child. What had happened in her life? What was she hiding?

"Are we gonna go yet?" Rosalie asked from the doorway of her room. She wore red stretch pants and a pink top with blue hearts.

"Sure," Brionney said.

"Yay!" The girls' feet thundered down the kitchen stairs.

"There was a day," Brionney said to Karissa, "when I would never have let my children leave the house in mismatched clothes. Now, I just hope what they are wearing looks mostly clean."

Karissa smiled, and Brionney was relieved to see her pain tucked out of sight. "She looks adorable," Karissa said. "Completely adorable."

The girls were waiting for them in Brionney's white four-door Ford Tempo. Karissa slid into the front passenger seat while Brionney settled behind the wheel.

"Are you sure you don't want me to drive?" Karissa asked. She spoke formally, as if to distance herself from her previous show of familiarity. Brionney was accustomed to the change in attitude, but she wished Karissa would trust her more.

"No. For long drives like this, I have to drive or I'll get carsick," Brionney said lightly. "It happens only when I'm pregnant."

Karissa nodded and looked out the window, where bright sunlight played over the landscape. Lush green sprang from the hills and valleys, replacing the former slushy carpet of snow.

"I love the green," Karissa said above the noise coming from the girls in the backseat. "I hate everything about this island except the green."

The vehemence in her voice took Brionney by surprise. "I thought you loved Kodiak."

"Malcolm loves Kodiak."

Ten weeks of living with this couple, and Brionney realized there was still much she didn't know about them. "So how did you get into plant collecting?" she asked, searching for safe ground.

"I've always loved plants," Karissa said. "But it wasn't until I'd been married about two years that I became serious about them." She laughed, and her eyes took on a faraway look. "I used to tell Malcolm to buy me plants for my birthday and Christmas, but he never would. He bought jewelry, clothes—anything but what I really wanted. When I finally confronted him, do you know what he said?"

"What?"

"He said he didn't buy me plants because since I always asked for plants, it wouldn't be a surprise. Imagine that! Doesn't that sound just like a man? I said to heck with the surprise, get me something I want! One more pan or bathrobe, and I was going to buy my own present!"

"So what'd he do?"

"Well, that Christmas he bought me the most beautiful weeping fig I'd ever seen. And ten other plants. I was so shocked, I almost couldn't speak. There I was, getting ready to knock him over the head with a cookie tray or a deep fryer, and he finally gets me what I want! I practically screamed with excitement. He's been getting me plants ever since."

Brionney chuckled. "I think I might try that with Jesse. Let's see; what shall I begin to collect? Diamonds, maybe?" They laughed together, and the tension that had been building dissipated.

"I've got another story for you," Karissa said. "My mother's one of those traditional types. She loves to cook and keep house. Everything has to be just so. My dad doesn't mess with the household chores much, or with making meals, but he loves those microwave dinners for snacks. He's an engineer, and someone at work put him on to them. Well, he wanted my Mom to get a microwave, but she wouldn't hear of it because she thinks it sucks out all the vitamins. Dad said he didn't care as long as the food tasted good. Anyway, come Christmas, Dad buys Mom a microwave so he can use it. She was so angry."

"You're kidding!"

"Nope. That was nine years ago, and she hasn't used the microwave once."

"You sound like you miss her," Brionney said.

"I do. And my brothers and sisters—especially my sisters."

"Not your father?"

She shrugged. "My father is a difficult man to get along with. He . . . well, he's always right for one thing. And he's hard, mean even."

Brionney thought of her own father, who had always been so important in her life. In many ways, he was softer than her mother. How many times had they cuddled on the couch and watched television together? Or worked in their garden? How many times had he given her sound advice? She felt sad that Karissa hadn't a father she could admire.

"Don't get me wrong," Karissa said quickly. "I love my father. I just don't like him very much. And he certainly doesn't approve of my life. I was the only child to get married out of the temple. For a man who's about to be translated, that's a hard thing to take."

"So you were raised in the Church?"

"Oh, yes." Karissa's voice grew bitter. "Every Sunday we were there in the first row, fifteen minutes before sacrament meeting started. If we didn't go for any reason at all—even if we were sick—he wouldn't talk to us for a week. Once he threw my twelve-year-old brother out of the house for missing his Sunday School class. It was snowing, and my brother quickly changed his mind about rebelling." Her voice held a mixture of awe and anger. "I never missed a meeting until I left home for college. And then I never went back to church again." She paused. "No, I don't miss my father."

Brionney felt there was more behind Karissa's anger than a parent's zeal for a child's faith, but she would wait until Karissa was ready to tell the full story. "You've really never been to church since?" she asked.

"Only a few times, when Malcolm's family has insisted. You know, for blessings or missionary homecomings."

"Do you miss it?"

The question seemed to catch Karissa by surprise. "Yes, I guess I do—sometimes."

They sat in thoughtful silence until they drove past the sprawling school building that was comprised of different sections for elementary, middle grade, and high school classes. There were tennis courts behind the school and a large ball field. Several blocks on, a track encircled a large field. There, a few children played on the swings and a jungle gym.

"The park!" Rosalie yelled. She bounced on her seat, straining at the seat belt.

The girls piled from the car as soon as Brionney pulled to a stop. "Now stay—" She had been about to tell them to stay together and not talk to strangers, but the idea of kidnaping was so rare here as not to make a difference. Kodiak was too isolated. In many instances, it was like going back in time. She let the words be swallowed by the light breeze.

For the next hour, Brionney was caught up in the joy of being with her children. She had no place to go, nothing more important to do. From time to time, she watched Karissa as the other woman pushed Camille on the swing or barreled down the slide with Rosalie on her lap, laughing. But behind the outside happiness, her pretty face held a quiet, desperate sadness.

"I'm getting as dirty as they are," Karissa said, taking a break. She slapped the dust off the leg of her jeans.

Brionney shook her head. "No way. You always look so put together. I used to spend a lot of time on myself, but now it seems like I barely have the time to put on makeup before Jesse comes home."

Karissa smiled. "I'll tell you the secret," she said, sweeping her dark-brown hair back from her forehead. "No matter what you do, wear lipstick. One of my sisters is a beautician. She taught me that even if you don't have time for anything else, lipstick will make you look finished. A little eye liner will add a lot too, if you have the time, but the lipstick is a must."

Brionney stared at Karissa. "Why, that's all you are wearing!"

"See? You didn't even notice that I had nothing else on. It's a trick. As long as you have lipstick on, people think you have the rest. It's almost as good as really having it." She laughed. "Look, I'll go to the car and get my purse. We'll put some on you, and you'll see." She bounded across the verdant grass on her long legs. Brionney watched her go until a voice caught her attention.

"They're five months," a woman was saying. "Mostly I don't do anything but tend them. I have to dress them, bathe them, feed them, and when I get all done I have to start all over again. I barely have time for my three-year-old."

"I can't imagine how you do it," another voice said. "My one baby keeps me busy. He's eight months now."

Brionney turned from where she pushed Rosalie in a swing and saw two women. One sat on a swing with a baby, and the other helped a little girl onto another black seat, giving her a gentle push. Next to the swing set stood a double stroller.

"Oh, I just keep plugging away," the mother pushing the little girl said. She left her daughter momentarily to peer into the stroller. Brionney followed her gaze. Two adorable twin babies dressed in dark blue stared up at her, uncertain smiles on their tiny faces.

Brionney had her mouth open, ready to tell the mother that things would get easier, at least physically, as the children matured. Soon they would dress themselves, however discordantly, get their own drinks of water, tie their own shoes. And twins would play well together as her oldest daughters now did.

But all at once the old pain returned with blunt force, and Brionney clutched at her stomach beneath her breasts, gasping for breath. She felt as if Rosalie had kicked her in the stomach as she swung forward in the swing, but that had not happened. Acrid tears stung Brionney's eyes and she blinked rapidly, turning away from the twin babies and Rosalie swinging in the air.

"Oh, Father," she mumbled. Still she struggled to breathe. She reached for the metal pole supporting the swing set, and it seemed to take forever to reach it. When she finally did, she clung to it, unseeing.

"Mommy, higher. I wanna go higher," yelled Rosalie. "Mommy, are you listening to me? I said I wanna go higher! Mommy, now!" Rosalie's plea had turned into a high-pitched wail, but Brionney only heard it on one level. She was all but in the past, remembering the pain that usually she recalled only twice a year. Once again she saw the dark-haired toddlers holding hands.

* * * *

When Karissa returned from the car, Brionney was standing by the side of the swing set. Her face was pale, and her hands clutched at the pole. Near her in the swing, Rosalie was yelling, her round face growing angrier by the moment.

"Brionney? Are you okay?" Karissa asked, reaching for her arm.

"Somebody push me!" screamed Rosalie.

"I'll be right back if you behave yourself," Karissa said sharply. Rosalie's open mouth shut abruptly.

"I'm all right," Brionney managed to say.

"What happened?" To Karissa's relief, Brionney's eyes focused on her and she began to walk in the direction Karissa led. She waited until they were seated on the bench near the edge of the sand before asking, "It's not the baby, is it?"

"No." Brionney took a deep breath. "I heard those women talking. One of them has twins, you see. And when I looked at them, I remembered my own babies. It's been so long since I thought about them. I just wasn't expecting it. And suddenly there those babies are, and they could have been mine."

"You had twins?" Karissa shook her head. She had thought Brionney's life so perfect, so trouble-free.

"I miscarried twin boys," Brionney said in a low voice. "I was four months along. Well, they had died a long time before I actually miscarried. I never felt them move. I don't even know if they were given spirits yet. I mourned for them a long time, but it gradually got better. I usually remember them only during the time they would have been born, or when I lost them." She gave a brief, strangled laugh. "It was last month, you know. When they were due, that is. But I hadn't even thought about them until now. I wasn't expecting it. Seeing those twin boys threw me off." She took another shaky breath. "Oh, I still want them!"

"I'm sorry," Karissa said, feeling inadequate. She didn't fully understand the heartache Brionney had endured, but she could imagine how she would feel if it had happened to her.

"No, it's okay, really." Brionney was breathing more easily now, and the white shock was slowly fading from her face. "I used to pray that I would have them, but now it's enough to know they'll be mine someday. I don't know how or when, but they will be."

Karissa didn't reply. Brionney spoke with a sound assurance, but Karissa's heart held no such faith. *If only it could be true,* she thought. A tingly feeling spread throughout her body, one she had begun to feel occasionally. In some ways it was familiar, but she still didn't understand what it meant. "What happened? Why did you lose them?"

"We'll never know for sure. But they shared the same sac. Not a good sign." Brionney's voice was soft with remembrance.

Karissa was surprised. "I thought all identical twins came in the same sac."

"Many people do. But it actually depends on when the embryo splits. The later it splits, the more they are likely to share and the more problems there are. Monoamniotic twins—where they share the same sac—happens in less than two percent of all twins. It means a higher death rate—fifty to sixty-two percent, if I remember correctly." Brionney gave a wry grimace. "You see, my sister's a nurse, and after I lost the babies, we did a lot of research. I needed answers. I'm sure the details don't interest you."

"But they do." Karissa briefly touched her friend's arm. "I should know these things. After all, I work in a hospital."

"As an administrator, not a doctor," Brionney said dryly.

Karissa shrugged. "I didn't know you'd ever gone through such a tragedy," she mused aloud. "I thought your life had been pretty smooth."

Brionney sat back on the bench and sighed. "We'll it's not something I go around announcing or anything. But I tell you—up until that point in my life it was the most traumatic thing that had happened to me. I wanted Jesse's baby desperately. I mean, he treated

Savannah like she was his, but our first baby together was special."

"You mean Jesse's not Savannah's biological father?" Karissa's asked slowly.

"No. He's not. I was married before. He left me."

"You don't sound too unhappy about it."

"Heck, no! Derek's leaving was the best thing for me and Savannah, though I didn't know it at the time. Jesse and I were meant to be together. He's a good father and husband. Derek wasn't either of those."

Karissa didn't speak for a moment, but watched the girls. Savannah, with her long, white-blonde hair, was pushing both Rosalie and Camille on the swings. "She looks just like you. Only with long hair."

"My ex-husband has blonde hair and blue eyes too," Brionney said without bitterness. "She does look like me, but I can see him in her also. But she's Jesse's now. My ex-husband even allowed him to adopt her."

They sat without speaking. The woman with the twins had taken both infants in her arms and was rocking them, love etched on her face. Karissa felt jealousy boil up in her chest.

"So you had the miscarriage before Camille," she said, looking away from the mother and her babies.

"Yes. I got pregnant with her about three months later. I hoped I was having the twins, but I didn't." There was a touch of melancholy in Brionney's voice.

"She's very special, that Camille," Karissa said. "It would have been good for you to have your twins, but then you wouldn't have had Camille, would you?"

Brionney was silent for a long minute. "I never thought of it that way. But you're so right. I wouldn't trade Camille for them. How could I? It's not a choice a mother could make. I'm glad I didn't have to. That sort of puts things into perspective." She turned to look at Karissa. "Thank you. Mostly, I'm fine with the past, but today I think I needed to be reminded of how special my little Camille is."

Karissa laughed. "Anytime. And who knows? If you really feel you'll see those babies again, maybe you'll have them this time."

"Oh, no," Brionney said. "I think I'm beyond that dream for now. I can barely handle the three I have. I can wait until the Millennium to have my boys."

Karissa thought it all nonsense. It was romantic to believe as Brionney did, but not realistic. Yet, it if was true, Karissa's own secret past could come back to haunt her some day—even more forcefully than it did now.

Oh, for a cigarette!

"You know," Brionney said, "we buried the babies beneath the cherry tree in my sister's yard—we were renting from her at the time. When we moved, I dug up the dirt, and of course there was nothing there. They were so tiny, and so much time had passed. Still, I put some of the dirt in a container, and on top of that I placed the two flat rocks we had used to mark the spot. I know it sounds strange, but it seems to help, having something tangible to remember them by."

Karissa had glimpsed the plant container and wondered at the contents. "That doesn't seem so strange to me," she said. "Working for the hospital, I've learned that it's good for people to have something they can use to focus their grief. It actually helps in the healing process."

"That's a relief," Brionney smiled, her cheeks dimpling. "I never told anyone besides Jesse because I thought I was losing it."

"I think you're doing just fine." Karissa wished she had something on which to focus her own grief. But there was nothing—except those terrible dreams of a mother causing her baby's death. Thankfully, those hadn't returned since she had stopped smoking.

"Come on," she said to Brionney. "Enough of seriousness. "Lets go find somewhere on this uncivilized island to buy ourselves an ice cream."

* * * *

Later that night, they ate baked halibut. The tasty morsels broke apart in Karissa's mouth as she chewed slowly. She hadn't liked fish before coming to Kodiak, but that was one more thing in her life that had changed.

"Next week, I want to take the girls with us," Jesse said enthusiastically. "I've never gone saltwater fishing before. I can't believe how big these fish are. Only one day, and we have enough for a week of fish!"

Karissa sighed. She liked halibut, but not *that* much. *Fish is healthy,* she consoled herself.

"I want to come too," Brionney said.

Jesse's dark eyes softened as they came to rest on his wife's face. "Are you feeling better today?" he asked. "I mean, you look really good, like maybe you haven't been so sick."

Brionney glanced over at Karissa, one blue eye closing in a wink. She wore the eye liner Karissa had put on at the park, along with the burnt sienna lipstick, now partially smeared from dinner. The extra color made her face more alive than usual. "I feel pretty good," Brionney said. "I think being on Kodiak agrees with me."

At least someone besides Malcolm likes this prison, Karissa thought. But her husband looked so pleased that she didn't say the words aloud.

Camille and Rosalie had satisfied their small appetites. "Can I take a bath?" Camille asked.

"Me too," Rosalie said. "Can I take a bath too? 'Cause I stink real bad."

Brionney laughed. "Of course you can. There's time before bed."

"Please do," Jesse said, plugging his nose and rolling his eyes. "Before my nose dies from the smell! Wow! How can such a little girl smell s-o-o-o-o bad?"

Rosalie giggled, her brown eyes dancing. "I smell bad!" she squealed. "I stink!" Camille leaned over to sniff her sister's arm, and Savannah pinched her nose shut. Karissa laughed out loud.

While Brionney and Jesse went upstairs to bathe their brood and settle them in bed, Karissa and Malcolm cleared the table. They worked side by side, so close that Karissa could smell her husband's freshly washed hair. She felt as if she needed a shower herself. During her outing with the girls, she had worked up quite a sweat pushing them in the swing and running around the park. Her thin T-shirt clung to her body, and a slightly sour smell reached her nose.

"I need a shower," she said as she rinsed the last dish and plopped it in the dishwasher.

"You look good to me," Malcolm said.

"I stink!" Karissa mimicked Rosalie's high-pitched voice.

Malcolm laughed. "You go ahead then. I'll wipe down the table."

Karissa kissed his cheek. "Thanks." She walked to the doorway. "Oh, I just remembered. You never told me that Brionney had been married before."

His eyebrows rose. "I didn't know. How 'bout that."

"She had Savannah with her first husband, and then married Jesse when Savannah was about one and a half."

"He never told me," Malcolm said. "Though I don't blame him. I wouldn't tell anyone if it was me."

"What do you mean?" Karissa's voice was sharper than she meant it to be.

"Nothing. Just that I wouldn't want people to know if my wife had been married to another man before me. It's a guy thing, you know."

It was all Karissa could do to keep her voice calm. "I don't think Jesse cares about her past. It's not her fault. Brionney didn't do anything wrong; her husband left her. I think Jesse's just grateful to have her in his life."

Malcolm shrugged. "But if that's so, why didn't he tell me?"

"Maybe it never came up."

"Maybe." Malcolm gazed at her with a question in his eyes. "What does it matter to us? We don't have any secrets like that."

Karissa nodded numbly. She had been right not to confide her secret to Malcolm. If he knew now, he would only look at her with disgust and anger. "I'm going to shower." She left him, feeling his eyes boring into her back.

She was in the shower a long time, scrubbing and scrubbing until her skin felt raw. Still she did not feel clean. Water could never wipe away her atrocious deed. Her face crumpled and she sobbed uncontrollably, letting the spray from the shower beat against her face and rinse the tears down to the tile and through the drain.

CHAPTER 10

When the girls were settled in their room, Jesse sat on the edge of his bed, staring out into the evening light. In Provo it would be already dark, but here in Kodiak during the summer, the days were much longer. Through the window, a group of young cottonwoods stood in the still air. Their leaves were a dark green, and the grass around them was even greener. A rough wooden bench sat under the trees, circled by the lighter green of perennials which were at differing stages of bloom. Lazy hills surrounded the manicured lawn. The whole setup looked like a paradise, but he knew that inside this house things were far from perfect.

"I saw Malcolm smoking this morning," he said.

Brionney dropped the nightgown she was taking from the tall oak dresser. Jesse wondered if the dresser was something else Malcolm had made in his youth.

"You saw him?" she asked, coming to sit beside him.

He nodded. "I walked into his studio to tell him I was ready to go, and he was standing with his back toward the door, staring at all those guns he has hanging on the walls. He was smoking, all right. All this time I thought the smoke smell was lingering around him because it was embedded in his clothes—like it is in their furniture. But he's still smoking."

"What did you do?"

"I did what I should have done in the first place. I went back into the kitchen and waited for a few minutes, then I yelled for him and made a lot of noise on my way through the garage. When I got back to the studio, he was sitting at his desk without the cigarette. I could still smell it, of course, but he didn't seem to notice."

"Smokers don't usually notice the smell," Brionney said, wrinkling her nose. Her blue eyes brimmed with the sadness she felt at this news. "Poor Karissa. She's so hopeful that quitting smoking will get them a baby. She's not going to like this."

"You won't tell her, will you?"

Brionney grimaced. "Not me. This is between them. But isn't there anything we can do? I thought by being here we could help. Maybe I was wrong."

"I know what you mean. It's so strange to me to be in this situation. Malcolm was the one who first taught me the gospel. I know he had a testimony. I felt it back then."

"Yet you weren't baptized until years later."

"That was my fault, not his. I was afraid to hurt my parents."

"I wonder what happened."

"From what I can gather, nothing really happened. He just let it go."

"So what can we do?"

Jesse's answer came after a long pause. "Just love him, I guess. Just love them both."

"I already do," she said softly.

"Me too." He stood, stifling a yawn. "I guess I'll go check on the girls."

* * * *

Karissa was taking a long time in the shower. Malcolm had finished cleaning the table and counter tops and now slipped up the kitchen stairs, past the room where Jesse and Brionney slept, to the girls' room. From the light coming in the window he could see Savannah in a bed on one side of the room and the two smaller girls snuggled together in the single bed on the other side. The room was painted white, now shadow-filled in the fading light, and bare except for the picture of a smiling Jesus surrounded by children of every nationality. A little boy with short tightly-curled hair and black skin sat on the Savior's lap. Of all the pictures Sister Goodrich had brought Karissa, this was Malcolm's favorite.

"I came to say good night," he said, glad they were still awake.

Each wrapped her chubby arms around him and kissed his cheek, laughing when his two-day old beard scratched her. When it was Rosalie's turn, he sniffed loudly. "I don't smell anything bad."

Rosalie giggled. "I got all clean."

"Where's Karissa?" Camille asked. Malcolm knew the dark-haired Camille was his wife's favorite. Since the Hergarters had come to stay, the two had spent long hours together making a list of all the plants in the greenhouse. Camille knew each by name, and carried her own copy of the list in a small notebook Karissa had bought for her. The child couldn't read the names yet, but pretended she could.

"She's taking a shower. I'm sure she'll be up soon to say good night."

Malcolm hated to leave them. He wished he could shut the heavy blinds to block out the light and tell them stories until each snored softly in her bed. If they were his girls, maybe he'd even curl up next to them so he could hear them breathing in the night, just to make sure they were safe. And he would take them camping and fishing, and make commercials with them. He would spend as much time as his dad had spent with him until their estrangement. And how had that happened? Malcolm knew it had begun with his wanting to marry Karissa out of the temple. Later, the breach had been perpetuated by his smoking and drinking, his savoring of the stuff humans were meant to enjoy. Well, he didn't need his father anyway. So what did it matter?

He spied a pile of socks on the floor, and picked them up to throw into the laundry chute. They felt heavy, and he tipped one upside down. Fine sand poured into his hand. He almost laughed. There had been a lot of sand floating around inside the house since the girls came. It hid inside shoes, socks, and rolled-up pant legs.

"Saving this to make a sandbox in here?" he asked.

The girls giggled. "'Course not, Malcolm," they chorused.

"Oh, I don't mind. But I think our cleaning lady might quit on us if we're not careful." More giggles.

He said good night and turned from the room. On the way to the back stairs, he passed Jesse. "They okay?" Jesse asked.

"Yeah," Malcolm said. "They're fine. I went in to say good night. They didn't come down like they usually do." He still held the sand in his fist, but he didn't show Jesse. That was between him and the girls.

"Brionney was anxious to get them in bed. It's been a long day for her."

"I bet. They have a lot of energy."

"They sure do." Jesse backed down the hall. "I like to check them before I turn in," he said as if excusing himself.

"I would too, if they were mine."

An unquenchable desire reared up in Malcolm's mind. *You need something,* it told him. *You shouldn't have to suffer your lack of children without some comfort.*

He went through the garage and into his studio. Three long strides brought him to the editing desk he had made himself in college. Oak again, his favorite medium. "Karissa won't be done for a while," he said aloud. "What she doesn't know won't hurt her." His tone was excusatory and Malcolm felt relieved, as if Karissa herself had said the words.

He drew out one of the cigarette packs from the carton he had bought earlier in the week. It was half-empty. He no longer told himself he would quit as he had two months ago; he knew he couldn't. The thought cut deeply.

The lighter sat in full view on the desk, and in an instant Malcolm breathed in a lungful of smoke and held it inside for a moment. It stung as if he had not smoked for weeks, and yet it somehow seemed to relieve his emotional aches.

He stood up and walked to the back of the room where his weapons hung on the otherwise bare wall. The Browning .300 Winchester Magnum was his favorite of the rifles. He ran a finger over the bluing and then along the smooth finish of the wood. Then his eye caught sight of the semiautomatic pistol his father had given him. He hadn't shot the Colt Mustang .380 for nearly a year, though he'd cleaned it only last week.

A sharp breath caught his attention. He whirled, instinctively hiding the cigarette behind him. Too late.

Karissa stood in the doorway dressed in an enticing black negligee and matching silk robe, her brilliant green eyes glinting with hurt. "You're smoking," she said needlessly. "I thought you'd stopped."

"I tried." Even to his own ears, the words sounded feeble. "I really tried. I couldn't."

"Having a baby didn't mean enough?" She wrapped the robe tightly around her body, crossing her arms over her chest as if she were cold.

"For heaven's sake, Karissa! My stopping smoking has nothing to do with our having a baby. You're the one who's going to carry it!"

"But it's wrong."

"Says who?"

"The Word of Wisdom."

He snorted. "That never bothered you before."

The muscles along her jaw tightened, and she blinked rapidly as if to stave off tears. The million excuses for his betrayal vanished instantly. He knew that he should have been honest about the difficulty he was having quitting, but he hated to admit failure, especially to Karissa. She had quit so easily, and he hated to appear weak before her.

"Karissa, I'm sorry."

When she spoke, her voice was without emotion. "I've been feeling so close to you. I thought we were working together, but all this time you were lying. No wonder we can't have a baby. We don't deserve one."

"That's not true!"

He wanted to tell her what good parents they would make, despite their weaknesses. Despite *his* weakness. Why couldn't he be strong like Karissa?

Before he found the words, she was gone. He went after her, but he heard the lock on their bedroom door snap into place as he strode down the hall. He leaned his cheek on the carved surface of the solid wood. It felt cool against his skin. Inside, he could hear nothing.

He thought she might leave Kodiak now. There was nothing holding her here, not really. Tears sprang from his eyes, and the agony in his heart was too much to bear. For a moment, he contemplated breaking the door down and pleading with her on hands and knees.

Would it do any good?

A sharp pain ate into his conscious thought. He glanced at his hand to see that the cigarette had burned down to his flesh. He crushed it between his fingers, ignoring the additional pain. Then he retraced his steps back to the cold and silent studio.

* * * *

Karissa slept badly. In the night, she awoke with a start, reaching over to the empty space where Malcolm should be. The hurt came back in a wave. Betrayal, that's what it was. She had smelled the smoke on his clothes and thought it was because of the men on his camera crew, or perhaps it came from clothes Maggie hadn't gotten around to cleaning on her tri-weekly visits. But no—he had lied.

She came heavily to her feet, glad sleep had a numbing effect on her emotions. Dark encompassed the room and hallway, but Karissa knew the way to the greenhouse without light. Many times when sleep eluded her, she would come here to think. Here she was free to wander among living things and wonder what might have been.

She sat on the cement curbing that surrounded the sand. Moonlight filtered in through the double layer of thick plastic, and the plants reflected a dark green color. Lush, verdant, living, growing—her womb could not compete. Though it had not started out so, the greenhouse was her private prison, her personal acknowledgment of the sin, and a constant reminder that she would never be whole.

And no one had ever guessed. Not even Malcolm.

A single tear watered the sand.

Faint steps sounded in the laundry room where she had left the door open. Karissa stiffened, thinking it was Malcolm.

"Camille?" a soft voice called. "Are you in here again?"

"It's Karissa. What are you doing awake?"

Brionney gave a low laugh and patted her bulging stomach. "I was hungry, what else? I came down to the kitchen, and saw something moving out here. I thought it might be Camille. I've found her here twice before in the middle of the night."

"We'll have to have a sleep out soon," Karissa said.

"They'll like that." Brionney paused. "Well, goodnight." Her feet shuffled, but she didn't leave. "May I ask what's wrong? "

"Yes. I think I would like to talk, if you don't mind." Maybe Brionney could help Karissa decide what to do about Malcolm.

Brionney nodded and sat beside her. In her hand, Karissa saw a piece of the deer jerky Malcolm had given them. The other woman saw her gaze. "I'm craving salt," she explained apologetically. "I always do when I'm pregnant."

"I don't like deer jerky much," Karissa answered. "Malcolm does." She wondered how to begin.

"You don't like Kodiak at all, do you?" Brionney said.

"No, I don't. I—I'm thinking about leaving."

"Oh, I thought Malcolm loved it here."

"He does. I'm thinking of going without him."

Brionney caught her breath. "You want to leave Malcolm?"

"He's smoking! He lied to me!" Karissa cried. To herself she wondered where all the emotion came from. Once, she had been able to handle things more calmly. "I don't know if I can take it."

"Is that all?" Brionney asked.

"You knew!"

"I found out tonight. Jesse saw him at it this morning."

"Malcolm knew how important this was to me. He knew! How could he do this?"

"I've seen him with the girls. It's important to him, too."

"Then why?"

"Maybe he's not as strong as you are."

"It doesn't matter. I'm leaving." Karissa stood abruptly. "There's nothing for me here."

"Wait!" Brionney jumped to her feet. Her white hair reflected the moonlight, giving the appearance of a halo. "So what if he's smoking? It's not as if that's the worst sin a man ever committed. He could be cheating on you, he could be abusing you, he could be a murderer, or worse. Give him time."

The words stung deeply. For all of Malcolm's deception, he was cleaner than Karissa. If it hadn't been for her sin . . .

"You have to do *anything* you can to save your marriage," Brionney continued passionately. "I know it might hurt. Believe me, I know. But you have to give it everything, or someday you may regret it. You'll ask yourself if things could have been different had you tried harder."

Karissa sighed and sat again on the cement curbing, reaching out for a handful of sand. "Did you try to hang on to your first marriage?"

"With all my heart," Brionney said. "I believed our sealing would last forever."

"It's not as if we were married in the temple." Karissa let the sand drop.

"So? Does that make your commitment to him any less? When you got married, did you say to yourself, 'Well, if it doesn't work out I can always get a divorce'? I hope not. That's not commitment. Commitment to marriage is doing everything in your power to keep things together. So what if you're not very happy with him at this moment? Maybe you even hate him a little. That's all right. But don't throw out your entire marriage on this one issue."

"But what if I don't love him anymore?"

"It doesn't matter," Brionney said, tossing her head back. Her hair rippled like waves of light. "The point is that you can love him if you try. Commitment brings an even stronger love, the eternal kind. But right now, it seems easier to walk away."

Karissa remembered how Malcolm's chiseled features had been harder than usual when she had caught him smoking. He hadn't seemed to care about her feelings at all.

Brionney looked down at her in the moonlight. "You may not be married in the temple, but you want to be. I can see that, even if you can't. And I don't know what's been holding you up—it certainly wasn't smoking—but I want you to know I'm here for you, that when you're ready to talk about it, I'll be here to listen. And I'll love you no matter what."

"I don't think Malcolm would."

"How do you know if you don't give him a try?"

"He wouldn't," Karissa said dully. "I know."

"Well, you can't leave him, not yet."

Karissa knew that Brionney spoke the truth.

"He's a smart man, Malcolm is. He knows what he's doing is wrong. Why don't you go back to bed and sleep on it? Things always look better to me in the morning." She grimaced. "At least they do when I'm not pregnant."

"I will," Karissa said. "And thank you."

Commitment and love. According to Brionney, they weren't necessarily the same thing. Was she committed to her marriage? She had been once. Was Malcolm? Maybe tomorrow they could find out.

* * * *

The house was silent when Karissa awoke Sunday morning. Brionney and Jesse must have taken the kids to church, and that meant she and Malcolm were home alone. The room was bright, despite the shades covering the window. Her heart didn't feel as heavy as the night before, as if the morning sun had burned away the shadows in her soul.

She showered quickly, not wetting her hair, and dressed in a gray sleeveless sweater and loose gray pants, pinstriped with alternating lines of white and jade. Then she brushed her long hair methodically and pinned it up. A few loose tendrils escaped along her jaw, softening her face.

"I'm ready," she told herself.

Malcolm was in the kitchen, sitting on a bar stool and staring at a bowl of the Grapenuts she had bought yesterday at Safeway. He stirred the cereal listlessly, as if waiting for the milk to soften the hard kernels. "You're leaving, aren't you?" he said, looking over at her. He hadn't shaved again, and his black-covered jaw worked as if trying to keep the words steady. Before he looked away, she saw a shimmer of tears in his eyes. "I don't suppose I can talk you out of it."

Karissa heard the plea in his voice, as well as a note of resignation. "I wanted to," she said slowly, rounding the bar until she was opposite him. "I don't like you very much right now."

His eyes met hers, waiting for the rest.

"But I am committed to our marriage. I made you a promise when we married, and I want to do everything to make it work. But I need to know if you're committed. You don't have to love me exactly, you just have to be committed."

Malcolm stood and took a few steps around the bar. "I am committed, Karissa. And I do love you." His tone seemed to imply that they were one and the same. "Don't you love me, Karissa?"

She lifted her hands helplessly. "I don't know. I really don't know. At this moment, I can't tell you what I feel, except numb. But I don't want to end our marriage, not without trying." There was pain in his face, but she couldn't take back the words. "You give up smoking if you want," she continued. "I want you to, but it's your choice. But if we . . ." She looked away from him. "If we decide to stay together and we have a baby, you have to promise not to smoke around him."

"I promise," he said immediately. "But does this mean you want to put off having a baby?"

"Maybe it would be better." Tears stung the back of her eyes, but she did not let them fall.

"That's some commitment," Malcolm said lightly.

She turned toward him. "What do you want from me?"

"I want you to love me again." His voice was choked. "I'm sorry I lied to you."

But she hadn't really loved him for a long time; the smoking had only been the proverbial straw that had broken the camel's back, or rather her commitment. At least until Brionney had glued the pieces back together.

"Oh, Karissa! I wish I could have stopped. I wish I could change things. Can't you love me a little?" He rubbed at his face, and his hands came away wet.

"I'll try," she said.

He approached hesitantly, and wrapped his arms around her, burying his face in her neck. His new beard, now dotted here and there with single white strands, was long enough to tickle without being sharp. Her hand went up and smoothed the gray at his temple. He'd always had those streaks of gray even before they were married, and she adored them.

"I know what," he said, drawing away. Karissa's neck felt moist where he had pressed his face. "We need to get away, just the two of us. You're up for vacation time soon, aren't you? Take it early and we'll go this week, as soon as you can get away."

"Where will we go? Camping?" she asked without much enthusiasm. Though she enjoyed camping, it was not her idea of relaxation.

"No, we'll go to an honest-to-goodness hotel right here on Kodiak." He snapped his fingers. "I know. We'll go to Kalsin Inn. It's right on Kalsin Bay, and it's beautiful. Yes! You'll love it there. It'll be like a second honeymoon. Say you'll go."

His excitement was catching. "Okay," she said with a smile. "But I'll have to go in tomorrow and get things ready to leave." She also had to have her blood tested in conjunction with Dr. Taylor's orders, though why he wanted the tests was beyond her. Something about early detection to see if her body was not making the proper levels of hormones to sustain pregnancy. Each time her ovulation cycle was over, she had submitted to the test only to find out absolutely nothing because she wasn't pregnant.

Malcolm practically ran to the phone, blind to her thoughts. "We'll have the time of our lives. I'll even teach you to fish, if you want."

Karissa laughed and felt the rest of her doubts evaporate. Maybe she had overreacted. Malcolm was a good husband. If only she dared to tell him the truth.

CHAPTER 11

Water rushing in the river filled Malcolm's ears. Occasionally another sound penetrated—the call of a bird or a rustling in the leaves made by a Sitka blacktail deer—but there was not a trace of another human being. In their chosen spot along the river, he and Karissa were completely alone.

The sky overhead was a bright, perfect blue, the kind of blue Malcolm liked to film before launching into a less pleasant aspect of nature in one of his documentaries. The blue stretched as far as he could see, until the green trees blocked the view.

Karissa gave a deep, throaty laugh, and Malcolm found it irresistible. It was as far removed from her tight, quick laughter of late as Kodiak was from her hometown in California. Knowing her so well, he recognized that the laugh signaled her happiness, deep in the essence of her soul. She had laughed that way once, long ago. When had it stopped? And why hadn't he noticed when it had stopped? Hooking his pole between two stones, he left his line dangling in the river and went to sit beside her on a large rock in the shade. The love in his heart had never been so strong; it seemed to even stem his desire to smoke. He was down to less than half a pack a day now and beginning to feel hopeful about quitting altogether. What a wonderful surprise for his precious wife.

"Hey, I thought we were trying to fish here," she protested weakly as he put a casual arm around her. In her slender hands she held his best fishing rod.

"We've done enough fishing." Today was Saturday, the last of their five days of vacation at Kalsin Bay. All week they had sailed, hiked, fished, and just plain sat together. Karissa had laughed at his jokes, had made a few of her own, and not once had either brought up his smoking or their possible separation. At times, Malcolm was sure there was love in her emerald eyes. But there was something else too, a hidden mystery in the way she acted, seemingly emphasized by the hollows in her cheeks. What could it be? She was quieter than usual, and several times he had caught her gazing off into nothing-ness, as if deep in reflective thought. When he called her back, she had stared at him in a sort of haunted fear. Was he only imagining it? When he tried to probe, she would become remote and almost hostile, so he backed off. What else could he do? He couldn't force her to share her feelings. He would have to wait until she was ready to broach the subject on her own.

"Stop jerking my line," she said.

"I'm not—" He broke off, seeing the way her line bent toward the water. "Uh-oh, it's a big one."

"Good!" Karissa jumped up from the rock, her ponytail swinging. Her long legs were tanned from a week of wearing cut-off Levis, and her face and arms were also kissed to a tawny brown by the ever-present sun. Malcolm thought the color looked good on her.

"Now pull back gently. Don't let the line snap." He wiped the sweat from his hands onto his shorts.

"I know, I know." The lean muscles in her arm flexed as she pulled back. "Oh, no! He won't come."

"Give him some line."

Karissa did as he directed, her smooth face scrunched with concen-tration. Minute beads of sweat appeared across her hatless brow.

"Now try to reel him in. Slowly . . . slowly. Why'd ya stop?" he asked.

"My cheek itches." She grinned at him.

"Here, give it to me."

She held the rod out of his reach. "Oh, no. This baby's mine. I'm going to win our bet. A week of back rubs is almost mine."

From the angle of the line, Malcolm knew she was probably right. "What about your cheek?"

"You scratch it. Right here, under my eye." She moved her right cheek to show him.

"Do you know how funny you look?"

"Scratch it," she ordered. So he did. "Thanks." She began to reel in the fish again.

"Not too fast," he warned.

"Who's got this fish, you or me?"

Malcolm laughed. Karissa had taken to fishing better than anyone he'd ever seen. She remembered what he told her and followed his advice exactly. Why hadn't he taken her years ago?

"There he comes," she said triumphantly. Malcolm could tell by the size that it outweighed his biggest catch of the week by at least ten pounds.

"It's heavy," she said.

"Can I help?"

She looked at him. "I still get the back rubs?"

Malcolm grinned. "You caught him." She nodded her consent, and he waded into the river to heft the fish. The water felt cool against his bare legs. "This'll feed an army."

Karissa watched him from the side. "I think we're going to need it."

"What do you mean?"

"I might be pregnant." Her green eyes glittered.

He stared at her, as though frozen in the water, too hopeful for words. And he also felt a relief; perhaps this explained the secret he sensed in her manner. Maybe now she would open up her heart to him.

"I took a blood test Monday at the hospital. It was positive. But I still have to take another test to make sure my body knows how to keep it."

Malcolm finally found his tongue. "Why didn't you tell me?" He wanted to drop the fish and go to her, but he wasn't sure what her waiting meant.

She looked down at the fish, then back to his face. "I wanted to be sure, that's all. About us."

"Did you find something about me to love?" he asked casually. Too casually. Both knew how important the answer was.

Karissa regarded him without speaking for what seemed an eternity, as if she weighed and measured him with her eyes. It occurred to him that he could choose to be offended, but he thrust the emotion away. At this moment, games or hurt feelings didn't matter. At least she was committed to making things work—for now.

She continued to study him. Suddenly the fishy smell of the salmon in his arms reached his nose, and he felt unclean and completely self-conscious under Karissa's penetrating gaze. A flush rose in his face, and it took great effort not to look away.

"I love the way you fish," she said. The words were measured like her stare, her voice serious. "I love the way you taught me to fish. I love your talent of making things out of wood. I love the way you are with Brionney's girls, and I love the way you're looking at me right now."

"But do you love *me*?"

She gazed at him blankly, as if not understanding the question. "You are all these things, and I love them."

Malcolm hesitated. Women liked to complicate matters. A man either loved a woman with his whole heart, or he didn't. At times he might not think about the love, but it was always there, sometimes blazing, sometimes banked like a fire in the night. To a woman, there were shades between love and hate. He didn't understand it, but there it was.

She saw his confusion. "I do love you, Malcolm."

He stepped out of the water, dropped the fish onto the ground, and hugged her. She hugged him back, laughing the throaty laugh again, and he laughed with her. He felt like dancing, like shouting his joy to the wind so it could be carried to the entire world. His wife, this beautiful, pure woman loved him—or at least parts of him—and was going to have his baby!

"Your mother was right," Karissa whispered. "I made my body healthy, and . . . and . . ." She didn't need to say more.

Maybe his mother had been right. Malcolm's own diet had changed, and his smoking was reduced by half. Who knew what result that might have produced? But one thing was certain: his mother would be overjoyed at the prospect of another grandchild. He would call her as soon as possible.

* * * *

They took a boat back to the city of Kodiak, where they picked up Karissa's Nissan. He wanted to drive, but she wouldn't let him. "I'm pregnant, not an invalid," she said. She smiled at him, a wide, happy smile. Malcolm knew he wore the same dumb grin on his own face, but he didn't care. He almost couldn't wait to get home to tell Jesse, Brionney, and the girls.

In the end, their news had to wait. At home they found Delinda Goodrich with three frightened little girls. Savannah and Camille had tears streaked on their faces, and their dinner sat on the bar before them, untouched. Rosalie had laid her head on her arms, refusing to look at Sister Goodrich or at her sisters. When the older girls saw Malcolm and Karissa, they bounced from their chairs, talking all at once. Malcolm glanced at Delinda, trying to make sense of the jumble.

"Brionney went to the hospital," Delinda said. Her blunt, muscled hand fingered the thick gold chain at her neck. On the fingers she wore three expensive-looking rings. "She had her doctor's appointment yesterday, and he thought there was something unusual; he didn't say what. He ordered an ultrasound, but Brionney didn't want to have it alone. They decided to do it on Monday so Jesse could be with her. Only this afternoon she started having contractions, and she was convinced her labor had started."

The color drained from Karissa's face. "Poor Brionney."

"I'm sure she's all right," Delinda said. "She's just nervous because of what the doctor said. That's what brought this all on. She should have just had the ultrasound yesterday to put her mind at ease. We all need to—"

"She lost a baby before," Karissa said, cutting off Delinda's babble. Malcolm saw the visiting teacher's eyes widen. He, too, was surprised; Jesse had never told him.

"Can we go see them?" Savannah said.

"Can we?" Camille echoed. Rosalie gave a loud sniff and gazed up at them beseechingly.

Karissa's eyes met Malcolm's. He nodded. "Let's all go."

"Thank you for coming out, Delinda," Karissa said. "We appreciate it." Malcolm knew she didn't like Delinda, but the words sounded sincere.

"Well, I'm Brionney's visiting teacher now too," the woman answered. "For as long as they're here. I was only too glad I could come and stay with the girls."

"Pile in the Jeep," Malcolm said. "Let's go see what's what." The girls cast grateful looks at him.

"Shoes first," Karissa said. "We'll need to go inside."

The shoe hunt began. Finally, Delinda found Rosalie's last shoe under the sofa in the living room. "I'm good at finding things," she said with a smile. "I've had a lot of practice with my brood."

Rosalie took the shoe and shoved it on her foot. "I all ready."

"So you are," Malcolm said, picking up the little girl. She snuggled into him, reminding him of Karissa and his own growing baby. Already the great news had become a part of him, had changed him somehow.

"I hope the baby's all right," Savannah said.

He did too.

* * * *

It was like a recurring dream from which Brionney couldn't escape. Memories boiled to the surface until she couldn't separate the past from the present. She clung to Jesse's hand so tightly that her fingers turned white.

"The bleeding could be because of your appointment yesterday," said Dr. Fairfax, the doctor on call. He was a young man in his mid-thirties with a quick smile, kind brown eyes, and dark hair. His body leaned toward heaviness around the middle, and he wore green tennis shoes and jeans under his white coat. "Did your doctor check you?"

"Yes, he was concerned about something. He didn't say what."

"I don't see any signs of labor." As Dr. Fairfax spoke the reassuring words, he spread a cold, clear jelly on Brionney's bare stomach. The baby inside her moved away from the cold. The movements at least were comforting.

"According to your records, the reason your doctor wanted the ultrasound is because you are measuring too large for how far along you are. That could mean problems, but it's just as likely nothing. There could be a multitude of meanings."

"Why didn't he tell her that?" Jesse's face was tense, his dark eyes brooding. Brionney knew he was worried.

"I should have asked," Brionney said.

Jesse shook his head. "No, he should have told you. Imagine, letting you go home as worried as you were. I think it's about time we got a new doctor."

Dr. Fairfax didn't give any sign of hearing their conversation. He rubbed the jelly around with the flat edge of the ultrasound wand that was connected to the monitor by a thin cord. "Uh-huh," he said after a few moments. "Oh, I see."

"What is it?" Brionney glanced from the monitor to the doctor's face, then back again. She stared at the image on the screen. When she had been pregnant with Rosalie, her doctor had taken a lot of time to explain the ultrasound, and the picture didn't look the same as it had then.

"Well, I see what's going on," the doctor said simply. "You're going to have twins."

The relief and shock hit at the same time. Brionney felt her eyes widen. She looked at Jesse. "We're finally having them!"

Dr. Fairfax looked puzzled. "You expected this?"

"No," Brionney said at the same time Jesse said, "Sort of."

"They're boys, aren't they," Brionney said. It wasn't a question. And she already knew that they would have Camille's brown, blue-tinged eyes and dark-brown hair.

"Yes," the doctor said after a minute. "They're definitely identical twins, and I can see that the one over here on the left is a boy. The other is turned so I can't see, but since they're identical, he has to be a boy too. There he goes. He turned. See?"

"They're not in the same sac, are they?" Brionney asked anxiously.

"No. I can see the division pretty clearly."

She breathed a sigh of relief. "Do you deliver twins?"

"Of course."

Brionney looked at Jesse, and he nodded. "We want you to be our doctor, then," she said. "We want to know what's going on, with nothing hidden."

"All right," said Dr. Fairfax. He wiped most of the jelly off Brionney's belly, gave her a cloth to clean it better, and retreated to the far side of the small room.

Jesse helped her sit up. His face could hardly contain his happiness. "I can't believe it," he muttered.

Neither could Brionney, yet they were going to have their twins. How or why was not important. The Lord had been so very good to them!

Then another thought forced its way abruptly into Brionney's mind. "Why now? I didn't think I could handle even one more right now."

Jesse fell silent. She could feel his eyes boring into her. "Are you sorry?"

She paused for a long time before answering. "No, but I am glad you're doing all the diapers for the first two weeks. You'd better clear your schedule. You're going to be awfully busy."

CHAPTER 12

Karissa had never been so happy. There weren't enough words in all the languages in the world to describe the sentiment in her heart. She couldn't wait to tell Malcolm. Too bad there wasn't a phone in the examination room.

"I admit I was a little worried," Dr. Taylor said. I wondered if the problem wasn't that you weren't getting pregnant," Dr. Taylor said, "but that your body wasn't maintaining the pregnancies."

"You thought I might be miscarrying each month?" Karissa shivered.

"Well, not every month, but something like that." He glanced down at the chart, and the flourescent lights reflected off his bald head. "But your hormone levels are right where they should be. I can't tell you why, but everything seems to be proceeding normally. I'll want your regular doctor to keep a close eye on you, but I don't anticipate any more problems."

"Thank you," Karissa said.

He shrugged. "Don't thank me. I didn't do anything. Except for the fertility pills."

Karissa laughed. "Maybe it was me. I quit smoking, you know. Let's see, it's the second week of July, so it's been over three months now. Plus, I've had no coffee, tea, or any medication at all. And I've been eating right."

"You sound like one of those Mormons, or something," Dr. Taylor said with a smile.

"Or something," Karissa agreed. "Maybe they know what they're talking about after all."

"Well, I don't think so. From what I hear, they are a very strange group."

For some reason, the comment rankled her. *What do I care?* she thought.

"Regardless, I'm going to keep your experience in mind and recommend a better diet to some of my other fertility patients. It'll be interesting to see what happens." He set his papers down, and his eyes met hers. "Now, don't worry about how much weight you gain, as long as you're eating a healthy diet."

"That's easy for you to say. You're thin as a rail."

He grimaced. "I forget to eat," he said, sounding apologetic. Karissa knew that his work had taken precedence in his life. She glanced at her watch.

"How about lunch and coffee?" she asked. "Or juice, since I'm not having any caffeine."

He nodded. "Thank you, I think I will. I've an hour before my next appointment."

She stopped by her office to call Malcolm on his cellular phone, but there was no response. "That's strange. He carries it with him everywhere."

"Maybe he's in the shower," Dr. Taylor suggested.

On the way to the hospital cafeteria, they met Damon Wolfe. Karissa hadn't seen him since they had finished their presentation of Jesse's new programs to the board last April. They had talked several times on the phone in the past months, but any problems that had arisen hadn't really been worth his notice. "There you are," he said. "I've been looking all over for you."

"I didn't know you were here, Damon. It's good to see you." Karissa shook his hand warmly. She'd missed seeing him over the past few months.

"I've just flown in today to see how my favorite hospital is doing." As he talked, Damon's feathery eyebrows moved expressively.

"You're checking up on me?" Karissa teased.

"No, but I have been hearing some interesting news." Damon's sharp amber brown eyes searched hers, missing nothing. "Is it true?"

Karissa laughed. "Oh, yes! Can you believe it? I'm finally going to have a baby! I was going to tell you, of course, but I wanted to make sure everything was going all right before I told everybody. I haven't even told my own parents or let Malcolm tell his. He's chomping at the bit to do so. But until Dr. Taylor here gave me the okay . . . You have met Dr. Taylor, haven't you?" They hadn't met, and Karissa made the introductions. "We're going down for something to eat. Want to join us?"

"Sure, I was headed there myself since I couldn't find you." Damon's narrow face glanced at her stomach, as if expecting to see signs of the baby already. "So does this mean I'm going to have to find a new administrator?" His fingers twisted the ends of his blonde mustache.

"I haven't thought that far ahead," Karissa said.

"Well, let me know." Damon shook his head again and gave her a smile that did not reach his eyes. "And I always thought I'd get you to leave Malcolm for me," he said jokingly. "Especially now that we've both quit smoking." There was something in his voice that didn't match the joviality he was trying to portray. Karissa suddenly understood that her pregnancy bothered him. Now that her dream had come true, would she have to worry about keeping her job?

"Not while you still have your moustache," she countered lightly. "But congratulations about stopping smoking. I wish I could get Malcolm to quit."

They arrived at the cafeteria and Damon motioned for her to go in front of him. "I stopped smoking because of my doctor's orders."

Karissa glanced at Dr. Taylor. "Are all you doctors against smoking?"

"Not all of us," he answered dryly. "The profession in general makes big bucks from smokers."

"That's sad," Karissa said.

"Not as sad as you not liking my moustache," Damon returned, feigning indignation. Karissa laughed.

Halfway through their meal, Karissa excused herself to call Malcolm again. There was still no response. She was tempted to call Brionney at the house to see if she had heard from him, but she didn't want to wake her or the two youngest girls from their naps. Since finding out about the twins, Brionney had been ordered to take things very easy, and that meant a lot of sleep and down-time. Besides, if she talked to Brionney, she would probably blurt out the doctor's findings, and she wanted Malcolm to be the next to hear the great news.

When she returned to the table, Damon and Dr. Taylor were in a tense discussion. Both smiled briefly at her and plunged once more into the conversation "The men are far too authoritarian," Dr. Taylor said.

"Why?" Damon replied. "Because they teach that the women should stay at home to raise their children? Because they believe that a man should carry the burden of earning a living and taking responsibility for his family? I think they have a very valid point. You've read the studies. Children are better off when a parent is at home with them, be it mother or father. And generally, if there is a choice to be made, I think a mother is a better, gentler choice, especially since men still tend to make a better wage, unjustified as that may be."

"I do agree with those studies," Dr. Taylor said, "but I think the ideal is far from realistic."

"Agreed, but it *is* a better situation."

"For the children," Dr. Taylor conceded. "But what about the mother? Why don't we ask Karissa how she feels about it?"

"Yeah, she's Mormon, even if she's not active. She can tell us how the women feel about staying home."

Dr. Taylor colored slightly and his smooth forehead wrinkled. "You're a Mormon?"

Karissa nodded. "But how on earth did you get to talking about this?"

Dr. Taylor's bare head nodded toward Damon. "Two young men came knocking on his door."

Damon's moustache twitched. "My son let them in a few months ago when I wasn't home. I let them come back because he was curious. With me present, of course. I was worried about brainwashing." He had the good grace to look embarrassed. "I find them interesting. A religion, definitely not a cult."

"Of course they're not a cult," Karissa said. "But some of them are overbearing, just like in any organization. Take my father, for instance. He—" She broke off, but the two men regarded her intently.

"What about your father?" Damon prompted.

"Never mind." Karissa dismissed her father with a wave of her hand. Suddenly, she had a headache. "Can we talk about something else?"

Damon stared at her for a moment, as if trying to wrench the information from her telepathically, then nodded slowly. He turned to Dr. Taylor. "You're a family man, aren't you?"

Dr. Taylor darted a glance in Karissa's direction before replying, "Yes, my wife and I have three children."

"Who watches them?"

"Why, my wife does. I—" Dr. Taylor nodded. "Oh, I see," he said. "Well, as a doctor I can afford to—"

"But that's just it. All men have the right to be able to support their families. One could argue that if women—no offense, Karissa—if women stayed home, more men would have good jobs available so they could support their families."

"That sounds rather chauvinistic," Dr. Taylor said. Karissa had to agree.

"I'm not saying I believe it," Damon countered. "I'm just putting it out for discussion."

"Well, I've got to get back to work," Karissa put in. She wasn't up to listening to their solutions to the world's problems. Even so, the discussion had opened a Pandora's box inside her own head—but one that she would deal with later. Right now, her work seemed unimportant in the face of finally having a child.

"But you've hardly touched your food," Damon protested. He reached out a hand to touch her arm, but pulled back before actually making contact. He looked at his hand as if wondering who it belonged to.

Karissa clapped him on the shoulder. "Thanks, but I'm not hungry."

"That will soon change," Dr. Taylor said with a grin.

"Don't I know it. My friend Brionney spends most of her time in the kitchen."

"With twins on the way, I wouldn't wonder," Damon said. "That reminds me, would you have Jesse call me? I've got some ideas for a partnership I want to run by him."

Karissa made her escape, but felt their eyes following her as she left. Why did she suddenly feel so uncomfortable around Damon? He had always been one of her best friends in Alaska.

For the rest of the afternoon she immersed herself in paperwork, marveling again at how much easier Jesse's programs made her job. Of course, she had been the one who decided they needed new programs, and Damon had been her principal support, even when others on the board had questioned the expense.

Thinking of Damon brought back the comment he had made about her leaving Malcolm. Could he have known how close she had been to doing just that? She found it interesting that Damon had stopped smoking while Malcolm hadn't. Both were strong, good-looking men, but obviously Damon had some inner resolve that Malcolm lacked. Why couldn't Malcolm be stronger? Did it really matter? Malcolm was a good man, and he would be a great father.

She was too happy with her life to dwell on the subject for long. Her hand fell from the keyboard to her flat stomach. "Hello, little one," she said aloud, then laughed at the silliness of it.

* * * *

Karissa arrived home later in the day, still smiling but feeling uneasy about not being able to reach Malcolm by telephone. The urge to tell him the good news about the baby burned inside her. As she exited her truck, she heard a car door slam in front of the house and someone call out, "Wait, Karissa!"

She turned to see Delinda Goodrich hurrying up the walk and into the open garage. Her daughter June came behind more slowly, holding the hand of a little boy about Camille's age. His red hair was an even brighter orange-red than June's. "How lucky you're home," Delinda said, puffing slightly at the exertion.

Luck, Karissa knew, had little to do with it. Delinda was nothing, if not persistent. "I'm just getting home from work," she said with a touch of coldness.

"Oh, good. Then you can just sit in on our lesson with Brionney. We're so glad to catch you both at home."

"Brionney knows you're coming?"

Delinda drew herself up to her full height, still a head shorter than Karissa. "Yes, she does."

"And we brought her something," June said, holding up a brown-wrapped rectangular package. Her pale eyes watered, but she didn't look away.

Karissa relaxed and turned back toward the kitchen door to hide her smile. "And who's this little boy?"

"That's my youngest, Germ," Delinda said, following her into the house.

"You call him Germ?"

"It's not his real name, but he won't answer to any other." Delinda shrugged, and her gold necklace caught the dim light in the kitchen, coming from the windows overlooking the greenhouse. "You gotta let them be themselves."

Before Karissa could reply, Savannah, Camille, and Rosalie raced into the kitchen, followed closely by Malcolm. "You're finally here!" exclaimed Rosalie. "We been waiting all day!"

"Come on," Savannah urged, her pale face flushing with excitement. Camille said nothing but danced from one foot to the other. She grabbed Karissa's hand and pulled.

"What's going on?" Karissa asked Malcolm. "I've been calling you, but there's been no answer. I was worried."

He smiled so she could see all his teeth, a row of stark white in his tanned face. "I've been working. I left the cell phone in the studio."

"I saw the doctor today," she said. The girls abruptly grew quiet, sensing the seriousness of the situation.

"And?"

Karissa glanced at the crowd around her. "Excuse us a minute?"

"No problem," Delinda replied. "Where's Brionney?"

Malcolm smiled. "She's in the greenhouse. Girls, will you show her the way?" Karissa opened her mouth to protest, but closed it again when Malcolm grabbed her hand.

"Well?" he asked when they were gone.

"Everything's going great. So far, it looks as though we're having this baby."

"Yes!" He jumped into the air. "I knew it!" He kissed her, and this time he tasted different, not as acrid as usual. A few moments passed until she realized that his breath was devoid of the customary smoke residue, and also of the mints he normally used to cover the smell.

"Why don't you go into the greenhouse for your lesson?" Malcolm said suddenly. "Brionney wanted me to stick one of her casseroles in the oven."

Karissa sighed. "I guess I'd better make sure Germ isn't destroying the plants."

"Germ?" he asked.

"It's a long story."

She wandered down the hall to the laundry room and through the door the girls had left open. What she saw made her stop and stare, her mouth falling open.

"Do you like it?" Malcolm came from behind her and wrapped his arms around her waist.

In the sandbox was the largest set of play tubes she had ever seen. It went up and over and down, and had dozens of nooks with Plexiglas windows where the children could wave down to them. Rosalie had her face pressed up against one of these, making her nose resemble a baby pig's snout. At the bottom end of one of the tubes, just outside the large circle of sand, there was a cage filled with hundreds of tiny balls. Germ was inside, laughing and throwing them about wildly. Overhead, Camille and Savannah swung back and forth in a huge round ball that vaguely resembled a spaceship. Rosalie pulled her face from the window and crawled up the adjoining flexi-tube to meet them.

"Jesse and I are putting up the swings now," Malcolm said, propelling her forward. "They go over the right side of the sandbox under that tube—see the empty space? Oh, yeah . . . we couldn't get the ball cage to fit inside the sandbox so we had to put it on the walkway outside—it was just the right size. Well, we did have to move a few of your plants to get it to fit, but we replanted them over on the other side. Camille watered them." He turned her around and held her close. "You do love it, don't you, Karissa? I had it especially designed after your first positive test. I paid extra to get it here so quickly. You're not mad about the plants, are you? Why don't you say something?"

She tried to swallow the lump in her throat, but it wouldn't go down. She wasn't mad about the play tubes being erected in the sandbox; she had designed the greenhouse with that very thing in mind. Nor was she upset about them moving the plants or not telling her what they had planned, though that had been her first inclination. What she did feel was an overwhelming love for Malcolm at his thoughtfulness and his excitement at the possibility of their children one day playing here. "I love it," she managed finally.

He hugged her joyfully. "Oh, Karissa," he whispered in her ear, "we're going to fill this place with children, just as we always planned."

They walked farther into the greenhouse. "So did the tests come back?" Brionney asked eagerly, turning from her conversation with Delinda. One hand rested on her growing stomach.

Karissa nodded. "The baby seems to be doing fine."

"A baby! Oh, landsakes! I'm so happy for ya." Delinda hugged Karissa. "Having a baby, why that's exciting! They're hard work, but fun."

Karissa looked at the children and smiled, pushing back her hair.

Delinda continued, "Pretty soon you'll be getting the Mormon Mommy Haircut—"

"The what?"

"The Mormon Mommy Haircut," Delinda replied, and Karissa heard the capitalization in her voice. The visiting teacher ran her hands through her short auburn locks. Her dangling earrings each held a shiny blue sapphire. "That's when ya finally give up your long hair. Usually somewhere around the fourth child."

Brionney nodded, touching the white-blonde locks whose ends barely brushed her shoulders. "I used to have even longer hair. And I'm going to cut it all off when the twins are born. It's in the way, especially with having a baby around."

"That's why I call it the Mormon Mommy Haircut. Once it's short, you'll never go back to long."

Karissa laughed. "Then I make a vow never to give in."

"Oh, it's not giving in. It's just going with the flow instead of swimming upstream." Delinda rubbed her blunt hands, looking back and forth between Malcolm and Karissa. "Landsakes, a baby! Pretty soon you'll be staying awake half the night and playing the 'I-can-clean-that-diaper-in-so-many-wipes' game. Yes, sir, good times are just around the corner." From her voice, Karissa couldn't tell if she was serious or teasing.

"I don't play that game," Jesse said, coming up behind them. "Brionney would win every time."

"To him, *all* diapers are at least six-wipe diapers," Brionney explained dryly. "You should see him piling them up in his hand so he doesn't get anything on him. We go through more wipes that way."

Jesse shuddered. "Six wipes is about right. It keeps my finger-nails clean."

Delinda chuckled, enjoying every minute of the exchange. "Well, with twins there'll be plenty to go around." Her brown eyes focused on Karissa. "But the haircut and the wipe game are only the beginning. Before long, you'll be rolling up your breasts like socks and sticking them in your bra—I read that somewhere, and boy, is it true!"

Brionney looked embarrassed, but she nodded in agreement. Malcolm and Jesse suddenly became interested in finishing the swing set.

"What about the casserole?" Karissa called after them.

Brionney started for the door. "I'll put it in."

"All this reminds me of our lesson this month," Delinda said.

I'll bet, Karissa thought as Brionney paused in her flight. Delinda was a master at weaving the lesson into any conversation.

"We have something for ya," June said, handing the package to Brionney with a shy smile. Despite her lack of friendship with the visiting teachers, Karissa felt odd at seeing that smile. June had never smiled at her. Not ever.

Brionney put her arm around the girl. "Thank you so much! I can't wait to see what it is."

Karissa already knew.

She followed the women slowly out of the greenhouse, glancing once more over her shoulder at the play equipment. Malcolm had stopped working and was watching at her, an enigmatic smile on his full lips. His gray eyes were softer than she had ever seen them.

"I love you," he mouthed.

But would he if he knew her secret? The happiness Karissa had held on to all day dissipated like heat in a strong breeze. Now she felt as though she walked a tightrope in a circus tent, and one false move would send her and their relationship, built as it was on falsehood, crashing to the hard dirt floor. Once it hadn't mattered, but now it did because she knew she loved him. She waved at Malcolm and turned quickly, hoping he wouldn't see her fear.

That night, the dream came as it hadn't since she had quit smoking. *The baby Karissa carried in her arms hit her head on the door frame and looked at her sadly. "Why? Why?" she asked. "I would have made you whole." And then she died.*

"No! It's just a dream!" Karissa screamed. "I didn't hit your head."

But the baby didn't hear.

CHAPTER 13

The late-September air held more than a hint of cold, and they conceded to the weather enough to wear warm jackets on their outing to Pillar Mountain. The little girls carried small tin buckets Brionney and Karissa had bought them at Safeway, and Jesse hefted the large picnic basket, filled to nearly overflowing with food and goodies. On his back he had also tied a blanket and a folding chair for his wife. Malcolm's arms were full, too, with plastic sacks of soda cans and old beer bottles. Over his shoulder he carried the Winchester Magnum, and the Colt Mustang rode in the holster around his waist. In his faded Levis and his old flannel jacket, he felt like something out of a cowboy movie. Even his worn leather hiking boots added to the effect.

There was a place for target shooting up ahead, and he planned to show the girls how it was done. He wished he had more bottles—they made a better show—but since he and Karissa had given up drinking, they had to make do with a few catsup bottles and what they had managed to collect from their remote neighbors.

The clear blue of the sky burst in on his senses, as if everything was sky, or wanted to be. There was a slight breeze whispering through the lustrous green of the bushes and long grass. He remembered the sound from his childhood. The wind and grass called his name and promised to show him wonders he had never imagined. And he had never been disappointed. Kodiak was everything a child could dream of. Part of him longed to lie in the green grass and stare forever at the sky.

"Is it far?" Savannah walked slowly by her mother with an arm around her for support, but looked longingly after her sisters, who danced on ahead, laughing and swinging their buckets.

"Not far now," Malcolm replied, squinting in the sun, which was still warm enough to keep them comfortable.

"I'm okay, Savannah," Brionney said, smiling down at her daughter. Her round eyes were the same color as the sky, certainly her best feature. She was quite heavy now, being eight months pregnant with her twins. "Don't worry. If I was going to go into labor because of the ride up, I would have done it by now. Go on ahead. I'll call if I need you." Brionney gave her daughter a gentle push. Savannah hesitated only a brief second before flitting away to join her sisters.

"Are you sure?" Hunched over with the weight of the picnic basket, Jesse looked worriedly at his wife.

"Landsakes," said Brionney, mimicking Delinda Goodrich. "I swear you people are worse than mother hens. I haven't been out of the house for nearly a month—or out of bed for a week. And you would have thought I was a piece of precious china, the way Malcolm crept up that road back there. For the last time, I'm all right! If I had stayed home one more minute, I would have gone insane!"

"Well, we had to go slow anyway with Jesse and the girls in the bed of the truck," Karissa said. "Either way, we'd hate to have something go wrong on our last outing before your babies come." Karissa was three months along now, but unlike Brionney, she didn't show in the slightest. She walked with an easy, relaxed stride, and her tanned face was happy.

Jesse shifted his load. "The girls'll be sad not to have you around so much."

"Are you sure you want to move to Anchorage?" Malcolm asked.

"Well, with having twins and all, we want to be closer to a hospital," Jesse said. "The doctor says the babies could come early. Besides, I've only got a few contracts left to finish before we head back to Utah—and most of those are in Anchorage. Damon Wolfe put me on to those. And we're thinking about starting our own software company. He's a smart guy, that Damon."

"They say everything he touches turns to gold," Karissa said. "The man is wealthier than I've ever cared to be."

Malcolm felt a twinge of jealousy at the admiration in her voice. "Money's not everything," he said quickly.

"Goodness, I know that." Her tone implied that Malcolm was missing the point. "I feel so sorry for him. His wife passed away just before we moved here, and he's lonely. He's got two great kids, too. Occasionally he brings them when he comes out." Malcolm didn't know Karissa had met Damon's children, and it bothered him that she had never mentioned it before.

A few puffy clouds like white marshmallows appeared on the horizon, giving relief to the absolute blue. A bald eagle swooped majestically overhead, and Malcolm wished he had brought his video camera instead of his regular one. He stopped and snapped a picture anyway.

"Here we are," Karissa announced. "Isn't this where you brought me last year?"

"More or less," Malcolm said, looking around. To the east he could see the ocean going forever until it curved out of sight over the horizon. Of course, there was land across that wide icy expanse, but it was too far away for him to see. The isolation was one of the reasons he loved Kodiak Island.

If they moved closer to the edge of Pillar Mountain, they would be able to see parts of the city of Kodiak in the northeast. "Did you ever see anything so beautiful?" he asked. The others nodded, and he was glad they didn't say anything to spoil the moment.

Then Karissa spoke, her voice a whisper in the crisp air. "It's very lonely."

"It's isolated," he answered, "that's all." There was a pristine beauty in this untouched world. Why couldn't she see that? He ached for her to understand why he loved this land, why it called out to his soul.

"Can we pick the berries now?" the girls begged.

Malcolm pretended to take offense. "Don't you want to go shooting with me?"

"After we pick berries," Savannah informed him gravely.

Brionney laughed. "Sorry, Malcolm. They've never picked lingan berries before."

"Cranberries," he corrected. "We call 'em cranberries."

"But they're much better," Karissa said, setting down the water cooler she carried. "Come on, girls, let's try those bushes over there." She pointed to the north. "If the people haven't picked them all."

"Or the bears," Jesse joked.

Other than the sudden frown, Karissa ignored his comment. Malcolm was glad he hadn't said it, although it had been on the tip of his tongue.

"Are there really bears?" Savannah asked, shivering deliciously. Her eyes opened wide.

"They like to stick to the wildlife refuge," Karissa said, moving off. "Hurry up. Maybe we'll find some salmon berries, too."

The girls scampered after Karissa, while the rest set down their gear. Brionney spread the blanket in a clearing where the grasses looked particularly soft. Jesse helped her, then placed her chair nearby and settled her into it. "Rest a bit," he ordered. "Please?"

Brionney laughed. "Okay, you nut, but I feel fine."

Malcolm turned away from their tender moment and went to pick berries with Karissa and the girls. To the north and slightly west, he could see the mountain range called the Three Sisters: Faith, Hope, and Charity. Beyond them and to the right he could see Monashka Bay. Although he was too far away, he imagined the rocky beaches interspersed by patches of soft sand. Wonder rushed through him as it always did when he was on Pillar Mountain. There were places on Kodiak that were more beautiful, but none that lived so vividly in both his present and childhood memories.

I'll bring my child here next year, he thought. As if sensing his thoughts, Karissa smiled at him. He realized that he had been wrong earlier; her pregnancy did show in the glow on her face and in the way the hollows beneath her cheekbones were filling in.

"What do you see?" she asked, gazing toward Monashka Bay.

"I'm seeing the past and the future," he replied. "I think next year they'll meet here." She couldn't possibly know what he was talking about, but he felt surprised when her face darkened a shade.

"The past is gone," she said stiffly.

"It's never gone, but always with us," he returned. "I can practically see myself here as a boy. I used to run and hide in the tall grasses and chase the rodents into their holes." He smiled. "That made me part of what I am."

A shadow leapt across her face and was gone, leaving a blank, hollow shell. "I guess you're right." Without another word, she turned and began picking berries. Malcolm picked with her, and after a while they began to talk like nothing had happened. He wasn't even sure the whole thing hadn't only occurred in his imagination. He wished he dared ask, but was unwilling to risk Karissa's wrath, or—even worse—her withdrawal. Better to leave it alone.

But what was bothering her? Did she hate the island so badly? Why couldn't she confide in him?

After they tired of gathering berries, they ate lunch. But the girls had eaten so many berries that they couldn't hold much more. Savannah stared at the macaroni salad her mother had made, picking at the kernels of sweet corn in the mixture. "I like corn better on that long straight thing."

"You mean the cob," Karissa said.

"Yeah, it's better that way," Camille agreed. "Only it gets stuck in your teeth."

"You just have to eat it the right way," Malcolm put in. "It's like this." He held up his hands with a pretend cob between them. "You eat one row at a time. Like a typewriter." He made the motions of eating a row, then he said, "Ding! And you start over."

The girls stared at him blankly. "What's a typewriter?" asked Savannah. Malcolm blinked at them in amazement before the laughter burst out of his mouth.

He slapped Jesse on the back. "What kind of an education are you giving these girls, anyway? They don't even know what a typewriter is."

Jesse grinned back. "What can I say? They're the children of a computer programmer. They've grown up with computers and laser printers. Is that so bad?"

"I think we still have a typewriter at the house," Karissa said. "We can show them when we get home." She shot a glance at her husband. "Malcolm used it in college, so it's probably a collector's item now." The girls giggled at Malcolm's growl of protest. He tickled Karissa until she took back the words.

In retrospect, Malcolm would wish they had simply gone home then, but he had been determined to shoot his guns. He walked a short way off and made a few practice shots, shattering the bottles into satisfying pieces. Then he helped Savannah shoot a can with the Colt Magnum. "I did it!" she shouted. "I'm really good, aren't I?" Malcolm said she was, though he had aimed the shot.

Jesse took a turn, but he didn't hit anything. "It's a good thing you're better at programs than you are at shooting," Malcolm said with a laugh.

Jessed grinned. "Well, girls, anyone else want a try?"

Rosalie shook her head and stuck her fingers in her ears, but Camille nodded. "But I have to go potty first," she said.

"Me too," the others added.

Jesse sighed. "Come on then. Let's go ask Mom where she set up the porta-potty." He rolled his eyes. "This is one of the side-effects of parenting that I'll never get used to."

All three girls ran with their father to where Brionney lounged in the chair. Karissa sat Indian-style on the blanket next to her. When the entire Hergarter family disappeared into the brush, Karissa arose and sauntered over to Malcolm, the long grasses brushing at her Levi's.

"Want to take a shot?" he asked.

"No." She looked embarrassed. "I'm afraid the noise will hurt the baby. I know it won't, but I worry a lot."

He held her close. "It doesn't sound strange at all. I'm tempted to put you in a glass room myself."

"Just try it," she threatened, raising her fist. He laughed. She joined in, but it wasn't the throaty laughter he loved. She hadn't laughed that way since their outing at Kalsin Bay.

"Come to think of it, I think I need to see a man about a dog myself." He released her and pointed to the knee-high rock where he had laid the weapons, the rifle in its case and the pistol in the holster he had removed from his hip. The bag with the extra ammunition was propped against the base of the stone. "Would you watch the guns while I go find a spare bush? They're loaded, and I wouldn't want the girls to get them by accident. And Jesse's not so good with guns."

She smiled. "Okay, but hurry. These things make me nervous."

"That's because you don't know how to use them. Once you learn, it'll be like fishing."

She wrinkled her nose. "Okay, I'll try it—next year."

He chuckled and moved off. At least there would be a next year for them. When Karissa was out of sight, he pulled a cigarette from the pack in his pocket. He lit up and slowly smoked the whole thing, killing the craving that had eaten at him all morning. Then he smoked another and began the third. Since the day he had built the play tubes inside the greenhouse his smoking had increased steadily, although he had been too busy that day to smoke at all. *I'm free,* he had thought after that successful day, but it had only been an illusion. The next day he had gone back to his films and had smoked twice his reduced amount, as if making up for the previous day. Now he was back to smoking nearly as much as he had before trying to quit. He hid his habit as best he could from Karissa, though she knew he still smoked. Something inside wouldn't allow him to ask for help—from anyone. But he knew he somehow had to find a way to stop smoking. He detested feeling so weak and out of control.

The third cigarette had burned nearly to the end when he heard the scream. It came out of nowhere and hung in the air, a bloodcurdling sound of stark terror mixed with a desperate plea for help. The voice was almost unrecognizable, but he knew in his heart it was Karissa. His legs felt weak as the fear oozed inside him, penetrating every cell.

"Karissa!" His scream was as equally loud as hers had been. The blood began to pump once more through his system and his feet moved back the way he had come, gaining speed as he went. Finally he was running, dodging through the berry bushes, uncaring as they grabbed onto his clothing, as though trying to slow him and prevent him from reaching Karissa.

She screamed again, words this time, but they were drowned in a ferocious roar that Malcolm recognized only too well.

A bear.

As his gaze took in the huge animal, facts came unbidden to Malcolm's mind. The Kodiak brown bear was famous among those who knew about bears, as was the Kodiak National Wildlife Refuge which covered three-quarters of Kodiak Island. The brown bear was one of only six native land mammals on Kodiak. The red fox, river otter, short-tailed weasel, little brown bat, and tundra vole were the other five, each smaller but just as important in the great design.

All this and more raced through Malcolm's mind like a section of his documentary. One part of him noticed how the bear reared on its hind legs and roared, its massive muscles rippling up the long, shaggy back. The bear's fur had grown long now, and would continue to do so until hibernation time. *What is it doing here?* In all his growing-up years on Kodiak Island, Malcolm had never seen a bear on Pillar Mountain, though as a child he had dreamed he would.

Malcolm pushed himself to run faster. He could see Karissa beyond the bear, backing slowly away, not taking her eyes off the creature that outweighed her many times over. Her face was drawn and pale beneath her tan, as if the blood had fled from her skin. Her hair streamed wildly past her cheeks, adding to her appearance of terror. One hand was pressed protectively against her flat belly.

As a child, Malcolm had been taught that when meeting a brown bear he should play dead, and the animal would go away. For a black bear, the victim should confront the animal, making a lot of noise to scare him off. For a white bear, the only chance was to run for dear life. Karissa didn't know any of this; besides, he would never want her to lie down and play dead. The bear might damage their unborn child as he sniffed and pawed at her body.

Karissa swiveled her head, looking off into the distance at something only she could see. Now Malcolm was close enough to hear the words she screamed: "Get back! Get back! Take the girls away!"

Malcolm heard more screams, fainter than Karissa's, but whatever made them—probably Jesse's family—was blocked by the bulky body of the bear.

The bear dropped to all fours and began to run toward Karissa. "No!" Malcolm screamed with an intensity that threatened to break his vocal cords. The bear hesitated, twisting his head to focus black, beady eyes on Malcolm.

In some distant part of his brain, Malcolm knew that going unarmed against an angry bear, brown or any other color, wasn't the most intelligent course, but there was nothing else he could do to save Karissa. There was no time for any strategem, just the knowledge that he had to protect his wife and the baby growing inside her.

The bear swung his head back toward Karissa, as if dismissing Malcolm completely. She backed away, more quickly now, with uncontrolled jerks. Several paces behind her, he could see the knee-high rock where he had laid the weapons.

"No, get me!" Malcolm yelled at the bear. He felt his side aching from the run and his lungs gasping for breath.

The huge beast didn't falter. Karissa tripped backward over the rock, scattering the guns. She fell hard into the sparse grass on the other side, back first. Malcolm was close enough to hear the loud thump and her low moan. He could also hear the panting of the bear. In one second, the animal would be on top of Karissa. She wasn't playing dead, but crying and struggling to get up.

Malcolm jumped hard and hit the beast from behind, grasping at his heavy coat. That got the bear's attention, and he whirled, tossing Malcolm sideways. Malcolm lost his hold on the bear's hide and fell over a short bush, then jumped back to his feet. The animal growled and opened his mouth to rip into Malcolm's unprotected flesh. Malcolm felt a rush of adrenaline, and for a brief second he wasn't afraid. Was this how his grandfather had felt when he had wrestled that other bear so long ago?

"Go away!" Malcolm heard Jesse shouting from somewhere.

A rock flew in the air, hitting the bear. The animal didn't appear to notice. He snapped at Malcolm, who tried to leap out of reach. He didn't jump fast enough. Sharp teeth tore into his right shoulder, but he didn't feel anything other than the initial agonizing pain. The bear slapped him down to the ground with surprisingly agile paws. Malcolm fell to his back, and the jagged rocks and dry brush bit through his flannel jacket, causing more pain than he now felt from the wound in his shoulder. He tried to lie still, faking death. Maybe it wasn't too late to make the bear lose interest. But the animal raised his paw and lashed out, dragging his black pointed nails down Malcolm's left shoulder clear to his waist.

That ended Malcolm's attempt to fool the bear. He brought his feet up in a swift motion, kicking at the beast with all his strength. The bear caught his right hiking boot in its mouth and shook its head furiously. Malcolm jabbed at the bear's face with the other heavy boot, smashing into it over and over. The bear clung to his prize, a ferocious growl emitting from his throat. The bone in Malcolm's right ankle suddenly snapped with a loud crack. A wave of nausea exploded in his stomach, and the world threatened to turn black with his pain.

"Go away!" Jesse yelled again. His voice was closer now, but tight with fear. He appeared in the edge of Malcolm's fading vision, carrying a large stick. With both arms over his head, Jesse smashed the end against the bear's skull. After the forth or fifth pass, the bear dropped Malcolm's ankle, but he didn't turn on Jesse or run away. He opened his mouth wide and started to go for Malcolm's defenseless stomach. There was nothing Malcolm could do to stop him.

* * * *

Even after he heard the scream and saw the bear, Jesse wasn't very worried. He had witnessed Malcolm's expertise with the guns, almost with envy, and though his friend was somewhat rusty after a few months without practice, his easy manner with the weapons appeared to return quickly. Besides, one shot in the air and the bear should flee back to wherever it had come from.

Then he saw with horror that Malcolm stood nowhere near the guns. Nor did Karissa, though she was the closest. Suddenly he knew that one of them might not make it home alive. He leaned his face close to Brionney's and echoed the words Karissa had just yelled at them. "Get the girls away!" he said fiercely. "Go back to the truck and get inside." If he knew Malcolm at all, the truck would be open. "Don't come back, no matter what!"

Brionney's eyes were wide with shock. "Come with me!" she pleaded.

Oh, how he wanted to! "I can't leave them," he said. He saw Malcolm running up behind the bear, waving his arms frantically and screaming at the animal like a lunatic. "You see that, don't you? I can't leave them."

Brionney searched his face with her eyes, seeming to capture each detail in her memory. "I love you," she replied, and the words showed her acceptance. He was glad she understood that he had no other choice. To run might mean leaving Malcolm or Karissa to die, and neither of them could live with that knowledge. Brionney turned away, dodging around a berry bush and lumbering awkwardly in the opposite direction, dragging the whimpering girls with her. But before she turned away, Jesse saw a glimpse of eternity in her blue, blue eyes, and it comforted him.

Malcolm had somehow turned the bear away from Karissa, but Jesse couldn't see her. Where was she? He felt the rock in his hand before he knew he had bent to pick it up. He threw it with all his force, praying it would find its mark. It hit the bear on the side of the head, but the animal didn't seem to falter. Jesse threw more rocks as the bear mauled Malcolm, knocking him like a rag doll to the ground with a single swipe of one powerful paw. There was a lot of red on Malcolm's body, but by his movements Jesse knew his friend was still alive.

The rocks are doing no good, Jesse decided. As if in answer to his silent prayer, he spied a big stick, as thick as his arm at its thinnest point and growing larger at the end. *A club,* he thought. *That might work.*

With the club in his arms, he ran at the bear, yelling and screaming as he had heard Indians do in the movies. It helped some, as his anger overcame part of his terrible fear. *What a great story this will make for my grandchildren,* he thought. But a more sobering realization followed on its heels: *If we all live.*

As he approached the bear, he saw Karissa on the animal's far side. She sprawled out on the ground, the guns scattered around her. *If only I could reach the guns,* he thought. But something told him every second counted. He raised the club and hit the bear over and over. Finally the animal released Malcolm's foot, and Jesse hoped the bear would run away. But it didn't. The dark eyes, no more than pinpoints compared to the creature's massive body, glowed with anger—dumb animal anger that would not desist.

Jesse jabbed the club at the bear's mouth. The animal tossed his head sharply, hitting the stick with such force that Jesse lost his hold. The branch flew through the air and clattered to the ground beyond his reach. Forgetting Malcolm, the bear whirled toward Jesse, its angry eyes focused murderously. But then one of Malcolm's feet came up again and stabbed at the bear's jaw. The beast growled and snapped at the boot, his spiked teeth closing on thin air. Jesse lunged for his stick, but he knew he would never reach it in time. The bear went again for Malcolm's unprotected stomach.

A shot rang out, pure and clean in the midst of the ugly turmoil. Jesse's gut wrenched with the sound, as if it was unsure of whether to be relieved or to prepare for more terror. The bear paused ever so briefly, and in that instant, more shots came. Jesse did not count them, but they seemed to never end. The animal moved with difficulty now, as if in slow motion. Blood dripped from a wound on its head. Then it gave a deep, tortured growl and lumbered away into the brush.

Jesse saw Karissa drop the pistol to the ground. Her face was stark white in contrast to the dark-brown hair that tumbled about her like a flowing veil. She walked toward them, a few rolling steps, a question in her eyes, and stood unsteadily staring down at Malcolm.

"I'm all right," Malcolm muttered huskily, pushing himself onto his left arm. "My ankle's broken though, and I—" He broke off. "I'm so sorry, Karissa. I shouldn't have left you alone." He stared down at the pack of cigarettes in his jacket pocket, which had spilled half its content onto the ground during the attack.

Karissa slumped to her knees. She didn't reach out to Malcolm as Jesse expected, but stared at the cigarettes on the dirt and grass. "You were smoking," she said. It wasn't a question.

Malcolm fell back onto the ground, groaning. Karissa slowly removed her flannel-lined denim jacket and pressed it to Malcolm's shoulder. "We have to get him back to the truck." Her voice was remote and calm. "There's a first aid kit there."

She's in shock, Jesse thought. "Maybe we shouldn't move him," he said.

"We can't let him bleed to death." Karissa's voice cracked slightly. "He needs a hospital."

"Okay then, let me run back to the truck and get the kit. We'll bandage him up before we try to get him down."

Karissa nodded and stared down at Malcolm's closed eyes. Jesse jerked to his feet, went to the fallen pistol, reloaded it, and handed it to Karissa. "In case the bear comes back." He didn't think it would, but it might pay to be sure. He removed the rifle from its cloth case and made sure it was also loaded before slinging it over his shoulder. "I'll hurry," he said. The words were unnecessary, as Karissa seemed not to hear.

Jesse ran. Now that the fight was over, he had time to worry about Brionney and the girls. Had they found the truck in this unfamiliar territory? Had Brionney overexerted herself? Had they run into the wounded, pain-crazed bear?

He found his family huddled in the cab of Karissa's Nissan, their eyes anxiously searching through the windows. Brionney opened the door and met him outside the truck. "Are they . . .?"

"They're alive," he said. "But Malcolm's hurt pretty bad. He's got a broken ankle, and he's bleeding in several places. We're going to try to stop the bleeding before we take him to the hospital. There's supposed to be a first aid kit in the car."

"I'll tell the rescue squad," Brionney said. For the first time, Jesse noticed she carried a cellular phone in her hands. "It's Malcolm's," she explained, seeing his glance. "He left it in the car. I called as soon as we got here. Someone's on their way already."

"Good." Jesse felt relief wash through him. Brionney talked into the phone while he found the first aid kit under the seat. Three scared little faces watched him gravely. "It's going to be all right," he assured the children. "Don't worry, but say a prayer."

"Is the bear gone?" Savannah asked.

"Yes. He won't be coming back, not ever." He managed to dredge up a smile.

Brionney took the phone away from her ear. "They say not to move him, that they'll be here by the time you finish the bandages. I'll show them where you are."

"You'd better wait for them inside the truck, just in case," Jesse said, his voice low so the children wouldn't hear. "I don't know where the bear went."

Brionney nodded. "Be careful."

"I will." He was always careful, and had always thought things out before acting—except for this once, when he had attacked the bear with a mere stick. Though he was safe now, he felt ill, and he knew the sickness wouldn't leave until the incident was long behind him.

Karissa had ripped open Malcolm's shirt and exposed his left side where the bear had clawed him. With one hand, she pressed against her jacket that covered Malcolm's damaged right shoulder. Already the blue material showed dark where the blood seeped through.

Without speaking, Jesse opened the first aid kit. Karissa directed him to pour antiseptic over the claw marks while she worked to stem the blood oozing from his right shoulder. Her face crinkled in concentration as she pulled a bandage around and around and tied it off. "I think that will work." She opened another package of cloth and likewise bandaged the claw marks. "These'll have to be stitched. And there's nothing we can do for his ankle. It's too swollen to take off the boot. Maybe it's just as well." Her voice was still unnaturally calm, though tears crept out of the corners of her eyes.

Malcolm moaned, but he had lapsed into unconsciousness.

"Brionney called for help. Someone'll be here soon."

"The cell phone."

"Yeah. Malcolm left it in the car."

They knelt in silence. Malcolm regained consciousness briefly, opening his gray eyes, then he was out again. "I want to give him a blessing," Jesse said. Karissa nodded, not looking at him. But Jesse had left his keys at home, and the consecrated oil on his key ring with it. There was nothing more he could do but pray.

"What's taking them so long?" Karissa said, her calm demeanor slipping. "He needs help."

"I'll go get the blanket," Jesse said. We can move him down in it."

He brought the blanket, but hesitated. Karissa was standing now, but moved with the cautiousness of someone who was broken inside. He recalled how she had fallen over the rock during the bear attack. How seriously had she been hurt? Regardless, she was in no condition to drag Malcolm down to the truck. They would have to wait for help to come.

Shouts drew his attention to where the mountain angled down in the direction of the parked truck. Soon three men came rushing toward them, carrying equipment and a stretcher. "Be careful of his right ankle," Jesse said. They nodded and took over. After a brief examination, they gave Malcolm a pint of blood before trying to move him.

"He's stable," said one of the men finally. "Let's get him down."

On the way back to the vehicles, they passed a group of five men, all carrying guns. Jesse couldn't tell if the guns used bullets or tranquilizers. "Which way did the bear go?" one of them asked.

"I'll show you." But before he did, Jesse took aside one of the EMTs. "You'd better check out Karissa, too," he said. "She fell. She doesn't look good. She's pregnant." The words came out short and sharp with a staccato effect. Jesse wondered for a moment if they even meant anything.

"I'll take care of her," the man assured him.

Jesse nodded his thanks and went back with the hunters to where the bear had attacked. "She shot at him a lot," he said. "It happened too fast to count. And I don't know if any shots went wild." He didn't see how Karissa could have missed any at that range. "Then he ran off that way."

"We'll find him." The hunters looked eager and ready. "We'll let you know."

Jesse slowly walked back to the car alone, struggling under the weight of Malcolm's guns and the picnic basket. Pillar Mountain was quiet now, with no trace of the attack except the dark stain of blood on the grass that Malcolm had left behind.

"It could have been much worse," he said. What could he have done differently? Not a thing, except to have brought his oil. Thinking of that gave him purpose. He had to get to the hospital.

CHAPTER 14

Karissa watched as Malcolm sat propped up on the bed, his face darkening in anger as he listened to Dr. Fairfax. He wore nothing but a pair of white boxer shorts, though his chest and part of his stomach were almost completely covered in protective bandages. His dark chest hair was still visible near the top of the bandages and on the slice of naked belly, and the sight made him seem vulnerable.

Karissa steeled herself against that vulnerability. Nothing else in Malcolm's appearance—not even the heavy white bandages—so much as hinted at weakness. Except the dark chest curls that suggested intimacy.

"I'm all right," Malcolm insisted. "I just want to go home." He swung his right foot off the bed, heavy with a calf-high cast. The doctor had cut the mauled boot off his mangled foot to set it. Karissa shuddered to think what his foot would look like if he had been wearing his Nikes instead of his boots.

"I'd like to give you a blessing," Jesse said from his place near the door.

Malcolm shook his head. "I feel fine. No use in bothering the Lord when I don't need help." After finishing all the stitches, the doctor had given Malcolm medication for the pain. He did act fine; maybe he really didn't need help.

"Are you sure?" Brionney asked. "Because your home teacher is waiting out in the hall with the girls."

"No, really. Thank you, but I feel fine. Like I said, I just want to go home."

Dr. Fairfax shook his head slowly. "You took some serious hits, Malcolm. I want you to stay overnight at least for observation."

Malcolm's face flushed, but he had heard the decisive note in the doctor's voice. He gritted his teeth and hefted his leg back onto the bed. "All right, but tomorrow I leave."

"We'll wait for you outside," Brionney whispered to Karissa.

Karissa didn't reply except to nod. She had expected to feel better once she learned Malcolm would be all right, but instead, a growing numbness filled her heart, spreading to her entire body. Jesse and Brionney said good-bye to Malcolm.

"Tell the girls not to worry. I'll see them tomorrow," Malcolm said as they left.

Karissa clutched at the bed.

"Karissa? Are you okay?" Malcolm's voice seemed to come from very far away.

Dr. Fairfax turned toward her. Karissa felt him touch her arm, but she was too busy fighting the sudden sharp pain in her abdomen. *No! It can't be,* she wanted to scream. *They took my blood pressure. They told me I was fine.*

"What's wrong? What's wrong with you?" Malcolm called out. There was frustration in his voice, a desperation that demanded an answer, but Karissa closed her eyes and the world went black.

* * * *

She saw the bear again, and though she knew it was a dream, she felt the terror flood her body. *The animal was larger than she remembered, its muscles strong and sinewy as it ran toward her. Her mouth opened to scream, but nothing came out. Next to her Malcolm calmly smoked a cigarette, laughing openly at her fear. "I could save you, but I won't," he said. She backed away, falling over the rock. For long moments she thought she would never reach the ground, just fall forever. Then the ground came abruptly, knocking the air out of her and breaking something inside far more important.*

She scrambled for the gun in her dream, as she had in real life, her hands shaky and dripping with sweat. The smell of terror filled her nostrils—and also the smell of blood dripping from Malcolm's body. In reality she had prayed at this point, and she did so again in the dream. "Father, help me please if You would. I know I don't deserve it, but

Malcolm and Jesse didn't commit the sin, I did. Help me save them."
Surely she would never be able to hit the bear, but rather Jesse or her
blood-drenched husband. But she fired six times, and each bullet found its
way into the bulky body of the bear. Only one hit the animal's head.

The bear turned to her and said, "Why did you kill me?"

"I didn't," she replied. "You ran off."

"You killed me," it said. "You didn't even give me a chance. I would
have loved you. I would have made you whole."

Karissa knew it wasn't the bear talking then, but the baby.

She awoke and found Brionney by her side, stroking her right
arm. "Oh good, you're awake."

"What happened?"

"You passed out. From shock, the doctor says."

"I'm losing the baby, aren't I?"

Brionney's smile dimmed. "It's too soon to tell. You are bleeding,
but there's still a chance that everything is fine."

Karissa had known, but hearing it made the agony slice through
the numbness in her heart. She turned her face away and sobbed.
Brionney continued to stroke her arm.

Malcolm appeared in the doorway in a wheelchair, pushed by
Jesse and the girls. They greeted her somberly. Brionney stood,
balancing her heavy body awkwardly. "We'll leave you two alone."

Jesse pushed Malcolm closer to the bed and followed his family
out the door. Karissa didn't speak, but Malcolm reached out to touch
her cheek and caught a tear on his fingertip.

"I'm sorry," he whispered.

"I haven't lost the baby yet."

"If you do, we'll try again."

Karissa clenched her teeth together and took a hissing breath.
"You were out smoking when the bear came," she said, staring at
him. And silently she added, *Because you just can't give up that filthy*
habit, our child will die. She didn't say it aloud, though doing so
might ease the hurt in her soul.

There were tears in Malcolm's eyes. "I didn't know. Please believe
me. I wish I could take it back." His voice was soft and full of sorrow,
and despite her anger and aching despair, Karissa felt her heart softening. She was glad someone had given Malcolm a gown, covering his

bandages and the hairy chest. She didn't want to feel anything for him—not pity, and certainly not love.

Sometimes sorry isn't enough, she thought. Oh, how well she knew that lesson! She made her voice calm and without emotion—anything not to give in to the brutal agony in her heart "Please, I need to be alone. I can't talk to you now."

His pain-filled face colored at her words. "What are you saying? That it's over?"

She didn't look at him. "I haven't thought that far," she said wearily. "I just want to be alone." If she talked to him now, she might say something she would later regret. Like she now regretted that long-ago decision. Besides, who was she to cast the first stone?

"It was a mistake, Karissa," he choked.

"Please." She stared at the bed, wanting to help him, but knowing she couldn't. She was too angry. Too hurt. Too guilty. "I need time."

If he had been able to walk, it would have made a great scene for a movie. He could have turned on his heel and thundered out the door, swinging his arms in wounded outrage at her words. As it was, he struggled to roll himself out the door, grimacing in pain. Karissa watched him leave, feeling numb. She had loved him this morning, or at least been committed to loving him, but now she didn't know what to do.

If only she wasn't losing the baby. If only he had been stronger.

Soon after Malcolm left, they brought a dinner tray and Karissa ate without relish. For the baby, she knew it was already too late.

She slept again, and when she awoke she could feel that she was not alone. A blonde man sat in the chair by her bed, scrunched over with his head in his hands, his elbows propped on his knees. In the darkness and without the moustache, she almost didn't recognize him.

"Damon?" she asked.

He started, rubbing the sleep from his eyes. "I didn't think you would awake till morning."

"Were you going to wait?"

He smiled, and Karissa noticed the moustache had hidden a well-formed upper lip that made him more handsome than she remembered. Why had he ever hidden behind a piece of hair?

"I have nowhere else I need to be. Jesse called Anchorage and told me what happened, and I flew in to see how you were." He laid his hand over hers. "I'm sorry, Kar. I know how much you wanted this baby."

His sincere attitude brought a breath of relief to her soul. "Thank you, Damon. That makes me feel better somehow."

"I wanted to be here for you."

"You shaved your moustache."

He grinned. "You like it?"

"I do actually. You look younger, and more handsome, I think."

"I'm glad." He paused for a second before asking, "How's your husband?"

"He'll be fine. But to tell you the truth, I'm finding it hard to care right now." She knew her words must sound callous, even mean, but she felt relieved to get her feelings into the open.

"You don't love him?" Damon's dark amber eyes bore into hers.

"He should have been with me when it happened. Not off smoking."

Damon frowned and sat back in the soft chair. His warm hand drew away from hers, leaving it cold. "Now, as much as I'm not a fan of Malcolm's, Jesse told me that Malcolm attacked a bear with his bare hands to save you. That shows courage. He could have run away."

"It should never have happened," she insisted. "I think this just proves the point. And now," she began to cry softly, "I'm going to lose my baby."

He grabbed her hand again, leaning his face close to hers.

"I waited for so long," she continued through her tears, "and now Malcolm's ruined everything. I know he didn't mean for it to happen, but there it is. I'm so angry and mad and sad and hurt. I can't even face him."

"I'm so very sorry," Damon whispered. "I wish I could take it all away." His voice was gruff, as though he was close to tears himself. "But things'll get better, Kar. They will. And once things settle down, you won't be so angry at Malcolm."

"Maybe." She sighed. "Thank you for coming. I really appreciate it. You've been a good friend."

"A friend," he repeated lightly, but his feathery eyebrows drew together as if in pain.

"What's wrong?" Karissa asked.

A blank look covered his face. "I enjoy being your friend, Karissa. I'll always be your friend." He patted her hand in a brotherly fashion. "Why don't you try to sleep now?"

Karissa closed her eyes obediently. But this time she dreamed again of the bear. She cried out, and Damon was there to pat her hand and to comfort her.

When she awoke the next morning, he was still in the room, and so were Jesse and Brionney. "Has she had a blessing?" Damon was asking.

Jesse shook his head. "We offered one to Malcolm, but he said he was fine. I was a little nervous to ask Karissa. I thought she'd ask if she wanted one."

Damon made an angry noise in the back of his throat. "Karissa isn't Malcolm, not by a long shot." He turned to the bed and found her watching him. "I'm giving you a blessing."

"But you don't have the priesthood."

"Yes, I do."

Karissa looked at Jesse, who nodded. "He was baptized several months ago. He just told us."

Karissa turned her gaze on Damon. "Why didn't you tell me sooner?"

"I—I don't know." He cast an embarrassed glance at Jesse and Brionney.

Karissa didn't need to hear more. "But this is happy news! I may not be active, but I know the Church is true."

"Then you'll consent to have a blessing?"

"Of course, though I don't know if it will matter." She felt the indifferent mask slip back over her face. *Will the Lord help such a vile sinner as I?*

Damon gave the blessing with a minimum of words. Karissa could tell by his voice and expression that he had not felt any particular way about the baby. She had not expected him to do so; she knew everything depended on her.

"Brionney, will you stay with me?" Karissa asked. The room radiated cold, reflecting the emotion in her heart.

"Of course."

Jesse left for church, where he had dropped off the little girls for Primary before coming to the hospital. Damon went with him, seemingly unmindful that his dress pants and short-sleeved white shirt were wrinkled from his night in the chair.

"How long does it usually take?" Karissa said. "I keep waiting, but I haven't felt any more pain. And the bleeding has stopped."

"It depends." In Brionney's eyes was the memory of her own tragedy. Karissa knew that her friend understood too well her thoughts and feelings, her denials, her thin hopes. "What does the doctor say?"

"He's going to give me another ultrasound today. To see if the heart is still beating. It was yesterday."

"We can't give up hope," Brionney said.

"But I don't have any hope, not really. It's as if all this time I've just been waiting for something like this to happen." Karissa met Brionney's eyes and saw that they held a multitude of tears. *Strange,* she thought. *My eyes are dry. The eyes of a sinner.*

"Tell me," Brionney said. "Isn't it time you trusted someone?"

"You said one day that I would be ready to tell you, and that you would still love me. I'm not ready. I can never be ready. But I need to tell someone."

Brionney leaned against the bed. "I'm listening."

Now that the moment was here, the words came easily. "I aborted a baby once." Karissa's eyes were still dry, but inside, her heart was drowning in the tears she could not shed. Brionney didn't gasp and pull away as she had expected, but reached out for her hand. Karissa let her take the hand, but she couldn't watch her friend's expression. Why wasn't there a window to stare out of? Instead she focused her gaze on a bouquet of white lilies someone had set by her bed.

"I was sixteen when I found out I was pregnant. I was so afraid my father would kill me, or disown me, or something. I didn't know what to do. I had absolutely no one I felt I could turn to. Everybody knew our family was above reproach, and my getting pregnant would have damaged our family's reputation forever. I knew my father would look at me with his terrible eyes and tell me I would go to hell and that he never wanted to see me again." There was a slight tremble in her voice. "Can you even begin to understand how I felt?"

"I can't, not really," Brionney said. "But I know you, and I think you must have felt desperate to do what you did."

Karissa nodded. "Oh, desperate doesn't begin to cover what I felt. But I am trying to excuse myself, really. Because I know that being desperate doesn't change what I did." Silent tears gathered in her eyes. "A million times I've looked back and told myself that there were other options. I could have run away. I could have confided in one of my teachers at church or school. I didn't have to kill my daughter."

"It was a girl?"

"They didn't tell me it was, but I heard two nurses talking, and I looked at my chart when the doctor left the room. They had it written there."

"What about the father?"

Karissa's brow furrowed, and she felt a stab of half-remembered pain shoot through her heart. "I loved him. He was a senior at my high school. He played football, and he was really good. He wasn't a member, and I never dared tell my family I dated him." She shrugged. "I could never date the boys at Church because my father would talk to their parents and to the boys. He would give us a lecture every time we went out, and haul us over the coals if we missed our ten o'clock curfew by even a minute. Ten o'clock on weekends! When everybody else was just beginning to have fun, we had to go home."

"He probably worried about something happening to you."

"To me?" The words came as a snort. She met Brionney's gaze briefly. "No, he worried about what effect we might have on *his* salvation. I don't think he really cared about me. Oh, I know that sounds like a child speaking, but even now I can't think of one time when he said he loved me."

"Well, he wanted your family to make it to heaven."

"Yes, by any means possible." Karissa laughed dryly, but tears still filled her eyes. "I used to compare him and Satan; they seemed to have the same motives—glory and force. But do you know something? I never once heard him bear his testimony. I don't think he really believes. I think he stays in the gospel because it looks good, or perhaps because that was how he was raised."

Brionney didn't reply, but Karissa saw the pity on her face. She plucked at the thin blanket on the bed before rushing on. "His name—the boy's—was Tyler, and I thought he loved me. I thought he would take me away from my life and from my father. But it was just a game for him, I think, and it was over before I found out about the baby. We were together three months."

"Did he ever know?" Brionney's voice was soft.

"About the baby? Yes. I went to him later. I was beginning to show, and I was so scared that my father would find out." Karissa took a deep, shuddering breath. " Tyler seemed glad to see me until I told him. Then he stopped talking all of a sudden. He asked me to meet him the next day at the mall. I did. He gave me money and the address of an abortion clinic. He said not to bother him again, and that if I did, he would deny it, or get a bunch of his friends to say that I was with all of them. I knew that whatever I chose, I was lost. Either my father would kill me, or God would. So I accepted the least scary option at the time. God wasn't real to me, but my father was. Only—"

"Only what?"

"I know I will have to pay for my sins, and I know that I chose badly, not just for my daughter, but for myself. My father could have killed me or raised a big fuss, but it would have passed. I understand that now. But what I chose instead was to deprive my baby of her chance for life, and myself of a chance for salvation." Karissa looked at her friend, her eyes wet and pleading. "Can you believe I did that, Brionney? Can you believe I killed a living person?" Her voice broke, but she continued unevenly. "What was I thinking? Sometimes when I'm really busy, I almost forget, but then it all comes back. If Malcolm knew, he would hate me. I don't think he would forgive me. And why should he, when I don't know if I can forgive him for not being there when I needed him yesterday?" She rubbed at her eyes with her hands. "Now my second child is gone, and I don't know if my commitment to our marriage is strong enough to take this second death."

Brionney gave her a little shake. "You can't think that way. There's a chance your baby will live! Oh, Karissa, you were just a child, a scared and lonely child when you made your mistake! You can't blame yourself any longer."

"But I *am* to blame!" Karissa exclaimed passionately. Then more quietly she added, "Please, let's not talk about it anymore. I've told you, and now you understand what this baby means to me. I thought maybe God was going to take pity on me, but I see that it's impossible for me to ever be happy in the way that you and Jesse are." She felt the tears envelop her, bitter and stinging, sliding down her face. "Why didn't my father bear his testimony?" she asked.

Brionney didn't know.

* * * *

After hearing Karissa's painful confession, Brionney's heart was in a turmoil. Karissa had aborted an innocent baby who had depended on her for life! There was a deeply ingrained part of Brionney that cried out at the injustice and claimed there was no redemption for such a heinous act. To her, pro-choice activists were people who wanted to spend their money and keep it at the same time. They claimed a woman's choice superseded that of an unborn fetus. But hadn't they made their choice when they agreed to a physical relationship? Brionney believed emphatically that they had. *If you don't want to be pregnant,* she thought, *you practice abstinence. That is the choice. Once a baby is conceived, then its rights must come first.*

There was another argument, Brionney knew, that women should have the same freedom as men to have relationships without responsibilities. But women, no matter how disguised, were not men, and they had, like it or not, the divine power of bearing children. Why would they want to be equal to men? To lose or transfer this power? Besides her eternal relationship with Jesse, Brionney knew there was no greater or more precious bond than that between mother and child. She remembered the miracle, the extraordinary feeling of newness, the responsibility that came with creating new life. How could someone destroy that glorious, unequaled feeling within the lifeless walls of an abortion clinic?

Yet there was Karissa, silently torturing herself year after year. Not even hell could exact a greater punishment. Compassion instead of condemnation filled Brionney's heart.

"I have to help her," she said to herself.

"Is she okay?"

Brionney hadn't realized she had said the words aloud until Delinda Goodrich spoke to her. "She's fine, but we won't know about the baby until later. The doctor's going to do another ultrasound."

Delinda simultaneously twisted two thick rings on the blunt index fingers of both hands. She used her thumbs, twirling the precious stones around and around. "Landsakes!" she exclaimed, darting a glance toward Karissa's door. Her long earrings swung back and forth. "Who could imagine such a thing happening? I can hardly believe it." She turned her soft eyes on Brionney. "Is there anything we can do? Meals? A blessing?"

Brionney shook her head. "I'm the one who cooks, and it's ridiculous for you to drive forty minutes when I'm perfectly capable. And she's had a blessing. We just need to wait now." Then she thought of something. "Look, Delinda, there may be some way we can help Karissa. She has some questions about God and forgiveness. When you come visiting teaching during the next few months, maybe you could focus on that. You know, forgiveness. Just a little at a time."

"Is there any particular thing you'd like me to discuss?" Delinda asked intently.

Brionney hesitated. No, she couldn't breach Karissa's confidence. "Follow the Spirit. I think Karissa is close to wanting to come back to church. Maybe we can help her."

Delinda nodded and disappeared into Karissa's room. As the door closed behind her, Brionney walked to the waiting room to see if Jesse and the girls had finished with church. One of the babies inside her stomach moved against her side, and she rubbed the spot, feeling an unidentified body part. The baby moved again.

This silent communication brought back Karissa's dreadful secret with undeniable force. Was there any forgiveness for what Karissa had done in her youth? *If it was in my power, I would forgive her,* Brionney thought. *But I could never forgive myself.*

It was always harder to forgive yourself.

CHAPTER 15

The ultrasound room was white, or at least it seemed so at first to Malcolm. When he looked closer, he could see the walls were papered and held a faint but intricate wheat design that was only visible if he concentrated on it. When he didn't, it faded again into a bleak white. But the whiteness of the room was nothing next to the look on Karissa's face when she saw the nurse wheel him through the door.

She said nothing, but her eyes pierced his as they had done when he had gone to her room yesterday. When she had asked him to leave. Obviously, she still didn't have anything to say to him.

He had prayed during the night as he remembered doing only on his mission. Like he had prayed for Jesse to come to know the truth. Jesse had, but his decision had come years too late for Malcolm to take him into the waters of baptism. Jesse had said it was because he didn't want to hurt his parents, but Malcolm still wondered if Jesse's delay hadn't been a reflection of a reluctant missionary's wavering faith—Malcolm's faith.

If only God would answer his prayers about the baby . . . about Karissa.

"I'm being released today," he said to Karissa, though she hadn't asked.

"If all goes well, your wife can go home with you," said Dr. Fairfax cheerfully, seemingly unaware of the undercurrents in the room. Malcolm knew that even if they were both released from the hospital, he wouldn't be going home with Karissa. That big house was too small for them right now. Maybe he'd go camping in one of the native villages for a few weeks—until Karissa either threw him out completely or forgave him. Of course, camping would be rather hard with his foot messed up so badly. Instead, he would have to crash at a friend's house in town.

The doctor was watching the picture on the screen now, a smile on his face. "See that heartbeat? It's still strong. I think whatever stress this baby endured yesterday, he or she has put it behind him."

Only when Malcolm let out his breath did he realize he had been holding it.

"And the placenta? Does it look all right?" Karissa asked.

"It seems fine," Dr. Fairfax replied, moving the wand to the left side where the placenta was located. "I was worried about the bleeding yesterday, but the placenta seems very firmly attached. From what the ultrasound can tell us, I think everything's going to be just fine. I'll want you to take it easy for a while, of course. Don't lift anything even remotely heavy, and get a lot of sleep."

Karissa's face held a trace of the shock she had shown yesterday before her collapse. The wide green eyes blinked unbelievingly, and Malcolm felt a sudden pity. She had fully expected to learn that the baby was dead! There had been not even a sliver of hope inside her heart. He laid a hand on hers, wanting to comfort her, and to his relief, she didn't pull away.

"I'll go sign the papers for you both to leave," Dr. Fairfax said. "I see no reason to keep either of you; though Malcolm, you have to be sure to take all your medication. I don't want your wounds getting infected." He crossed to the door and paused, turning a warm grin on them. "And stay away from those bears, would ya?"

Malcolm chuckled to be polite and even Karissa smiled, but her eyes were unfocused, as if looking at something far away, or perhaps inside herself, to the baby.

"It's going to be all right," Malcolm said tentatively.

Karissa came out of herself to ask, "Do you have a place to stay?"

Malcolm grimaced. "I thought you were committed."

Her eyes darkened and her forehead wrinkled. "I am," she retorted, "but are you? Are you really?"

Her words made Malcolm angry. He felt a hot flush creep up his neck and face, and his wounds started to ache. "I love you, Karissa. I want to be with you."

"Look, I care about you, but I can't be with you right now," she said, and her expression was so devastatingly sad that Malcolm wanted to gather her into his arms and comfort her. If only he could get out of the stupid wheelchair!

"What is really wrong here?" he asked. "I know you're mad at me, and I feel I even deserve it." That much was true. Why couldn't he be a stronger person? Why couldn't he stop smoking as easily as Karissa had? Why couldn't he have been with her when she had needed him the most?

Her face tightened. "Nothing's wrong," she nearly yelled at him. Her voice sounded angry, but her brown eyes were huge and scared.

"Tell me. Be honest." At his urging, she grew pale and her eyes flashed.

"It's nothing!" she nearly hissed. "I just need some time. I gave you time when you needed it. And you still didn't stop smoking, and look what almost hap—" She broke off and turned her face away from him.

What is she not saying? He wanted to wrest the truth from her, but didn't want to upset her further, fearing it wouldn't be good for her or the baby. Instinctively, he knew she was speaking more from her fright or from mixed-up hormones than from any feeling of hatred she harbored toward him. If they could get past this day, this experience, maybe she could open her heart to him. "What do you want me to do?" he asked simply.

The fear in her eyes lessened. "I want you to stop smoking."

He fought anger and resentment, knowing that the feelings stemmed from his own guilt. "I will try."

Her lips fell in a frown, and he knew his "try" wasn't good enough. But he didn't dare say more for fear of another failure. Above all, he was being honest. Didn't that count for something?

"Look, you'd better get home and get some rest," he made himself say. "We'll talk later. In a few days. You have my cell number if you need to reach me."

Karissa nodded calmly and slid off the examining table. "Take care of yourself," she said coolly. She left him there alone. He sat silently and watched her leave, his head held erect by his hurt and pride. What if after a few days she wouldn't have him back?

She has to, he thought. *I love her.* Then why couldn't he stop smoking? He had asked himself the question a hundred times, berating his lack of willpower. *I should be able to do it for her, if not for myself.*

A long time later he emerged from the room, struggling with the chair and feeling suddenly more sick than he had let on to either Karissa or the doctor. He could have called a nurse for help, but was determined to find his own way back to his room. Doubtless both the nurse who had brought him and Dr. Fairfax had believed that Karissa would take care of him. Malcolm almost snorted. He wouldn't ask for her help, not after what he had done. Ultimately the whole bear episode had been his fault, and he knew it. But he couldn't change things now.

"Mr. Mathees, let me do that." A young nurse with blonde permanented curls came up behind him. "I'm sorry I wasn't back earlier. I got a phone call." Her pretty face turned pink. "From my fiancé, you know. He's flying in from Anchorage tomorrow."

"Will you be leaving Kodiak?" Malcolm asked, glad to think of something else.

"What?"

"When you get married, will you be leaving the island?"

"Oh, yes!" she said emphatically. "I can't wait to be out of here! Kodiak is so tiny, and there are so few opportunities here. Fish, fish, fish, and that's it. I'm sick of it all."

The vehemence in her voice took him back in time to when he had left the island. He, too, had been in awe of the real world. Yet in the end the cities held nothing for him, and he had returned to the island, vowing never to leave again, no matter what. Of course, he had to leave temporarily from time to time to wherever his work would lead, but he had become adept at arranging things to spend as much time as possible on Kodiak.

"I feel so trapped here," the young nurse continued. "There's just nothing to do, and sometimes I feel like my own thoughts are all that exist." She laughed self-consciously. "I think that may sound stupid."

But it made some kind of sense. "I like my thoughts," he said. "I have a clear conscience." *Usually.*

"Yeah, but you're old. I mean older than me. You're married, and—" She shrugged. "Maybe someday I'll return."

Malcolm doubted she ever would. Unless her husband was in the fishing business, it was unlikely he would agree to confine himself to a small island that held no place and certainly no love in his childhood memories.

"Well, here we are," the nurse said. "Do you want help getting into bed?"

"No. I'll be leaving soon, one way or the other." This last was a mild threat, but she appeared not to notice. She left hurriedly, her thoughts already as far away from Kodiak as her heart wanted to be.

He sat with a brooding frown on his face. What to do now? Where would he go?

"Hey, Malcolm." Jesse appeared in the open doorway. "How is my bear-wrestling buddy?"

Malcolm grinned. "We did it, didn't we?"

Jesse nodded. "We did."

Malcolm felt his smile fade into seriousness. "Thanks for not leaving me. That was a really brave thing you did."

"You would have done the same for me."

"I'd like to think so."

"I knew the risks. Brionney did, too. It was the only choice." Jesse sat heavily on the bed and looked down at Malcolm in his wheelchair. "But I admit, I was scared. The only thing that kept me sane was thinking that regardless of the outcome, I would still see my family again. Sometimes I forget that, but it was as clear as a bell at the moment the bear turned on me." He shrugged and fell into silence.

Malcolm remembered the terror he had felt when he saw the bear going for Karissa. The comfort Jesse spoke of had never come to his heart. Of course, their marriage had not been sealed in a temple of God.

"Man, you should have seen yourself whacking that bear with that silly stick," Malcolm said to lighten the moment. "I would give almost anything to have it on film."

Jesse chuckled. "Great story for the grandkids, I'll say. The day I fought a bear with a club." He eyed Malcolm enviously. "But your story is something else. I can just hear your grandchildren now, saying how you barehandedly wrestled a bear and saved your wife's life."

"Ha! She saved us by shooting the bear," Malcolm put in.

"Yeah, but in a hundred years no one'll remember that, just you wrestling the bear. Malcolm Mathees, legendary bear-wrestler."

Malcolm raised his arms carefully and tried to flex. Pain rippled through his wounds and he grimaced. "Some hero. I can barely move my arms."

"Give it time."

"I've got a documentary to finish."

"Does that mean you're going home today?"

"I think I've convinced the doctor to let me out. Karissa's going home now, too. The baby's doing all right."

"I heard. I'm really glad for you both."

"Thanks, Jesse."

"I wanted to ask if it's okay for us to stay on for another week. Brionney refuses to leave Karissa alone until she's sure she's all right."

"Uh . . ." He paused, wondering how to tell Jesse about their separation. "I'd like it if you could stay," he said slowly, "to keep an eye on Karissa. I'm going to stay in town for a while. She's a little upset at me right now, and we're going to let things cool off."

Jessed frowned. "That's tough, man. I'm sorry. But sometimes there's not much else to do but back off when faced with pregnancy hormones. As long as it's temporary."

Malcolm didn't know what to say. He hoped it was temporary. But he feared that Karissa wouldn't take him back unless he quit smoking, and he had already tried so hard.

Hadn't he?

A lump formed in his throat. Karissa and their baby had almost died because of him. And the worst thing was that he still didn't know how to overcome his addiction. Some hero he was.

Jesse stood and took a few steps toward Malcolm. "What about your wounds? You shouldn't be alone. What if you start bleeding or something?"

"All the more reason to stay in town. Karissa's in no condition to take care of me. I'll crash at someone's house for a while. One of the men on my camera crew lives nearby." Malcolm shrugged.

"I'll take care of him," said a crisp voice behind Malcolm.

"Mother!" Malcolm turned his head to see her coming through the open door.

As she bent to kiss him, her straight black hair swung forward against his chest, smelling of strawberries. "To think that we had to read about the attack in the newspaper. I can't believe you didn't call me." Her black eyes regarded him seriously behind the round glasses.

"I, uh . . . I've been a bit busy, Mom."

"So I heard," she said dryly. "I talked to Karissa this morning before I came. She told me what wasn't in the papers. She asked me to take care of you for a week or so. My friend Sally's moved over to the mainland, and she's letting us use her house until you patch things up with your wife."

"You'll be bored, Mom. I'll be working." Despite his words, Malcolm was glad to have his mother here, and especially glad that Karissa still cared enough about him to worry about his care.

"That doesn't matter. I'll be busy enough seeing old friends. It's been too long since I've visited with the ward members here. Now that you're finally giving me a grandchild, I'll have to visit more often—if you make it up to your wife. Whatever did you do to make her so mad at you?"

So Karissa hadn't told his mother *all* the ugly details. That sounded more like his wife.

"Well?" Faith prompted.

Malcolm groaned. "You don't even know what it is, and you're taking her side."

"You're a man," Faith said, as if that explained everything. She shifted her black eyes to Jesse. "Do you know what this is all about?"

Jesse smiled. "Hey, I just live with them." He glanced at his watch. "I've got to get back to my family. It was nice to meet you, Sister Mathees."

"You're a member?"

"Yeah. In fact, Malcolm was the first missionary to teach me the gospel."

Faith's full lips curved into a smile. "It's good to meet you,—"

"Jesse," Malcolm supplied.

"Jesse." Faith offered a deeply tanned hand and Jesse shook it firmly. With a last sympathetic glance at Malcolm, Jesse took his leave.

Faith stood behind Malcolm's wheelchair. "Now, let's see about getting you out of here."

They went to the nurses' station, where Malcolm was surprised to see Damon Wolfe talking to the head nurse. "I'm glad you're all right," he said, shaking Malcolm's hand. "That was a brave thing you did, protecting Karissa. From what I hear, you saved her life."

Malcolm wished Karissa could see it that way. "I just did what I had to do," he said brusquely. He knew he didn't sound very friendly, but he didn't care. Something about this man irritated him.

"She's a special woman, Karissa is. I'd hang on to her if I were you."

Malcolm bristled at the thinly veiled warning in the other man's voice. "I mean to," he said coldly.

Damon smiled. "I gave her a blessing, did she tell you? And I hear her baby's all right."

"Yeah, she told me," Malcolm lied. "Thanks. And *our* baby is doing fine."

"I'll be staying in town to cover for Karissa. She's on sick leave as of tomorrow."

Malcolm nodded, not wanting to thank the man again. Didn't Damon have some other life besides watching over another man's wife? And since when had he become a member of the Church? There seemed to be a lot Karissa wasn't telling him.

CHAPTER 16

Laughter filled the greenhouse as Karissa had always imagined it might. Savannah, Camille, and Rosalie giggled as they pelted each other with the light plastic balls in the cage Malcolm and Jesse had installed. Rained drizzled from the darkened sky onto the plastic of the greenhouse, running down its sides in steady streams. A smell of damp leaves and grass came through to Karissa, though she knew it wasn't from the plants in the greenhouse—which she now kept drier than usual because of the children—but from the lush land around the house. The leaves were falling from the trees and packing down under the week-long rain, rotting and giving off a slight musty scent. The smell came through the plastic and through the vents in the greenhouse's heating and cooling system. The odor was pleasant, bringing to mind a cold day spent lazily before the fire, tucked safely inside against the weather and the darkness that came earlier each Alaskan night.

Karissa was happy that Brionney and the children had stayed with her. Without them around to occupy her time, all she had were her thoughts of self-recrimination. In the week and a half since the bear attack, they hadn't talked of her confession, and Brionney hadn't treated her any differently. Between the two of them, they had managed to get more rest than they needed. Maggie came in daily to clean now, and she also made dinner.

"Those kids act like crazy nuts," Brionney said, rubbing her hands gently over her distended stomach. They sat on two lounge chairs, with a small table of goodies and drinks between them. Overhead, the artificial lights already glowed brightly.

Karissa smiled, but her thoughts were on Malcolm. He hadn't called her once this entire week, though his mother had telephoned her yesterday when he had his stitches removed. "He works too much, in spite of his foot," Faith had said. "Can't you talk to him?"

"The next move is his," she had replied.

Faith hadn't said anything for a long time, and then, "Does it matter whose move it is?"

"This time it does." But her heart cried out for her husband. Had she been too hard on him? The attack hadn't been his fault, not really. Nor her fall. But why hadn't he called? Was he only giving her time as she requested? Or—and this thought scared her deeply—had he glimpsed her dreadful secret in her eyes?

Karissa had been relieved to hear from Faith and to know that Malcolm was all right. Still, last night, lying there alone in their queen-sized, bed she had wondered how his wounds were healing, and if he needed her. She missed him more than she would admit to anyone—even to herself.

"Karissa, did you hear me?" Brionney's voice brought her back to the present. "I said with all our snacks, I won't be hungry for Maggie's dinner."

"I will be," Karissa said. "I'm always hungry now."

She glanced toward the kitchen window, where she could see Maggie cleaning before beginning the evening meal. The old woman had been born on Kodiak and was rather proud of the fact that she had never left the island. She was as native as a person could be and not have Aleutian blood. She lived in Dell Flats with her nephew, his wife, and their six growing boys. On good days, Maggie used her ancient bicycle to come to work. On rainy days such as today, or when there was snow on the dirt road, one of her nephew's sons would come in a battered red Ford pickup to bring their aunt, and return later to collect her. Karissa and Malcolm had offered her the use of a vehicle, but the old woman stubbornly refused to learn how to drive.

Before the Hergarters had come to live with the Mathees, Maggie would let herself in at two and be gone by five on Mondays, Wednesdays, and Fridays. Karissa had rarely seen Maggie, as Malcolm took care of her pay. He had also been the one to employ her. Once when Maggie had been ill, Karissa had stopped at the small wooden house in Dell Flats to see how she was doing. The woman had been surrounded by her nephew's children, who treated her with an air of reserved affection—the same attitude the old woman had toward Malcolm. Karissa liked her instantly, and she felt an unspoken bond with her as well. They had been two women destined never to hold their own newborns to their breasts.

After Brionney had found out about the twins, she had asked Maggie to come two extra days a week. Maggie had complied willingly, for money was always in short supply in the derelict house in Dell Flats, where all six young boys shared the same room—except sometimes in the summer when it didn't rain, and they could sleep out under the stars—and where Maggie herself slept in the living room. These past ten days the old woman had agreed to stay an extra hour to make dinner, but today was her last late day. Karissa felt good now and knew that she could return to work and her normal life. Her only regret was that Brionney and her family were leaving the island.

"Just wait until you get the backache," Brionney said, pushing one hand underneath her to rub at her back. She sighed. "I'll be glad when this is all over."

Karissa didn't share the sentiment. "Except for the mornings, I like being pregnant. So far."

"You must be one of the lucky few."

Karissa laughed. "We'll see, later on."

"Yeah, when you're as big as an elephant." Brionney made a face, and Karissa laughed again.

Like Maggie's extra days, this quiet peaceful time with Brionney was coming to an end. Tomorrow the Hergarters would go to Anchorage to await the birth of the babies, and after a few months more they would return to Utah or wherever Jesse's work took them. Karissa would be trapped once more on the island with no one but Malcolm and the elusive Maggie for company.

If she let Malcolm return.

I miss him, she thought. *I want him to come home.*

"Ow," Brionney groaned.

"Another kick? I can't wait until mine gets old enough."

"No, it wasn't that. It's this backache. Only it's shooting pain now." Brionney grimaced.

Karissa sat up. "Are you in labor?"

"Naw, can't be. Probably false labor."

Karissa sat on the lounge chair in the greenhouse for another hour, alternately listening to the children's laughter, the rain on the thick plastic roof, or the sound of Brionney's fluid voice. Soon Brionney stopped talking, and her breath came more quickly.

"Karissa, I think I *am* in labor," she said finally. Karissa nearly jumped from her chair. "Don't panic," Brionney added. "We have plenty of time. The fastest baby was Rosalie, and she took four hours to come."

"You shouldn't have stayed out here with me," Karissa said, helping Brionney to stand.

"Yes, I should have." Brionney groaned and slumped back on the lounge chair. "I think I'll wait right here until you get my hospital bag. Do you think Maggie will mind watching the girls, or should we take them with us?"

"Let's leave them here. We'll have enough to worry about without them bouncing off the hospital walls."

"Good point." She closed her eyes and panted softly.

Karissa patted her shoulder. "I'll call everyone and get your bag. I'll be right back to help you to my truck."

"What time is it?"

"Twenty to five."

"Then Jesse's still at the cannery, working on his new program. He left the number by the phone."

Karissa came into the kitchen so quickly that she startled Maggie. "Brionney's in labor," she explained. "Will you stay with the girls?"

Maggie's round face crinkled as she smiled. "I'll be glad to stay. I'll call my neighbor and send him over to tell Jake not to pick me up." Maggie's nephew didn't have a phone, but their closest neighbor did.

"Tell him we'll take you back when it's over," Karissa said. "We really appreciate it."

Karissa picked up the phone and left a message for Jesse to meet them at the hospital, then she carried Brionney's bag out to the car. There was a chill in the unheated garage, and she started the Nissan to warm the interior of the cab.

The girls gathered around Brionney, smothering her with kisses and good luck. She was walking on her own, but closing her eyes at the pain of the contractions.

Karissa drove as quickly as she could down the dirt road, dodging the worst of the washboards with the confidence and instinct that came with driving a well-known route. "We'll be there before long," she murmured.

Brionney nodded and said nothing. From the way she breathed, Karissa knew the contractions were growing harder, and her watch said they were coming closer together as well.

Rain still came down unremittingly, and the gray clouds blocked out most of the light. Without a clock, she would have guessed it was much later. The weeks of continuous rain on Kodiak had always bothered her, and now the weather seemed to cast an eerie feeling over the truck, not warm and safe, but something menacing. The road had turned to mud, and Karissa strained to see through the steady movements of the windshield wipers.

It was then she caught sight of the gasoline gauge, and her heart nearly stopped. When was the last time someone had put gas in the tank? She'd filled it a day or so before they went to Pillar Mountain on the day of the bear attack, but she hadn't driven home that day or since. Jesse had driven the truck to the hospital and later home, and there it had stood, forgotten.

"Easy, babies," Brionney whispered, hugging her stomach with her arms.

The truck lurched a few more paces, then came to a stop. Karissa looked over at her friend, seeing her eyes widen with sudden understanding. Now what were they going to do?

* * * *

Malcolm received Jesse's phone call at ten after six. "I'm at the hospital," he said without preamble. His voice was strained and thin. "Karissa was bringing Brionney in, but they should have arrived at least thirty minutes ago. I've called the house, but Maggie said they left right after they called the cannery. I'm worried that something's wrong."

"I take it Brionney's in labor."

"Yes. Didn't I say so?"

"What do you want me to do?"

"Do you mind going to look for them? Meantime, I'll wait here and call you if they arrive."

"I'm leaving right now," Malcolm said. "I'll call when I know anything."

"Thanks, Malcolm. It's just driving me crazy not being able to do anything."

"Don't worry, they'll probably show up any minute now." Malcolm flipped his phone shut and stood abruptly from his borrowed desk. Several pages of text he had received from the writer he had hired to help him with the documentary fluttered to the floor. He left them where they lay and walked to the door as quickly as his cast would allow him. Faith looked up from her knitting, a question in her eyes.

"I'm going out, Mom." He picked up the crutches by the door, along with his flannel-lined denim jacket.

"In this rain? But you filmed all last week. I thought—"

"Jesse's wife's in labor, but she and Karissa haven't shown up at the hospital. I'm going to look for them."

Faith put down her tiny knitting needles and arose. "I'll get some blankets."

He raced through the wet, nearly-deserted streets of Kodiak as Faith watched him with a worried stare. "I'm all right," he said, pushing his cast more firmly against the gas pedal. She had volunteered to drive, but Malcolm knew that even with his cast he would get there a lot faster than she would. He ran a red light at the only stoplight in town, almost wishing a policeman would pull him over and offer to help find Karissa and Brionney. But no one noticed his hurry. Rain beat at the plastic top of his Jeep, driving him into the unnatural dark caused by the heavy clouds.

"She probably can't call," Faith said, answering his unasked question. But Malcolm wondered if Karissa would call him even if she had a phone. He had betrayed her trust. Could he ever win it back? There seemed to be only one way, and he wasn't sure he was capable of quitting smoking.

They made their way past the airport and the Coast Guard base in silence. When the paved road ended at Dell Flats, Malcolm began to relax. "They must have already made it to the hospital," he said. His voice was rough from lack of use.

"Wouldn't your friend have called?"

He cleared his throat before replying. "Maybe he got busy. They're having twins, you know."

"I didn't."

They both saw Karissa's Nissan at the same time, sitting in the middle of the road as if she hadn't been planning to stop.

"Are they inside?" Faith asked.

Malcolm shook his head. He wondered why the women had left the truck. The tires had sunk into the mud, but with the four-wheel-drive, Karissa could have made it out.

"We have to find them!" Faith said. She peered into the dark.

"Which way should we go?" he asked, hating the feeling of helplessness that overwhelmed him. Had he been so intent on driving that he had passed the women in the dark? Was Brionney even now giving birth on the side of the road in the rain? Why on earth did they leave the truck?

Of course he knew the answer. They had left the truck because they knew no one would come.

CHAPTER 17

No one would come for them until it was too late. Karissa debated silently for only a few minutes before turning to Brionney.

"How bad is it?" she asked. "Can you walk at all?"

"I think so. But where will we go?"

"We're right in the middle between Dell Flats and home," she said. "We could continue on to Dell Flats. Someone's bound to be home, and some of them have phones."

"And if they're not home?" Brionney asked.

"We break in."

"Or?"

"Or we could go back home and call the ambulance."

Brionney thought for a moment. "Let's go home. Maggie's there."

Karissa didn't see what Maggie's presence had to do with anything, but she felt a pure calm fall over her as they made the decision. What was that feeling?

"Let's go." She bent down to retrieve the umbrella under the seat next to the first aid kit.

Brionney buttoned her jacket over her huge stomach, grimacing as another contraction took her. Karissa helped her from the truck and held the umbrella firmly over them, one arm around Brionney's back. How long would it take them? Half an hour? Forty minutes? An hour? Did they have that long?

"How do you feel?" she asked after a long while. Brionney had to stop walking during the contractions now.

"When I was a little girl," Brionney said as they walked slowly on, "I sometimes dreamed of romantic things. You know, like having a baby in a perilous situation with only my handsome, dashing husband to help me. Of course, he knew all about delivering a baby, as he was some famous—not to mention rich—doctor. But now that I'm actually in this position, I can see that dream was pretty stupid."

Karissa couldn't help the smile that came to her face. "I'm sorry I'm not Jesse."

Brionney snorted softly. "Him? Jesse's a wonderful guy, but he doesn't know much about having babies. He gets a little green in the face each time I deliver. The nurses always ask him if he wants to leave, but he just stays there and clings to my hand. I wonder who's helping who. No, in this situation, I'd much rather have another woman. Especially you, Karissa. You keep your head during a crisis. I saw you with that bear."

Karissa shuddered. "Don't talk about him."

She had dreamed several more nights about the bear, and each time he looked at her with sad brown eyes and asked, "Why did you kill me?"

"I didn't, I didn't," she would insist. But he would only nod his head, his eyes wise. "You didn't even give me a chance. I would have loved you. I would have made you whole."

Brionney gave a little cry, shaking Karissa from these macabre thoughts. "My water! I just felt it break. At least I think that's what it was. Oh, dear Lord, please help me!"

Karissa echoed the prayer. "It'll be all right," she found herself saying. "It's not far now." She scanned the darkness, but there were absolutely no lights ahead.

"I don't think I can make it," Brionney wailed.

"Of course you can! You have to! I felt it." It came to Karissa vividly now what the calm feeling had been: the Spirit confirming their choice. She hadn't experienced it for so long that she had forgotten what it felt like.

There had been a time in her life when she had often felt the Spirit. When she had been a little girl, nine or ten, she had borne her testimony each fast Sunday. She had believed then with her whole being, and each time she said the words the Spirit had confirmed the truth with its unmistakable touch on her soul. Then there had been the fateful Sunday which now stood out in her mind like a day alone, somehow apart from all the others, as if lived by someone other than herself. Her father had touched her shoulder as she came back from bearing her testimony at the pulpit, an indulgent smile on his lips. "It isn't necessary for you to go up each Sunday," he said to her, and nothing more. And suddenly her testimony, once pure and untarnished with a child's unquestioning faith, seemed dirty, something dark she had forced upon the rest of the long-suffering ward members, tolerated because they were in a church, but laughed at behind closed doors.

Karissa had never borne her testimony again.

Brionney was crying now, and Karissa hugged her, desperation seeping into her being like the rain that oozed through her jacket and saturated the clothes beneath. But with the desperation came another emotion, a feeling of determination and strength. She didn't know how they would make it, but they would. Was this how the pioneer women of old faced their troubles? With this curious mixture of desperation and resolve?

She felt cold. Neither of them were dressed for this mad flight in the early October rain. Maybe they shouldn't have left the truck. But they couldn't have stayed there doing nothing, could they? They had to make it! At least it wasn't snowing—yet. *Walk,* Karissa told herself. *Keep moving.* She took more of Brionney's weight upon herself, urging her friend forward.

When she saw the headlights coming from behind, it took Karissa a moment to realize that she wasn't hallucinating. She pushed aside her wet hair—somehow it was wet despite the umbrella—to blink in the glare. Leaving Brionney at the side of the road with the umbrella, she plunged into middle of the road, nearly tripping in the muddy potholes, and waved her arms crazily above her head. The vehicle stopped and Karissa ran forward, getting ready to plead her case. Freezing rain stung her cheeks and nose.

The door opened and Malcolm's arms were around her. Karissa felt her strength drain as she realized that her immediate worries were over. "Malcolm," she whispered. He didn't appear to hear her over the rain, but his strong arms tightened.

"Get in," he said, his voice rough with emotion. He stood only partially out of the Jeep, with one foot sinking into the dark mud and the one with the cast still inside the cab.

"Brionney—" But Karissa saw that Faith had gone out into the rain and was now helping Brionney into the backseat of the Jeep.

Malcolm drove quickly, but with a back-and-forth motion as he circumvented the water-filled holes in the dirt road. Faith sat with Brionney in the back seat, positioning blankets over and around her laboring body.

They arrived at the house in five minutes and drove into the dry and comparatively warm confines of the garage, sealing the door behind them. Malcolm jumped out of the truck and opened the kitchen door, wincing as he banged his cast on the stair. "I'll call Jesse and the hospital."

"There's not going to be time," Faith said calmly. "Is there any place on this floor for her to lie down?"

"My room," Karissa said. She and Karissa helped Brionney into the house.

"Hi, Maggie," Faith said as the surprised woman turned from the stove. "We'll need some clean sheets for Karissa's bed, and a large sheet of plastic. A shower sheet will do if there's nothing else to put over the mattress. We'll need a lot of towels, some plastic garbage bags, a heating pad. You know the drill."

Maggie nodded and made her way down the hall. Karissa found an unused sheet of plastic Malcolm had bought during the painting phase of their house and spread it over the mattress. Then Faith put on the fitted sheet before helping Brionney ease onto the bed.

"I'll go boil the water," Maggie muttered.

What for? Karissa wanted to ask.

"Get her a nightgown," Faith said in that same calm voice. Brionney had no sooner laid back against the mound of pillows, than a contraction came, harder than all the rest.

"I can't do this," she cried, drawing a shuddering breath. "It hurts too much!"

"Nonsense," Faith returned. "Women have done it for years without drugs. You'll be all right. Now, breathe with me. Concentrate on letting the pain flow through you. Think about your little babies."

Brionney did as she asked, her hand gripping Karissa's painfully. Malcolm came in, limping because of his cast. *Why didn't he use his crutches?* The thought flashed through Karissa's head and then was gone.

"Jesse's coming with an ambulance," he said. He looked almost fearfully at Brionney, who clutched at her stomach with her free hand and moaned dismally.

"They won't make it," Faith said implacably. "I'll need the first aid kit, son. The big one I gave you for Christmas a few years ago."

Karissa saw Malcolm move decisively into the hall from the front room. His cast made a clumping sound on the hardwood floor in the hallway.

"I have to push," Brionney said.

Faith paused, her face thoughtful, as if pondering some deeper significance that Karissa didn't understand. "Do it," Faith said finally, "but just enough to take the edge off the pain. We're not quite ready."

Brionney clenched her teeth and pushed, grasping Karissa's hand even tighter. "It feels better when I push," she gasped.

"That's because you are probably fully dilated,." Faith explained.

"The baby's head is down?" Karissa asked.

Faith nodded. "Yes, I think so. I'll check her in a minute to be sure. But I need the things Malcolm went to get. Hold on a bit more, Brionney."

Maggie came into the room before Malcolm returned, carrying a pair of scissors, and four new shoelaces on a clean dishtowel. "They're all boiled and ready to go," Maggie said, setting them on the bed.

They heard Malcolm's step in the hall. Faith slid off the bed, and for the first time Karissa noticed the streaks of gray in her black hair. Maggie took Faith's place on the bed near Brionney's feet while Faith rifled through the first aid kit Malcolm had set on the edge of the bed. Both older women moved without speaking, as if in a silent dance—rusty perhaps, but well-remembered.

"You've done this before," Karissa said.

Maggie nodded. "All six nephews," she said. "And Faith and I have helped others."

The fear ebbed from Karissa's body. Women had given birth for many years before hospitals were invented. Even Jesus Christ had been born in a manger without a doctor.

"You all need to wash with this soap," Faith said, drawing a small bottle from the first aid kit. There was a quiet urgency in her voice.

"You too, Malcolm," she said as he was about to leave. "Afterwards, you take Karissa's place with Brionney. Up there out of the way, but here in case we need you. We're having twins here, remember. We'll be as modest as we can."

Beside the shoelaces and the scissors, Faith laid a packet of plastic gloves, a stack of sterile gauze, and a new bulb syringe she found in the first aid kit. "We'll boil that after the first baby, if there's time," she said. "If not, we won't."

"The water's still on." Maggie shifted to let Faith back on the bed.

"Where are the girls?" Brionney asked between contractions. Beads of sweat slid down her forehead until Karissa wiped them away.

"They're in the greenhouse playing," Malcolm said. "I checked on them. Savannah's watching the others." He sat at the head of the bed where Karissa had been before going to wash her hands with the small vial of green antiseptic soap.

Faith shoved the opened syringe into Karissa's hands. "You clean them out when they come, because I may need Maggie to help me with Brionney. Wipe off the face with this gauze and then use the syringe in the baby's mouth with a steady, sweeping motion. Maggie will help you if you need it."

Faith had on one of the gloves, and she checked Brionney gently beneath the draping of her nightgown. "Yes, you are ready to go," she said. "And that's definitely a head I feel coming. Let's hope the other baby also turns before he decides to follow." It was Faith's first admission of concern since they had entered the house. "Although once the way is open, a breech delivery is not so dangerous."

"Can I push now?" Brionney panted. "Oh, I have to push! It hurts so bad!" Taking a big breath, she bore down, emitting a high wail of pain.

Karissa didn't think it was supposed to happen so fast, but even after the contraction, Brionney still pushed. On the next contraction, more of the head emerged.

"Wait just a minute," Faith said. She held the little head in one hand now, and with the other checked the baby's neck for a cord. "Okay, whenever you're ready." As Brionney pushed, Faith hooked a finger under the baby's arm and helped ease the body out of its confinement. Karissa watched in amazement as the baby turned, making his way into the world to lie face-up on the bed.

The newborn was not letting out a sound. Even as Brionney gave a sigh of relief at the abrupt absence of pain, Karissa squeezed the syringe and sucked the mucus from the baby's nose and throat. "Farther inside," Maggie directed.

"He's not breathing," Karissa wailed.

"Sometimes they don't right away," Maggie said. "There's time. He's still receiving oxygen from his mother through the cord. Do it again."

As Karissa obeyed, Malcolm reached over and rubbed the baby's feet. "Come on, now," he said, more tenderly than Karissa had ever heard him speak. "Do I have to hold you upside down and spank you? Do I, little guy?" The baby opened his mouth and let out a scream entirely too loud for anything so small. Malcolm grinned. "That's a good boy."

Maggie checked the baby. "He looks good," she said. "Strong. And loud. See?"

Now that they had gotten the baby to breathe on his own, he wouldn't stop crying. Maggie handed Malcolm a soft towel that had been wrapped around the heating pad, putting another in its place. Malcolm helped Karissa cover the still-sobbing baby.

"It's okay," Karissa said. She hugged the baby to her breast. He seemed so tiny that she was afraid he would break or scream himself to death, or both. "Oh, I know what you want: your mother." She eased onto the bed and laid the infant in Brionney's arms.

Her friend put her face close to the baby. "Shh, there. Mommy's here. Don't cry." Upon hearing Brionney's voice, the baby quieted.

"Who says they don't recognize their mothers?" Malcolm asked.

"No one," Faith said, sounding amused. Malcolm's mouth rounded in an O. Maggie laughed as she stuffed some wet towels into one of the empty garbage bags.

Brionney ran a finger over the white vernix on the baby's head. "It's like hand lotion, only thicker," Faith said. "It protects their skin from the water." Watching mother and baby brought a feeling of longing to Karissa. One day soon, she could be holding her own baby. Her hand fell to her stomach. Malcolm put his arm around her, saying nothing, but communicating so much.

Maggie asked Malcolm to tie two of the shoelaces around the cord. "Leave space for a real clamp," she directed. "They'll want to put one on when they arrive. Make sure the laces are real tight," she added. "It's not the ideal thing, but we use what's available." The women let Malcolm cut the cord between the laces as the baby lay on his mother's chest.

After a few minutes, Brionney's face contorted. "They're coming again," she said. She handed the baby to Malcolm, who sat next to her at the head of the bed. "Is he coming right?"

Faith nodded. "I saw him turn after his brother came out. And I can feel the head now. Don't worry."

The second baby came more quickly than the first, and the aftermath also went more smoothly now that everyone knew their jobs. Karissa was ready with the syringe, but this time it proved almost unnecessary—at least so far as the baby's breathing was concerned. As soon as his body cleared his mother's, he began to cry. Karissa suctioned him out, just to make sure the mucus wouldn't choke him, causing the baby to scream even louder. That started the first baby crying again, and together they chorused their complaints. Both tried to suck their fists as they cried.

"I think they're hungry," Malcolm said.

Faith gave him a smile. "They're babies; they're always hungry."

"A baby's instinct to nurse is the strongest in the first half-hour or so of life," Maggie added.

Malcolm gave the first baby back to Brionney, who sat staring, relieved from her pain now, as if bemused by the miracle that had taken place. "You'd better nurse," Faith said. "It will help your uterus to contract; you've lost a bit more blood than I like to see. And I'll make you a cayenne mixture to drink. That'll help."

"I'll go get the girls," Malcolm said. He went reluctantly to the door, and Karissa knew it wasn't because of his broken ankle that he went so slowly, but because he was loath to leave the new babies and the miracle of their birth. She gazed at the baby in her arms, so soft, so tiny, so . . . helpless. One minute they weren't there, the next they were. Karissa felt like laughing, singing, and crying all at once. Not the sad kind of tears, but those that came from uninhibited joy.

Everyone arrived in Karissa's room nearly at once. Jesse, Dr. Fairfax, a nurse, and the ambulance workers came in the front door and down the hall just as the girls burst into the room. The medical people carried bags and equipment; the girls brought hugs and kisses. All were anxious to see the babies and Brionney. Only Malcolm did not return.

Karissa handed baby number two to Jesse as reluctantly as Malcolm had relinquished his place in the room. "He came second," she murmured. "Just so you don't get them mixed up."

"As long as they came out safely," Jesse said. His eyes met his wife's. "And as long as Brionney's all right, nothing else matters." He sat on the bed and leaned over to kiss his wife, sharing a private moment even among the excited, giggling girls and the other adults who looked on. The baby in his arms began wailing again.

Karissa backed away from the bed and toward the door. Where was Malcolm? After having been in the room during the birth, and even having been an important part of getting the first baby to breathe, was he now suffering from embarrassment? Or feeling unneeded, as Karissa herself now felt?

"So you're making house calls now," Brionney joked as Dr. Fairfax approached the bed.

"It isn't the first time," he said. "And it won't be the last. Too many people live too far from the hospital." He glanced over at Faith and Maggie. "But I see you've been in capable hands. These women have been helping deliver babies since before I left the island to attend medical school, and more than once we've run into each other."

"Tell the rest," Maggie said with an indulgent smile.

Dr. Fairfax laughed. "Okay, okay. Maggie here delivered me herself."

"How about that," Jesse said.

Karissa left them then, the happy family and those who would examine both mother and infants. They would weigh and dress the new additions, and finally clean up until there was no trace of the divine miracle that had occurred. Karissa was no use to them now, but the thought didn't make her sad. For a few moments she had helped a baby take his first breath of air. Her exhilaration at the experience was tinged by bitter pain and sweet hope. What would her life have been like if her first baby had lived? Would this new baby inside her womb heal her from that aching guilt and longing?

She found Malcolm on the porch, the last place she looked. He stood at the top of the stairs, staring out into the dark night. The rain had worsened into a genuine storm, and the wind whipped her hair around her face. She heard a crack of lightning and a short time later saw a jagged flash in the distance, illuminating the angry tumult of clouds in the sky.

"Isn't it beautiful?" Malcolm asked without turning.

Karissa had always preferred quiet, peaceful nights when she could hear the grasshoppers calling and smell the earth cooling from the heat of the day. She stepped up to the edge of the stairs and looked out in the direction where Malcolm stared, searching for the beauty that fascinated him. The wind rushed at her, bringing a tumult of fresh, stimulating scents, some comfortingly familiar, some wildly different and intoxicating. The blast of air spiraled around her, playing with her hair and making her think of a nymph set free to dance in the night where no protruding eyes watched or arms threatened to seize. It was incredible!

The lightning flashed in the sky and Karissa saw the clouds shifting, driven by the wind-nymph in her untamed dance. Then the thunder came again, pounding through her body, summoning reactions she had never before noticed. "It's more than beautiful," she agreed simply.

He turned to her, smiling. His eyes met hers, but she couldn't read the thoughts written there in the gray that now seemed black in the stormy night.

"I've been an idiot," he said. "I can't believe I've let so many years go by being a complete and utter idiot." Karissa gazed at him without speaking, not understanding his words.

"I've never seen a baby so new," he said, touching her arm. "Suddenly there he was, squeezing his eyes shut and refusing to take a breath, and I knew I could spank him or give him mouth-to-mouth and make him breathe, but then I thought how much better if he did it on his own, so I rubbed his feet, and then he took that first breath and everything was okay. Oh, Karissa! Now I know what my parents have been doing all these years; they've been rubbing my feet and praying—as hard as I prayed to find you on the road tonight—that I would breathe on my own."

"What are you saying?" Malcolm occasionally talked in metaphors and Karissa had chalked it up to his creative nature. But this time she wanted plain language.

"That baby is from heaven, Karissa. From heaven! Where our baby is. I want us to be a complete family, an eternal family. And here I have separated us because I wasn't willing to sacrifice for our child as much as you were. I'm not worthy of a child, but I will be. So help me, I promise you I will be!"

The wind blew her hair in her face, and she tossed it back impatiently. "You'll quit smoking?"

He nodded. "I don't know how, but I know why. I can't let a pure, perfect child of God into my home unless I'm worthy. By the time our child comes, I'll be ready."

The lightning blazed, closer this time, and in that flash, Karissa saw that he was serious. "What are you say—?" She broke off, recognizing that she didn't know if she wanted to hear the answer.

"It's time we decided what's really important in our lives," he responded to her unfinished question. The wind tore his words from his lips, but instead of tossing them into the night, it planted them deep in Karissa's heart. His eyes were awash with love and purpose. "You've been hinting at this all along, haven't you? With all this talk of the Church and eating right. I was just too blind to see it."

But she had mixed feelings about this sudden change of heart. Over the years she had told herself that it would never come, even knowing all along that it would. Malcolm was a good man, and in her heart she had always felt that one day he would want to search for a deeper meaning in life, one that wasn't connected to material gain or professional recognition. Yet she had looked forward to the change with trepidation, not joy, even though in her heart she yearned for the freedom it would give her. For embracing the gospel would entail great changes, and she knew she wasn't capable of changing herself— not completely. She couldn't admit her unforgivable sin, not to anyone but Brionney, and certainly not to Malcolm, who would never understand.

"Let's take this one day at a time," she said softly. "Start first with the smoking." *Maybe he won't be able to quit,* she thought. *He couldn't before. And then the point of further spiritual progression won't matter. I can't lose him now.*

Fear and regret grew in her heart. Why had she insisted? The very thing that had kept Malcolm from the Church had kept him with her. Why hadn't she realized that until this very moment? What did she really want? Why did things have to be so complicated?

One thing stood out clearly: Malcolm, whether he liked to admit it or not, came from a spiritual family, and their ideas were engraved upon his heart and mind. Worse—or better, depending upon the viewpoint—he had felt the Spirit tonight. Latent roots, planted firmly in the soil of his youth, had sprouted; now they had only to grow.

Karissa too had felt the Spirit, but her secret made redemption impossible. Her roots had been cut off permanently because of her past. *Malcolm, I committed a sin,* she could say, and have it over with. But she wouldn't—she couldn't. She knew he would turn against her.

He pulled her close and rested his cheek against hers. "Can you believe those two little babies? And soon that will be us."

"I'd prefer a hospital, if you don't mind," she said, marveling that her voice could be so calm when her heart ached so badly.

"I love you," he whispered.

She couldn't say it back. Her emotions were so volatile that even if it were true on this stormy night, it might not be tomorrow. More important than love was the commitment. The love could come and go, blaze or dim, but regardless, she needed her husband.

"Stay with me?" she asked.

"I'll never leave you again."

Karissa hoped he spoke the truth.

CHAPTER 18

"Help! It's the unidentified flying diaper!" Jesse called laughingly. He threw a disposable diaper over Camille's head and into the short garbage can they had kept in the family room since the day after the twins' birth. Savannah and Camille echoed their father's laughter. Baby number one, or Gabriel as his parents called him, blinked lazily as his father fastened the tabs on his new diaper, his dark eyes an undefined blue-brown.

"Pass me Forest," said Jesse, pulling on Gabriel's tiny pajamas. "I might as well get this over with in one nose-plugging swoop."

Karissa laid Forest on the baby blanket next to his brother. As Jesse opened the myriad of tiny snaps on his soft pajamas, she picked up Gabriel and returned to the sofa, where Delinda Goodrich eyed him intently.

"They look exactly alike," Delinda said. She moved closer, just to make sure, and the plastic sack on her lap crinkled noisily.

"They're identical twins," Malcolm reminded her. He sat in the easy chair, his cast resting on an ottoman.

"Can I hold him when you're through?" Savannah asked.

Forest started to cry. It seemed to Jesse that Forest was always crying, just as he had the moment he had come from Brionney's womb.

"Of course you can. But for Pete's sake, get the pacifier before he wakes up your mother and Rosalie." Jesse's face held a tint of green as he eyed the contents of Forest's diaper. Savannah scrambled for the pacifier and obediently poked it in the baby's mouth. He promptly spit it out and cried more loudly.

"You need some tape to keep it in his mouth," Malcolm suggested.

"What, you don't have Crazy Glue?" Jesse returned. Grimacing, he fished into the container of wipes and came out with a small stack.

"Landsakes!" Delinda said. "Let me do that. You're going to use a whole pack of wipes on two diapers!"

"Oh, no," Jesse said. "I made a deal with Brionney to change all the diapers for two weeks. I've only got two more days to go, and then I'm free."

Delinda sighed. "It's good I brought ya these then," she said, dumping the contents of her sack onto the floor: a mound of diaper wipe refills. Malcolm, Karissa, and the girls nearly choked on their laughter, but Jesse looked at Delinda gratefully.

"Thanks, Delinda," he said. "Whoever invented these must have been a father who hated changing diapers."

"Or a mother who was sick of doing all the work," Karissa said wryly.

Delinda laughed. "That's more likely."

"Are we going to have family night?" Camille asked.

"Well, I don't know. We don't have a treat," Jesse said to tease her.

"Uh-huh." Camille looked at him seriously. "We have burnt cookies."

Karissa colored. "Oh, you weren't supposed to tell them about that."

"But they're good." Savannah licked her lips.

"My motto is that if they got sugar, kids'll eat 'em," Delinda said. "Now pass me one of those little angels. Not the one that you said came out screaming—goodness, I'm too old for that. Give me Gabriel; isn't that his name?"

Jesse finished the diaper and let Savannah hold the screamer Forest under Karissa's watchful eye. He went into the kitchen to wash his hands, and Malcolm followed.

"Ya got a minute?" Malcolm asked.

"Sure, what is it?" Jesse turned on the water.

"Well, about that night, when the babies were born."

Jesse turned, leaving the water running. "I appreciate what you did, Malcolm. Without you searching for Karissa and Brionney, things would have been a lot worse. As it was, everything turned out great—except for my missing the birth."

"It's not that. I feel partly at fault for Brionney even being at the house instead of in Anchorage or in Kodiak, closer to a hospital."

"It was me who forgot to fill up Karissa's gas tank," Jesse said. "I don't blame you for anything."

Malcolm went on without acknowledging Jesse's possible guilt. "There I was at the head of the bed, wishing I could help Brionney, thinking that if you were there, you would have given her a blessing. But I couldn't do that. I gave up my right to do so long ago. I hadn't missed my priesthood before that night, not even when Karissa threatened to miscarry. Someone else would be there and would certainly give her a blessing—and did, as it turned out."

"It was Damon."

Malcolm shook his head as if he could shake the name out of the conversation. "Someone was there, it didn't matter who, just that it didn't have to be me. But that night with Brionney, there was only me, and I couldn't do it."

Jesse felt a leap of excitement in his heart. "It could be you. It was once. You gave me a blessing when you were on your mission. You still have the power; you just need to be worthy."

"I know, I know," he said, his voice low and tense. "But I've got to quit smoking. I went and got a patch." He pulled up his sleeve to reveal a blue nicotine patch, then covered it again and began to pace awkwardly with his heavy cast. "It's not working. I've tried and tried, and I know it's no longer a physical problem, really, but a psychological one. Despite this stupid patch, I've smoked every day since the babies came, even though I tried so hard not to. I can't tell Karissa; she'd be so disappointed. It doesn't help that she quit the first time she tried." He slammed his fist in his hand. "Darn it all, I've just got to beat this, but how?"

Jesse wanted to make a suggestion, but something held him back. *Let it be Malcolm's idea,* he thought. He squeezed soap from the flowered bottle near the sink and methodically washed his hands under the running water. Turning it off, he shook his hands in the sink the way Brionney hated, before remembering the hand towel hanging from the ceramic holder. As he dried his hands, he turned back to where Malcolm had stopped pacing and stood staring, waiting.

"I'd love to help," Jesse prompted. "What can I do?"

Malcolm's thick eyebrows drew together, wrinkling the skin on his forehead. He clamped his lips tightly together before opening them to say, "Could you give me a blessing?"

The words hadn't come easily, and Jesse quickly squelched any sign of triumph or amusement that might have come to his face. "That might work," he replied more calmly than he felt. "I'd be glad to do it. Can you think of anyone else that you'd like to assist me?"

"Can't you just do it alone?"

"You know how it is, Malcolm. It should be two. One does great in an emergency, but we have time here."

Malcolm sighed. "Okay, then. Jud Kennedy's my home teacher. I don't know who his companion is now, but Jud's always trying to come and teach me something. I think he'd be glad enough to assist." His face turned sheepish. "I don't know how I'm going to call him, though. I've spent so long trying to avoid him that I don't even know his number."

"I have it on the ward list. I'll go get it."

"Wait."

Jesse paused on his way out the door.

"Do you think we could keep this between us men?" He shrugged. "I just don't want to worry Karissa now. She's been through enough in the last few months."

"Sure, Malcolm." Jesse wondered if Malcolm's real reason for not telling Karissa was that he was embarrassed by his inability to stop smoking on his own. "We'll invite Jud to come home teaching, and afterwards you can show off your studio. We can do it then."

The crease went out of Malcolm's forehead. "Thanks, Jesse. I appreciate it."

"No problem."

* * * *

Jud came that night, without a companion but promptly and with a lesson. During the discussion he ducked his blonde head nervously, and the flaccid cheek beneath his left eye twitched furiously. But when he bore his testimony, both the nervous ducking and twitching stopped. His round face seemed firmer, and his eyes burned with the strength of his conviction.

Malcolm listened intently, as did Karissa, but Jesse noticed that her face was pale and the hollows in her cheeks more pronounced. *She's not happy about Malcolm asking Jud to be here,* he concluded. The Spirit confirmed his thought. *But why?* Jesse had always thought it was Malcolm holding Karissa back, but now he was not so sure.

Later, as he gave Malcolm a blessing, a strong prompting came to Jesse's mind: "Pray every day to keep from smoking, and the strength will be given you at the very moment you are in need. But you must also love your wife and remember that she is a special daughter of God. Cleave unto her and to no other."

The two things didn't match, but neither of the other two men seemed to think it strange. Jud shook Malcolm's hand. "I'm really glad you asked me to come out."

"Thank you for coming," Malcolm said. "And on such short notice."

"I enjoyed being here. But what about Sunday? Will you be coming to church?" The twitch had relaxed after the lesson was over, but now came back in force. Jesse felt a burst of admiration for this man, who forged ahead regardless of his insecurities.

"I'll talk to Karissa," Malcolm said. "I just might be there."

* * * *

"It's time for us to leave the island," Jesse said to Brionney as they readied for bed.

"You think we've outstayed our welcome?"

He crossed the room and took her hands. "It's not that. I just think Malcolm and Karissa need some time alone. I think they're on the right track, or almost are. And Delinda and Jud will watch out for them. I don't want to be in the way."

"Maybe you're right," Brionney said.

"Besides," he added, "the other guys and I have finished up every scrap of business I had lined up in Kodiak, and even some of the contracts in Anchorage. To keep working, I'd have to leave you and the kids alone too much. I wouldn't be able to fly home from Anchorage every night."

She pulled away and walked over to the crib next to the bed. The twins were nestled together, sleeping—Gabriel soundly and Forest with tiny grunts and sighs. "Do you want to leave Alaska?" she asked.

Jesse leaned against the crib. "I don't think we should go that far—just to Anchorage. I have some contracts to finish there, and Damon and I still have plans to make. I think his idea of marketing my hospital program for national use is going to be a great success."

"Then can we go home?" There was longing in her voice.

Jesse laughed. "I thought you wanted to stay on Kodiak."

She shook her head slowly. "I love it here, but it's not home." Her blue eyes focused on him, turning his insides weak, despite their seriousness. "But I think I'm ready to settle down. We have five children now; they need a house, someplace stable. And I miss my family."

"You're right. We'll go. Right away if you want."

"No. I'm not sure I should leave Karissa completely just yet. I'd like to stay in Alaska until her baby is born. There are things that—" She broke off. "I just don't feel we should go right this minute. But soon. Let's see this thing through with Damon, and finish your other contracts."

"It's a deal," Jesse said. "And I'll tell Damon we'll have to base our company in Utah. It won't be the first software company there—not by a long shot."

Brionney frowned suddenly. "I don't know if it will be that easy to convince him. He has a lot of ties here."

Did she know something Jesse didn't? Women always seemed to communicate by undercurrents.

Brionney sighed deeply.

"Is something wrong?" he asked.

"Oh, I don't know. Despite my homesickness for Utah and my family, I think I'm going to miss it here.

* * * *

A few days later, Jesse and Brionney drove to a deserted bay before leaving Kodiak Island. The girls crowded around Brionney as she stood on a rock outcropping over the water. Jesse watched from the beach, the twins cradled in his arms.

In her hands she held the green plant container. Brionney removed one flat rock from the container and tossed it into the clear water. The second rock followed, skipping three times before sinking out of sight. Then she shook out the dirt from the container, watching it fall and disappear into the ocean.

With the twins in her life, she no longer needed the pot of dirt and rocks for a reminder. They had served their purpose, but now there were no wounds left unhealed. *Thank you, Father,* Brionney prayed. She and Jesse had come a long way. It hadn't been easy thus far, nor would the future be without challenges, but they would make it together.

She turned back toward the beach, grabbing Rosalie's hand so she wouldn't slip from the rock. The other girls followed, their laughter rising on the breeze.

Would Karissa ever reach the point where she could give up the past? Brionney hoped so. One thing she knew: the Lord loved her friend despite her sin. She only wished that Karissa would let Him show her that love before it was too late.

CHAPTER 19

Malcolm urged the jeep into the curve as fast as he could, feeling it plow through the slushy late-March snow. His mind was alive, and he reveled in the freedom he enjoyed. The best two years of his life, his mission, had finally been supplanted by the growing joy in his heart. Looking back, he could see that the night Brionney's twins were born had been the beginning; from there he had set about changing his life with a vengeance. Since he quit smoking, five months ago after Jesse's blessing, he hadn't missed a day of church or felt a craving that he couldn't conquer with a prayer.

When had he lost sight of the importance of the gospel? He didn't know or pretend to understand. Now the gospel of Jesus Christ filled the emptiness he had felt in his heart for so many years.

He glanced at his watch. Nearly thirty minutes since Karissa had called from the hospital. He wouldn't miss the birth of his first child, he just wouldn't! And he wanted to be with Karissa, to support her. Maybe he would even give her a blessing. He hadn't used his priesthood yet since his return to church, and he was only beginning to feel worthy of doing so. Now he would be able to name and bless his own child! Tears came to his eyes, and he blinked them back to focus on the road.

Returning to church had been much easier than he had imagined. People had welcomed him, and he found joy in seeing them and sharing in their lives. Some of the single sisters had thought him a bachelor, and he had many interesting conversations with them until they realized that he was completely and totally in love with his pregnant wife.

Malcolm's smiled died on his face. Karissa hadn't returned to church with him, despite his gentle urgings. But then, she had been sick with her pregnancy. "I can't stay for three hours," she had said. Or, "driving in the car makes me sick." This last, at least, was true. If Karissa didn't drive herself, she would throw up repeatedly. Even when she did drive, she would feel faint.

He had schooled himself to be patient, sure that things would get better after the baby came. Karissa still worked full time, which drained all her energy, but maybe that would change, too. She had mentioned that Damon had found a temporary replacement for six months until she decided what she wanted to do.

To Malcolm, there was no decision to be made. He had just sold his documentary, and his commercials had made such an impact on the market that he had the funds to think about turning completely to movie-making, his childhood dream. One of his clients had given him a movie script by a young author who Malcolm was sure would make the grade, and it was set on a remote island that sounded very much like Kodiak. Malcolm already had backers for the film. It would be a success, and Karissa would never need to work again.

Malcolm didn't say any of this to Karissa, but he thought about it every day. He planned how the rooms in their house would be filled with children, and Karissa would be as happy as she had been while caring for Jesse's girls.

The hospital parking lot was just ahead, and he turned in and came to a quick, slushy stop at the parking space nearest the building. Not bothering to lock the Jeep's doors, he plunged through the melting snow and into the hospital. "Where's Karissa?" he asked the nurse on the maternity floor.

"What? No 'good afternoon?'" She winked. "Come on, Mr. Mathees, I'll take you there."

Karissa was lying on a bed, looking calm. She held out her hands for him. "Malcolm."

He hugged her and kissed her forehead. "I made it."

"Not by much," she said. "They say it's going quickly for a first baby. They're giving me an epidural now."

Compared to Brionney's delivery that stormy night, Karissa's seemed easy. She had sweat on her forehead and occasionally grimaced during the contractions, but the pain was kept at bay by the epidural. The baby came quickly and with no complications.

"It's a girl!" Malcolm said excitedly, glad they had waited to find out. "Oh, she's beautiful!"

He watched Dr. Fairfax clean and suction the infant and wrap her in a soft blanket. "A textbook delivery," he said, handing her the baby. "Congratulations."

Karissa's face shone with perspiration, but her hair and makeup seemed untouched. She cradled the baby with wonder in her eyes, the same wonder Malcolm felt on his own face. He put his arm around her and snuggled up close, caressing the baby with his hand. Karissa tore her gaze away from their daughter to glance at him. "She's all ours," she whispered.

"You did a great job."

She smiled. "It was hard, but easier than I expected," she admitted. "Though for a while before the epidural, I thought I was going to scream. If it's this easy, maybe we can have some more." It was the first time Karissa had mentioned the possibility of other children, as if wanting more would jinx the baby they had been given.

"You just say when," Malcolm said.

She sighed in contentment. "I'm so happy."

Malcolm was happy, too. Maybe now Karissa would see how good the Lord had been to them and search for the deeper meaning in their existence. He prayed for this daily.

"Let's name her Stephanie." Karissa shifted the baby on her chest and turned her head to see his face.

"Why Stephanie?" he asked. They had discussed names, but this one had never come up. "I don't know anyone by that name."

"Exactly. It's just her. She seems like a Stephanie." There was a thinly veiled intensity in her voice.

He slid a hand down her long hair. "Karissa, is something wrong? You can tell me."

"Nothing. I just like that name. What do you think?"

He looked down at the little baby with the mass of black hair and wide, dark eyes, slightly swollen and squeezed shut now against the light. "It fits her," he said, smiling. "Besides, after going through that, you can name her anything you like."

Karissa laughed the deep, throaty laugh Malcolm loved and laid her head back on his chest. Malcolm knew life couldn't be any better than it was at this moment.

It wasn't until weeks later that Malcolm's world fell apart.

* * * *

The first time Stephanie threw up, Karissa didn't think much of it. She had seen Brionney's babies do it many times, and had learned that babies spit up—sometimes a lot. She simply took the week-old Stephanie from her breast and wiped her mouth with the cloth diaper she kept handy, then laid the baby on the sofa next to her. She adjusted her bra and pulled down her shirt, wincing slightly at the soreness she still felt at nursing time. "That's all for you, my dear. It looks like you've had too much already."

She picked up the manuscript she had found on the coffee table. Its storyline took place on a remote island very much like Kodiak. She wondered where Malcolm had found it and why he had kept it. The words kept drawing her back to the page and she read on, fascinated. Every so often little Stephanie would make a small noise, and Karissa would hurriedly check to make sure her daughter was all right.

When Malcolm came into the television room, she tore her gaze away from the manuscript and looked up, noticing that he still had the glazed look he had worn since Stephanie's birth. She chuckled. "Run into any more walls, Malcolm?"

He picked up Stephanie and sat beside her, placing the baby's head on his knees with her little feet pointing to his stomach. Next to his left eye, beginning at the end of his eyebrow, an inch-long cut scarred his face. He fingered it gently. "Not since this."

"It's not every day a man becomes a father for the first time."

Malcolm snorted. "That's what the doctor said when he stitched me up. But it was embarrassing, I tell you. Embarrassing." He poked gently at Stephanie's stomach as she watched him complacently with her overlarge eyes.

"Did you remember to take Delinda's dishes back?" Karissa asked. Delinda and some of the other ward members had brought dinners for several days after Steph's birth, and she had been asking him to return their pans and Tupperware™ containers.

"I finally remembered." His eyes glanced at the manuscript, then stared as he recognized it.

"It's really good," Karissa said. "It'd make a wonderful movie. With a few changes, it could have happened on Kodiak."

"I want to make it into a movie," he confessed. The new scar near his eye made it droop slightly, and Karissa thought it added character and a sense of mystery. "Do you think I could do it?"

Was he asking for her permission? "I think it's a wonderful idea. You would do a great job. And I'd even like to help, if you want."

"I'd love it!" Malcolm seemed pleased. He jumped up and did a little dance with the baby, favoring his right shoulder as he had since the bear attack the previous year. "Oh, it's going to be great!" Stephanie chose that moment to lose the rest of her dinner. Karissa tossed him a new cloth, since the one she had used a few minutes before was wet.

"Yuck," Malcolm said, mopping his shirt. "Why did you do that to your old dad?"

"I think we'll both have to get used to it," Karissa sighed.

Malcolm eyes shone, and Karissa knew he didn't mind. He loved Stephanie no matter what she did. Karissa felt happier than she had felt in a long time.

Only Malcolm's renewed interest in the Church threatened Karissa. Over the past months, as his devotion to the Church deepened, Karissa's resistance to it had increased. She felt as if he were being ripped away from her and taken to a place where she could not follow. But today they were joined by their love for their daughter and their excitement over the film Malcolm would make. He put his arm around her, and she leaned her head against his shoulder, feeling closer to him than she had ever felt.

Then Malcolm glanced at his watch. "Oops, I've got to get going. I have home teaching in a few minutes." He handed the baby back to his wife, kissed her, and rose from the couch, leaving Karissa to stare after him.

* * * *

When Stephanie was ten days old, Karissa took her in for a checkup with Dr. Fairfax. His eyebrows drew together anxiously. "She seems healthy," he said. "But she hasn't gained any weight. In fact, she's lost six ounces since birth."

"But don't all babies lose some weight?" Karissa asked.

"That's true, but she should be gaining by now."

"Well, she's been throwing up some. But I didn't imagine it was too much."

Dr. Fairfax met Karissa's steady gaze. "Now, you know I'm a big advocate for breast feeding, but some babies take a little longer than others to catch on. I want you to supplement two bottles a day until she starts gaining weight. And I want to see her again in two days. It's a Saturday, but I'll be here seeing some other patients. We don't want to take any chances."

"Thank you," Karissa mumbled.

During the next two days, Stephanie began to throw up a short time after each feeding. It was so much that Karissa would have to change the baby's clothes, and often her own as well. Malcolm was working, but every few hours he called to see how Stephanie was doing.

"She still hasn't gained any weight," Dr. Fairfax said at the next visit. Stephanie was twelve days old and weighed six and a half pounds, still six ounces less than she had at birth. "I think we'd better go strictly to formula," he said. "Maybe she's allergic to something in your milk. I'll want to see you in another two days."

Karissa felt as if her heart would break.

Dr. Fairfax touched her arm. "She still seems healthy. We'll get through this." His words hadn't calmed Karissa's heart, but his manner had. Whatever was wrong with her daughter, they would find and fix it.

Stephanie continued to throw up the formula a half hour to two hours after eating. Karissa experimented with every formula on the market, and even with fresh milk from Maggie's goat, but Stephanie's stomach rejected everything. Afterwards she would begin crying, a thin, wailing sound that ate at Karissa's heart.

"I'm so sorry, Steph," Karissa whispered.

The night before they were to return to the doctor, Malcolm rubbed Karissa's back as they sat together on their bed, a thick towel between them for the inevitable loss of milk from their daughter's stomach.

Karissa felt the tears slide down her face. "I feel so bad for her, not having anything in her tummy. She doesn't know that life isn't supposed to be like this. It's supposed to be better."

"Let's pray," Malcolm suggested.

They prayed together, more fervently than they ever had before. Surely God would heal their baby.

At fourteen days, Stephanie had lost two more ounces. Since she didn't keep down the formula any better, Karissa began to nurse her again, feeling some relief that her milk had not been causing the problem. The lactation consultant at the hospital began working with Karissa to single out a possible allergy Stephanie might have to something in both Karissa's milk and the formulas. They began by cutting out all dairy products in Karissa's diet.

"I'll be honest with you, Karissa," Dr. Fairfax said. "I don't know what's causing this, but if she loses any more weight I'm going to have to admit her to the hospital. For now, try to give her small amounts of milk many times during the day. Perhaps that will help. The important thing is to make sure she doesn't become dehydrated."

Karissa drove slowly away from the hospital. It was mid-April now, and the snow was nearly melted by the continuous rains. Karissa remembered how at this time last year she and Malcolm had gone to see the fertility doctor, and how envious she'd been of Brionney's daughters. It seemed like a long time ago.

Tears flooded her eyes, dropping from her face and soaking into her jeans. She pulled off the road a few minutes from Dell Flats and put her head in her hands. "Oh, Stephanie," she murmured.

When she was sixteen and had thought that Tyler might marry her and take her away from her life, Karissa had picked out a name for their baby. Stephanie had been her choice. She had always wanted a little girl to dress up and to put bows in her hair.

Heat rushed to Karissa's face. What had she been thinking? That first Stephanie was gone, and naming this precious new soul after that old dream couldn't bring her back. What's more, Karissa was losing this Stephanie, too.

The baby woke up now that the movement of the car had stopped, and she began crying in a voice that seemed to accuse Karissa. "Dear God," Karissa prayed aloud, "it's not her fault. Please help her!"

Stephanie cried most of the last twenty minutes to the house, stopping when Karissa took her out of the car seat. She rooted around, trying to nurse on Karissa's sweater.

"Just a minute, Steph." Karissa fed her daughter, counting the swallows the way the doctor had told her. Ten swallows was approximately an ounce of milk—the small amount she was supposed to give Stephanie at each feeding. But when the ten swallows were up, Stephanie still nursed strongly, fussing when removed, and Karissa didn't have the heart to stop her. Afterward, the baby was happy and lay contentedly in her mother's arms while Karissa prayed.

"Karissa?" Malcolm came in from the garage and found them in the television room. His face was red from the cold, but his grin radiated warmth. "Well?" he asked, reaching for the baby.

Karissa pushed his hands away. "I just fed her. Don't jiggle her."

The throwing up began suddenly, as it always did, with Stephanie crying between each gush. Karissa held her while Malcolm mopped up the carpet. He slumped down on the sofa, circling his arms around his family.

"I don't know what to do," Karissa murmured. "It's all my fault."

"Don't say that," Malcolm ordered gruffly. "It just happened, that's all. Years from now, we'll look back on this with a different view."

Karissa knew that Malcolm didn't understand her culpability the way she did, and she was too afraid to tell him the truth. She held her secret to her, feeling alone despite her husband's presence. Part of her seemed to die each time Stephanie threw up.

That evening, Malcolm's mother called and suggested several native herbs that might help. Since Dr. Fairfax didn't know what caused the problem, Karissa was willing to try anything.

"And has Stephanie received a blessing?" Faith asked.

Karissa blinked. "No."

"Then get her one."

"Why didn't I think of that?" Malcolm fumed aloud. "I know better now."

But Karissa knew they had been so busy trying to save Steph that they hadn't thought of the religion that had been of so little importance in their life together. Malcolm called Jud Kennedy, and they gave Stephanie a blessing. This time Karissa didn't resent the religious interference, but prayed fervently for the Lord to hear their prayer.

Two days later, Karissa returned to see Dr. Fairfax. "How is she?" he asked.

"She's keeping down about every other meal." Karissa knew the hope showed clearly in her face.

"Five ounces. She's gained five ounces!" Dr. Fairfax smiled. "It looks like whatever we're doing is starting to work."

Could it have been the blessing? Karissa didn't know or care; it didn't matter as long as Stephanie was going to be all right.

"Let's see," Dr. Fairfax said. "Today is Thursday. Why don't you bring her back on Monday, and we'll see how she is."

That night, after putting the sleeping Stephanie in the crib Malcolm had made for her, Karissa curled up in Malcolm's arms. The crib was in their room so they could hear if the baby needed them.

"I told you it would be okay," Malcolm said.

"We don't know that yet."

His arms tightened. "I think the Lord just was just testing us. I think He wanted to show you that He could heal her. Maybe He wants you to come back to church."

"So He plays games with babies' lives?" Karissa said, turning her back toward him. "I don't believe that, Malcolm."

"Well, maybe not," he conceded.

He continued to hold her rigid body. Finally, Karissa rolled back over and looked at him. "There's no maybe. Stephanie shouldn't have to suffer for our sins, you know that."

"Will you come back to church with me?" Malcolm stared into her eyes, and she felt trapped. "I want us to go to the temple soon. Now that we've quit smoking, there's nothing holding us back."

Karissa stifled a wild urge to laugh. Malcolm was nothing if not persistent, and she didn't know how much longer she could avoid the issue. "I've been through a lot," she said. "Steph's only sixteen days old, and I haven't exactly been getting any sleep. Birth's hard on a woman, you know. And with Steph's problem, could you imagine the mess she'd make at church?"

Remorse bathed his face instantly. He touched her cheek in the lazy way she adored. "I'm sorry. You *have* been through a lot. I forget that sometimes. You're a very strong person."

"I don't feel strong."

He kissed her brow slowly, working his way down to her neck. "You are, though. And I love you."

Karissa settled into the warmth of her husband's arms, her back cradled against his chest. *Maybe returning to church wouldn't be so bad. Provided Stephanie continues to get better.* It was her last thought before sleep took her.

That night she had the dream. *Karissa fed Stephanie and the baby shook her head. "No more. No more."*

"You have to eat."

"You gave me too much. Why did you do that?" Then she was still.

Karissa awoke and checked on Stephanie. She was sleeping soundly and peacefully. *Dear Father, help me!* Karissa prayed. Feeling better, she wiped the tears from her cheeks and returned to bed.

* * * *

Little Stephanie threw up only three times in the next two days, and Karissa's hope grew with each feeding. But her hope turned to agony on Saturday afternoon when her daughter began to throw up almost continuously. Throughout the night and the next day she and Malcolm tended and fed Stephanie, fearing that each episode brought their daughter closer to death. Malcolm didn't go to church, but stayed home to help Karissa.

Sunday night after Stephanie was finally asleep, Karissa changed her clothes for the sixth time that day. She threw the milk-soaked T-shirt and jeans into the dirty hamper, already full of at least eleven of Stephanie's tiny outfits—all of which had been clean at the beginning of the day.

She locked the bathroom door and turned on the shower. Then she sat on the cold tile floor in her underwear and cried, tears flowing from her eyes in an unending stream. Her body felt more weary than she had ever remembered. Her back and arms ached from holding Stephanie, and her legs throbbed from pacing. Inside, her womb felt sore.

All this pain was nothing compared to the agony in her soul. What if Steph died from losing so much weight? Or from dehydration? What if she had some awful disease that the doctor had missed with all his tests. What if it was something not yet discovered? Something horrible and deadly? Her shoulders convulsed violently as she sobbed out her fear.

Worst of all, Karissa knew that she deserved the pain. But not Stephanie. Never her precious Steph. When would it all end?

CHAPTER 20

Monday, after a long, sleepless night, Karissa went to the Nissan and settled Stephanie in the car seat. The baby opened her eyes for a moment, and her little hands moved erratically in the air. Karissa sat beside her, smoothing the dark hair on her head. "It's okay, Steph. I promise." She knew the words meant nothing, but the baby slept again.

Malcolm's face creased in a worried scowl as he drove them to the doctor's office. Karissa said nothing to him. She wished she could cry to let out some of her terror, but after last night there were no tears left.

Dr. Fairfax examined Stephanie almost immediately. "We're going to have to admit her. She's becoming dehydrated. We'll get her an IV and that should help."

Karissa nodded stoically, grateful that at last something was being done.

Malcolm's jaw dropped, then closed with a snap. "You can't admit her," he protested. "She needs to be with her family. She *has* to be all right. The Lord will heal her."

Dr. Fairfax shook his head. "She's too bad off not to be admitted. She's lost too much weight."

"But what's wrong?" Karissa asked. "Why can't anyone tell us what's wrong?" She started to cry, and some distant part of her wondered where the new tears came from. An ugly, painful knot formed in her stomach.

"I don't know what's wrong," said Dr. Fairfax gently. "None of us knows. Right now, I'm going to call Anchorage to see if they have a bed for Stephanie. We're simply not equipped on Kodiak for this situation. It's too severe."

"What about calling in a specialist?"

Dr. Fairfax shook his head. "This is too serious to wait for such an opportunity. You'll have to go to him."

They sat in silence until the doctor returned. "They have no beds," he said. "We'll just have to keep her in the hospital here until something comes up."

"What about the other hospitals?" Karissa said. She desperately tried to act like an administrator instead of a frantic mother. Many times she had faced and solved similar crises. Of course, the difference this time was that it was her life that would be affected.

"I'll keep checking." The determined way Dr. Fairfax spoke renewed the fear in her heart.

"What about Lucy?" Malcolm asked.

Karissa snapped her fingers. "I'll put her on it." Technically, Lucy wasn't her secretary anymore—or at least for the six months Karissa was taking off as director of the hospital—but that didn't mean she wouldn't help.

"I'll talk to her," Dr. Fairfax said. "You go with Steph to the hospital. I've ordered another urinalysis, a culture, and an upper GI series That will get us on our way. I'll be there before the tests are finished."

At the hospital, Stephanie cried with all her frail strength when the nurse inserted the catheter. As there was so little fluid in Steph's stomach to begin with, there was no urine to collect, and they had to wait for her bladder to fill. It took a long time. Karissa tried to feed her to help the process along, but Stephanie refused. She lay weakly in Karissa's arms, her skin sagging loosely on her body, making her appear unnatural. The stark realization came to Karissa that there was absolutely nothing she could do for her baby, and she had never felt so utterly helpless. When she could finally bear no more, a welcome numbness spread over her heart and mind, dulling the terrible guilt and sorrow.

"We're done here," the nurse announced much later.

Karissa cuddled Stephanie to her chest and began to leave the room with Malcolm.

"You're not taking that baby anywhere," the nurse said tersely.

Karissa's eyes flicked to the woman's name tag. Didn't she know who Karissa was? "My child is being admitted," she returned icily. "You don't have to act like I'm doing something wrong by holding her." There was a deep fear inside of Karissa that they would take her baby away and she would never see her again. It had happened once. Of course, that time she had signed the papers permitting the procedure.

The doctor came in and waved the nurse away. "Still no bed in Anchorage," he said. "But at least with an IV, she'll get the water and food she needs."

"How long will it be before we know about the bed?" Malcolm asked. His face had lost much of its color, and he looked as scared as Karissa felt.

"Damon," Karissa said abruptly. "He'll be able to help. He knows people."

Malcolm's face darkened. "So do you, for crying out loud! You talk to the directors at the other hospitals, don't you?"

Karissa whirled, letting her frustration tear into him. "I've been a little busy, if you haven't noticed!"

He stared, but slowly began to nod. "Okay, call him."

"Stay with Stephanie?" Karissa asked. "Please? I don't want her to be alone."

"Of course I'll stay. She's my daughter, too."

Relief flooded Karissa. At that moment, she couldn't face seeing Steph in any more pain. She needed to escape, if only briefly. She quickly called Damon, but his secretary answered. Then she dialed his home phone—to no avail. Finally, she called Brionney's number in Anchorage.

"Karissa!" Brionney sounded happy to hear from her. "I've been going to call you, but these twins are keeping me busy. How are things going with Stephanie? I bet she's growing like a weed. You'll have to send me a new picture."

"She's not growing," Karissa said.

There was a shocked pause. "What's going on?" Brionney asked slowly.

"Steph isn't keeping her milk down. The doctors here don't know what's going on."

"Oh, Karissa, I'm so sorry! Why didn't you tell me?"

"I just thought it would go away, or fix itself. Dr. Fairfax hoped it would. He thought at first that she just had a tender stomach or something. Maybe an allergy. But now he thinks it's something more serious. They're putting her on an IV now."

"I'm so very sorry, Karissa. What can I do? I could fly out and stay with you."

"No," Karissa said. "You couldn't do anything that we're not doing now. But thanks anyway. I do need to know if you know where Damon is. He's not at home or at his office."

"He's with Jesse. They went somewhere. Business."

"If you see him before I catch him myself, can you tell him to call me?"

"Sure, but Karissa . . ."

She thought Brionney's voice sounded uneasy, but maybe it was just the long distance between them. "Yes?"

"If you don't mind my asking, why do you need Damon?"

"To help find a good hospital for her. So far we can't find a bed at the pediatric hospital. Damon's been here a lot longer than I have; he'll know what strings to pull and who's the best out there to take care of Steph."

"Oh. All right. That makes sense."

Karissa hung up, wondering at Brionney's reluctance. What did she think Karissa wanted with Damon? Shrugging off the thought, she went to find where they had put Stephanie.

"We have a private room—for now," Malcolm said, looking up from an easy chair and smiling weakly. Stephanie was asleep on her father's chest, but her eyes fluttered at his voice. A portable metal crib stood nearby.

"Did she cry when they put the needle in?" Karissa asked, glancing at the IV in her daughter's small arm and then back to Malcolm.

He didn't meet her gaze. "Yes. I'm glad you weren't here to see it."

"I shouldn't have left her." Karissa smoothed Stephanie's dark hair.

"I held her," Malcolm said. "I took care of her."

Of course he had. "I'm sorry." She blinked back tears. "I know I couldn't have done any better."

"So what did Damon say?"

"I couldn't reach him. I left a few messages, though."

Malcolm jerked his chin toward the rocking chair next to him. "Have a seat."

But Karissa shook her head and slumped on the arm of his chair. "I need to be closer to her."

He nodded, and after a few minutes said, "What will we do next?"

"We wait. There's nothing to do but wait."

They took turns holding Stephanie, feeding her occasionally and cleaning up after her. Karissa was glad the other beds in the room were vacant, giving them privacy to deal with their daughter. Minutes ticked painfully into hours.

Well into the afternoon, a nurse stuck her head in the door. "There's a phone call for you, Mrs. Mathees. He wanted me to make sure you were here. I'll have it transferred."

Karissa glanced briefly at Malcolm's unreadable features before rushing to the phone. It rang, and she picked it up.

"Hello?" Karissa said.

"Kar, it's me, Damon." His voice was intense.

She felt a rush of relief. "Thank Heaven! I need to talk with you."

"I know. Brionney told me. I'm sorry I didn't call earlier."

"That's all right. You couldn't have known. It's Stephanie, she—"

"I've talked to Dr. Fairfax," he interrupted. "I've found a bed for Steph at a hospital here that has a great pediatric department. They have a doctor there, Robert Schmidt, who is one of the best pediatric doctors in Anchorage, and possibly in the entire United States. They are waiting for you now. I'll meet you at the airport on this side with an ambulance."

Tears stung at Karissa's eyes. "Thanks so much, Damon."

"It's nothing. I'm always going to be here for you." His voice sounded strangely gruff. "Now hang up and get down to the airport. I've already told them you're coming."

* * * *

Malcolm contemplated Karissa's face during the flight to Anchorage. She looked more weary than he had ever seen her. On her lap she held Stephanie, staring at her as if afraid to look away. In the next seat, a nurse from the hospital checked the baby's IV.

He worried about Karissa. There was an undeniable connection between her and their daughter. As much as he feared losing Stephanie, he thought he could eventually come to terms with her loss. But not if Karissa followed her; he couldn't lose them both.

As promised, Damon met them at the airport after the hour-long flight. He was only slightly shorter than Malcolm, and his blonde head was visible above the small crowd. "Kar, this way!" he called. Karissa waved and turned in his direction.

Malcolm hated the familiar way he addressed Karissa, though he admitted to himself that the man had done nothing to evoke his suspicions during the past months.

"The ambulance is over here," Damon said. "I'll follow you in my car." Next to the ambulance, Malcolm noticed a dark blue Mercedes.

Karissa refused to relinquish the baby to anyone in the ambulance, but continued to hold her. On the way to the hospital Stephanie cried, and Malcolm and Karissa tried uselessly to comfort her. The ambulance driver drove rapidly through town in the failing light, plowing headlong through the melting snow. *Where has the day gone?* thought Malcolm.

"You'll like Robert Schmidt. He's a good man," Damon said when they arrived. He talked easily, and his words seemed to soothe Karissa's nerves. Malcolm sized up the blonde man with the odd yellow-brown eyes, finding it difficult not to like him.

They hurried into the emergency room—the most filthy Malcolm had ever seen, with papers and bits of plastic spread over a floor that looked like it hadn't been cleaned in a month. Karissa's nose wrinkled. "Maybe we should go somewhere else," she whispered uncertainly when Damon left them briefly.

She sounded frustrated and close to tears. In the face of her need, Malcolm felt his own strength increase. "I think there might be a reason we're here," he said. "Let's give it a chance."

Dr. Schmidt appeared after a tedious forty-five minute wait. He matched Malcolm's height inch for inch, but he was larger boned. He had nondescript brown hair and eyes, yet his eyelashes were the longest and curliest Malcolm had ever seen on a man or woman.

"I'm Dr. Schmidt," he said easily, his wide face cracking into a smile. "This must be little Stephanie." He turned to the baby, who was lying on an examining table. "Hi there, Stephanie." As he spoke, he pulled up her shirt and touched her stomach gently with his large hands. Then he pulled his hands away and lowered his face close to her body, studying it.

"Look at that," he said. "There appears to be a rolling movement. That's her stomach trying to push the food through the pyloric valve to the duodenum—the first part of the small intestine." He straightened. "From what I see here and from her symptoms, she probably has pyloric stenosis. That's when the muscle around the pyloric valve is too big and won't allow the stomach to empty through the small intestine, instead causing the food to come back up. If that's the case, we can correct it with minor surgery. We can't be sure, however, until we do a few more tests."

"Then it's not too serious?" Malcolm asked.

"Not the surgery itself. But like I said, we have to make sure that's what's really wrong."

He transferred Stephanie from the emergency area to a room with four large metal cribs. One stood empty, but the other three were filled with babies—all crying and coughing while their parents looked on miserably. The frequent beeping of the various machines and monitors added to the dismal feeling in the room.

Karissa settled into a comfortable chair next to Stephanie's assigned crib, but she wouldn't put the baby inside.

"Have you guys eaten?" Damon asked when he came to check on them.

Karissa didn't reply.

"Not since this morning," Malcolm said.

"Why don't you get something to eat?" Damon suggested. "I could stay with Stephanie."

"I'm not leaving her again," Karissa said, looking up at him. "I left her when they put in the IV back on Kodiak. I couldn't stand another test or to hear her cry again." Tears squeezed out of the corners of her eyes and made a wet trail down her white face. "Do you think I'm awful for leaving her?" she asked. Before either of them could reply, her words tumbled on. "I deserted her once before, but I won't do it again. Not now."

Damon nodded, shifting uneasily. Malcolm touched her shoulder. "It's going to be all right," he ventured.

Karissa didn't reply.

"I'll be back later," Damon said. There was reluctance in his voice. "Please call me if you need anything. Anything at all."

Dr. Schmidt came in as Damon left. "I've ordered a blood draw, and in the morning we'll have some more tests." He smiled confidently.

A nurse appeared and led them to a treatment room. Karissa held Stephanie as the nurse tried to take the baby's blood. The first time she was unable to take anything, and the second time, she withdrew only a little. "That's not enough for the tests," she said, and tried again. The third time the blood clotted. "That's a problem with dehydrated babies. The blood is very difficult to get out, and when you do get some, it tends to clot." She poked Stephanie for a fourth time and took a little more blood.

Malcolm felt pity wrench him as he watched his daughter burst into tears for the fourth time since they had entered the room. Karissa tried to soothe her, but he wondered how long it would be before the baby didn't believe in her comfort anymore.

"I don't think that's enough blood." The nurse wanted to try again.

"It has to be enough," Karissa said sharply, pulling Stephanie to her chest. Her face was an angry red. "I'm not going to let you poke her again. I won't. Not tonight, anyway. You do the tests with what you have."

The nurse contemplated Karissa's determined features. She glanced at Malcolm. "No more tonight," he confirmed. "Let her sleep." He meant Karissa as much as Stephanie.

They returned to Stephanie's room and sat together, watching their daughter drift off to sleep after nursing at Karissa's breast. The cries of babies, bleeps of the machines, and soft voices of the other parents filled the gap between them.

With no warning, Delinda Goodrich flounced into the room. "Oh, here you are." She carried a large paper sack, and her gold bracelets tinkled together as she set it on the floor. "There's food, magazines, books—everything you'll need for a hospital stay except clothes."

"You flew all the way from Kodiak to bring us this?" Karissa asked. She looked as if she was going to cry.

"Landsakes no!" Delinda said. "When I heard about what happened, I decided to come and visit my oldest daughter. She lives near here, you know, and she's always complaining that I don't get to see my grandchildren enough."

Malcolm grasped her hand. "Thanks, Delinda. We're grateful you're here." He was touched beyond expression.

The woman sniffed. "Oh, go on with you. I told you it's not because of you; my daughter just needed a visit."

But they all knew the truth. Delinda bent and put an arm around Karissa's shoulders as she sat in the chair, giving a slight squeeze. "I'm here for you," she whispered. "And so is your Father in Heaven. He loves you."

Karissa bit her lip to keep it from trembling. "Thanks, Delinda. I mean it."

"I know you do, dear." Delinda touched Stephanie's head with a soft hand before leaving.

Malcolm and Karissa stared after. "She's a good woman," Karissa said.

CHAPTER 21

At six the next morning, a nurse came into the room. "We'll have to take some new blood," she said. "All the blood we took last night clotted."

Karissa's face drew tightly, but she didn't refuse. "Can I nurse her first? She hasn't eaten since three, and she threw a lot of it up."

"No, don't feed her anything," the nurse said. "She's scheduled for an ultrasound at ten, and she has to have an empty stomach."

Malcolm helped Karissa to her feet, noting the dark circles under her eyes. This time she let him carry Stephanie to the treatment room.

The first two times she tried, the nurse succeeded in withdrawing a little blood. The third time she took nothing. Stephanie cried in hopeless wails, and Malcolm blinked back the tears forming in his eyes. *The pain she must feel!* he thought. *And no way to understand why. Dear Lord, please help my daughter!*

As the nurse prepared another needle, Karissa scooped up the crying Stephanie. "No!" she yelled at the nurse through her tears. "Not again. No way! You only have to do three tests for electrolytes. You should have enough blood. For goodness' sake, she's only a baby!"

Karissa headed out the door with Stephanie, and Malcolm followed her, relieved that for the moment at least, Stephanie was safe from the needle.

"The vampires," Karissa muttered in the hall.

Malcolm pulled her to a stop and wiped the tears from her eyes. "My wife, the warrior," he said lightly. "I never knew you were so strong."

Her emerald eyes, made even brighter for the sheen of tears, met his gaze. "There's a lot you don't know about me, Malcolm." Her voice was neither light nor teasing, but deadly serious.

Malcolm felt a shiver crawl up his back. *It's just this situation,* he told himself.

Karissa started again toward Stephanie's room, but Malcolm went more slowly. He felt as if he saw the stark hospital walls and the clean tile through a hazy dream lens. Maybe he would wake up, and this nightmare would be over.

"Malcolm!" Jesse and Brionney waved to him from the nurses' station. He waited for them to approach. "We would have come sooner," Brionney said, "but the kids . . . Where's Karissa?"

"She's in the room," Malcolm said.

"How's she holding up?"

"I'm not sure," he admitted. "She seems strong."

Brionney grimaced. "What she should be is in bed. This is too much for anyone three weeks after giving birth. She'll get sick."

That was what Malcolm feared. "Can you convince her to rest, do you think? I tell her I'll stay with the baby, but . . ."

"Get used to it," Jesse said, his voice full of pity. "To women, that's not as good as being there themselves." He looked after Brionney, as if expecting a comment, but she was intent on reaching Karissa. "And maybe they're right," he added as if in afterthought.

Malcolm, remembering the way Karissa had fought to save Stephanie pain, thought so too.

"Oh, Brionney!" Karissa exclaimed when she saw them. The women drew their heads close together and talked in quiet, urgent voices. Malcolm and Jesse listened without speaking.

"I'm so sorry," Brionney said.

"Three weeks. She's three weeks old today and in less than twenty-four hours they've poked her with a needle ten times—not to mention that horrible urine test where they have to stick that tube in her. How can she stand more?"

"She's got a strong spirit."

"They keep wanting more and more blood."

"Do they know what's wrong?"

"Not yet. Maybe today."

"More tests?"

"An ultrasound. I think I'm beginning to hate these people."

"They're just doing their jobs."

"I know, but Steph doesn't."

"One day she will."

"Yes, but I found out today that this is a teaching hospital. It makes me so mad to think of them practicing on my baby!"

"But it was the only place available," Malcolm put in. "And Dr. Schmidt, at least, is experienced."

"It still makes me mad!"

Brionney rubbed Karissa's arm sympathetically. "Tell me, what can I do to help?"

"No one can help. It's my fault. You and I both know I deserve this."

Brionney drew back slightly. "No. That's not true. No matter what, that's not true."

"Yes, it is."

Malcolm wanted to ask what they were talking about. Why would Karissa feel so strongly that Stephanie's problem was her fault? She had mentioned this to him once before, but he had dismissed it as a normal tendency for mothers when their babies were not born perfect. Now Karissa's feelings seemed to go beyond all reason.

"At least we're off the island." Karissa spoke vehemently, but a shadow of guilt passed over her pale face as she glanced at him. With a flash of understanding, Malcolm realized that despite their closeness in the past few months, Karissa still felt imprisoned on Kodiak, not free and alive as he did. The realization brought a deep sadness.

The Hergarters left shortly, promising to return later. "Please call if you need me," Brionney begged.

"I will," Karissa said. Malcolm knew she didn't mean it. He could at least read his wife that well.

The same nurse who had drawn Stephanie's blood that morning came into the room. Her expression was wary. "We are going to need a urine test to check for a bladder infection."

Karissa closed her eyes, as if gathering strength. "She had one yesterday on Kodiak," she said calmly. "Those results should be in sometime today. You can use those."

"I'll go check with the doctor."

"Thank you." Malcolm could see Karissa was holding back her anger.

The doctor confirmed that the results from the first test could be used, as well as some of the other tests Dr. Fairfax had ordered on Kodiak. Malcolm felt grateful that Karissa had asked, saving little Stephanie further pain.

After eleven, the nurse still had not come to take Stephanie for the ultrasound. "What's taking them so long?" Karissa asked as she paced near the metal crib with the crying baby in her arms. "Steph hasn't eaten since three this morning. She's hungry. I can't believe this!"

"I'll go and ask them to hurry," Malcolm said, grateful for something to do.

For all his efforts, it was noon before they took Stephanie for her ultrasound. She was cranky and hungry, but the nurse was very gentle and the baby didn't cry. Karissa's face relaxed, and she let Malcolm take her hand.

"Everything looks normal," said the nurse.

Malcolm wasn't sure if that was good. If Stephanie's problem wasn't pyloric stenosis as the doctor suspected, then what was wrong? Could it be even more serious?

By one-thirty they were back in Stephanie's room, and Karissa nursed the baby. "Look how happy and content she is," Karissa said, love etched unmistakably on her face.

"And she hasn't thrown up," Malcolm added.

"Not yet."

The doctors and nurses left them alone for the afternoon. When Brionney and Jesse returned later that night, Malcolm took a taxi to his parents' house to shower, shave, and change into some clothes borrowed from his father.

"How is she?" Faith asked.

"We don't know, Mom," he said. "They're still trying to find out what's wrong."

"Could I go and stay with her while you and Karissa get some rest?"

He shook his head. "No. Karissa won't let anyone stay with her."

"I can hardly fault her for that," his mother said. "But tell her we are all praying for Stephanie. We're having a family fast."

"Thanks. I'll tell her."

She hugged him before he left. "I'm proud of you, son. I know it hasn't been easy coming back to church and getting your life in order. I know Karissa will join you soon."

Karissa's church activity was the farthest from his mind at that moment. "For now, we just need to get through this," he said.

"Of course. And we are here to help you. Your father and I will come over in a while to see how you're doing."

Malcolm drove back to the hospital in his mother's car. Jesse and Brionney had left, but Damon was with Karissa. "It doesn't seem fair for Steph to have to go through this," Karissa was saying. "I don't understand it."

"I don't either," Damon said, "but maybe we will later." He saw Malcolm and rose from the chair. "I'll leave you two alone now." He touched Karissa's arm. "You call me if you need anything. It doesn't matter what time."

Karissa smiled. "Thanks, Damon."

Damon shook hands with Malcolm before leaving. "See if you can't get her to sleep a little," Damon said softly. "She needs it."

Malcolm felt his mouth tighten. Why did everyone seem to think that he wasn't doing his best to take care of Karissa? "I will," he murmured.

Damon flashed him a wide smile. Malcolm caught sight of a gold tooth far back in his mouth. It sparkled, making Damon's grin appear even wider. Malcolm was glad to see him go.

Richard and Faith arrived shortly after for a brief visit. Karissa said little to them, but Malcolm saw that she was more relaxed with his parents than she had ever been. She even let Faith hold Stephanie while she visited the restroom.

Later, Malcolm kissed Karissa and tried to take Stephanie from her arms. "Let me hold her while you sleep a little."

"But—"

"No buts. She's my daughter too, and I can take care of her tonight. You need to keep your health up for her. Lie down on the blanket. I'll wake you when she needs to nurse."

"Or if the doctor or nurse comes in? Promise?"

Malcolm couldn't help his smile. "Of course."

He passed an uncomfortable but peaceful night in the easy chair. His neck ached from holding Stephanie, and he wondered how Karissa had managed in her weakened condition. Despite the fact that he was holding Stephanie, Karissa seemed to sleep little. Each time he gave the baby to her to nurse, she was already awake and waiting. When her breathing had once told him that she slept, she had suddenly jerked and cried out.

"What is it?" he asked.

"Just a dream," she murmured. "Give Steph to me, would you? I need to feel her breathing."

She held the baby for a long time before giving her back. Malcolm settled Stephanie on his chest. "She doesn't seem to be throwing up as much as she normally does," he commented.

"Maybe her body will heal itself."

Malcolm prayed for it to be so.

Morning came too soon for all of them. At six-thirty Dr. Schmidt came in with some papers in his hands. "The ultrasound has ruled out pyloric stenosis."

"That's good, isn't it?" Karissa asked.

"It depends on what's really wrong," Dr. Schmidt said. "We'll have to wait and see what the X-rays reveal. That's one of the reasons I came by—to remind you not to feed Stephanie. We need her to be hungry enough to drink the barium before her X-rays today."

"How many will she need?" Karissa asked. "I don't want her exposed to too much radiation."

"Three or four," Dr. Schmidt said. "At low dosages. Don't worry, we'll take good of your daughter."

Later, they fed Stephanie the white chalky fluid that would show up in the X-rays, allowing the doctors to trace the path of her digestive system, and took her to radiology. After twenty X-rays, Malcolm lost count. Karissa's face drooped, and her eyes were desolate. "They don't seem to be finding anything," she whispered.

When they were allowed to return to Stephanie's room, Karissa said nothing. She held and nursed their daughter as if each moment were her last. Malcolm prayed as fervently as he knew how. *I promise to face anything you throw my way, Father,* he said silently. *Just please help Stephanie.*

At one in the afternoon, Dr. Schmidt and another doctor entered the room, serious expressions on their faces. Malcolm and Karissa stood up to meet them. "The X-rays show a blockage between the duodenum and the small intestine," Dr. Schmidt said. "We're not sure exactly what it is, but we feel the only way to correct it is through surgery."

Karissa slumped to the chair, holding Stephanie tightly. "Oh, no. I've been so sure her body would get better on its own. She's gained nearly half a pound in two days." Her watery eyes met Malcolm's. "She's only three weeks old!" She studied the doctor for a full minute without speaking. Then, "Are you sure she needs the surgery? We'll want a second opinion, of course. And I want to see the X-rays."

Malcolm saw a flash of irritation in Dr. Schmidt's face, but it was squelched quickly. "I knew you would want that," he said coolly. "Which is why I brought my colleague, Dr. Mizra. He will tell you himself that he agrees with my diagnosis." The brown eyes behind the curly lashes narrowed. "But the bottom line is, do you want your daughter to die?"

Karissa gasped at his insensitivity and began to cry. Malcolm grabbed Dr. Schmidt's arm and pulled him to the door. "That's enough," Malcolm said. "I appreciate your work with Stephanie, but we need to be alone now."

Dr. Schmidt's broad face showed remorse. "I'm sorry I had to say it that way. I felt she didn't understand the seriousness of this situation. If Stephanie doesn't have the surgery, she will die."

Malcolm looked at the other doctor. "Is this your opinion as well?"

"Yes. The sooner she has the surgery, the better," Dr. Mizra said. He was older than Dr. Schmidt by at least ten years, and graying hair framed his kind face.

"Dr. Mizra has practiced pediatric surgery for more than thirty years," said Dr. Schmidt. "He would be my choice for assisting me with the surgery, if you agree to it."

"I think Karissa and I are worried about unnecessary surgery," Malcolm said. "You said you *think* that is what's wrong. How can we be sure?"

"We would never do any unnecessary surgery—especially on an infant as young as Stephanie," Dr. Mizra said. "In fact, we've ordered a few more X-rays to see how the barium has been digested. The results will show conclusively whether or not surgery is our only recourse."

Malcolm liked this man, and thought Karissa would too, given the chance. "All right," he said.

"Dr. Mizra or I will check in with you after the X-rays, and if they confirm our suspicians, one of us will explain the surgery in detail," Dr. Schmidt added. "Your wife will have time to get used to the idea by then."

"Thank you."

Malcolm returned to Karissa. He massaged her shoulders while explaining what the doctors had told him. He spoke quietly so the other parents in the room wouldn't hear. "I feel they're honest men," he said. "And we've tried everything else, haven't we?"

"I guess so." Her voice sounded oddly detached and lifeless.

"Darn it all, Karissa, we knew it was something serious. At least I did. And now we'll get it taken care of so that Stephanie can have a normal life—so that we can have a normal life." He touched her chin, drawing her haggard face toward him. Even now, she was beautiful to him. "We can pray, Karissa. I know God will listen."

Instantly, her face became livid. "Where is God now?" she screamed at him. "Why isn't He healing my baby?"

Malcolm felt the eyes of the two other parents on them. Though the room was large and there were white curtains between the cribs, Karissa's voice carried easily. Both averted their eyes, and one left the room with her baby. After a minute of silence, the other mother also left. "Karissa," Malcolm began.

"No, you listen," she said. "You don't understand. This is all happening because I deserve it! God is punishing me for my sins."

"Your sins? You've done nothing wrong."

She nodded, her eyes sadly triumphant. "Oh, yes I have. I'm a murderer. I murdered my own unborn child."

Malcolm's jaw dropped. "What are you saying?"

"You heard me. I murdered—"

"Our baby? When?" He was unable to keep the horror from his voice. Never had he felt so betrayed. But things abruptly grew worse.

"Not our baby," she said ruthlessly. "It happened before we met. She was a little girl too—or would have been."

In her simple words, a lot of things became glaringly clear—Karissa's real reasons for leaving the Church, her strangeness of late, the odd comments, and even the nightmares she suffered.

"It's not true," he muttered. He felt utterly desolate, as if his entire world had fallen in around him and he couldn't find a safe place to set his feet. He stared in bewilderment at the woman he had thought he knew.

Karissa hung her head. "Poor Steph is suffering because of me," she whispered. "What kind of God would do that to a baby?"

It was difficult for Malcolm to think about Stephanie or God at that moment. He waited for Karissa to beg for his forgiveness. Could he give it? He wasn't sure.

But she didn't speak again, and in her eyes Malcolm saw the guilt. He knew then that Karissa wouldn't ask for his forgiveness, because she believed that there was none for her—not in this life or ever.

Sudden rage blotted out all the other emotions. His wife had lied to him for ten years! And she had committed not one but both of the gravest sins anyone could ever commit! Their marriage was a mockery. Revulsion washed over his body, forcing him to take two steps back from her. "You!" His voice was brutal.

Karissa released one hand from Stephanie's body and brought it to her mouth, sobbing. Her eyes pleaded without words.

Malcolm shook his head and strode from the room. Karissa—the sweet wife he had known—was gone forever.

CHAPTER 22

The room was strangely silent, as it had been since Malcolm had walked out on her an hour before. For the first time since Stephanie's admission to this hospital, the other cribs were all empty. The other sick children were either in surgery or still out in the halls with their mothers. The monitors were also silent, except for the occasional beep from Steph's machine.

And now I've lost Malcolm, Karissa thought. Her agony over Stephanie's condition had plummeted to new depths when Malcolm had stared at her, his burning accusation hanging in the air between them.

"What have I done?" she whispered. The words mocked her.

The nurse came to take Steph for new X-rays, and when Karissa returned to the room she found the other parents there also. They smiled at Karissa as if nothing had happened.

"I'm taking Randy home," one of the mothers said. "The doctor says he's well enough."

"That's good," Karissa responded automatically.

Randy was soon replaced by another sick infant who coughed repeatedly. Karissa worried that her daughter would contract some new disease and wouldn't be able to make it through her surgery. She wished she could talk to Malcolm about the possibility, but he didn't return.

Karissa's mind replayed her confession and the look in Malcolm's eyes. Did he hate her? Would he divorce her immediately?

Just when she could bear no more, Brionney called. "What's wrong?" she asked after Karissa's sorrowful greeting.

"Steph's probably going to have surgery," she said. "It's more serious than they first thought, though the doctor insists that it's still minor surgery. I just feel like I'm all alone."

"Where's Malcolm?"

"He left. I—I told him about . . . about . . . the . . ." Karissa let her voice fade away. "He's upset."

"Give him time," Brionney said sympathetically. "Look, you hang on tight. I'm going to call Delinda to stay with my kids, and I'll be right down."

"You don't have to do that," Karissa murmured.

"We'll see you in a few minutes."

A short time later, Malcolm returned with Dr. Mizra. He kissed Stephanie and stroked her cheek, but didn't meet Karissa's eyes or greet her.

"The X-rays prove that the surgery is necessary beyond any doubt," said Dr. Mizra. "The best way I can explain it to you is that your daughter has what is called a duodenal web that blocks the food from going into the small intestine. We'll have to remove this web. If all goes smoothly, as I believe it will, we should have her back at home in less than a week. So what do you say?"

Karissa glanced at Malcolm. "Okay."

"Yeah, go ahead," Malcolm agreed.

"Then I'll have the necessary papers sent to you this evening," said Dr. Mizra.

"When will you do it?" Malcolm asked.

"Dr. Schmidt has tentatively scheduled the surgery for Friday." He smiled and left.

Friday, thought Karissa. *Today is Wednesday. That means we have to wait two more days.* Now that she had agreed to the surgery, two days seemed like an eternity for Stephanie to continue her suffering.

Karissa and Malcolm sat in silence. She wanted to reach out to him, but his angry eyes told her what he would say.

"So what was his name?" he asked.

"Who?"

"The father of your baby."

The question disconcerted her. "Tyler," she said. "But I didn't love him, I just thought I did. He—"

"You loved him enough, evidently."

Karissa shut her eyes, fighting the tears. She deserved this. She deserved everything. "Yes," she whispered.

Malcolm's face showed no pity or compassion, only hurt and betrayal. She knew he would dredge up everything now, and doing so would only make things worse between them.

Salvation came in the form of Brionney. She walked into the room carrying a small blue and white cooler. Without permission, she boldly took Stephanie from her mother's arms, careful of the IV and the white wires attached to her chest, and handed her to Malcolm. "Karissa and I are going somewhere," she said firmly. "Delinda has sent along a nice dinner for you, Malcolm," she added, kicking the cooler. She put an arm around Karissa and nearly dragged her to the door. "Let him watch Steph," she whispered. "Whatever his feelings toward you, he'll take care of her."

Karissa had just fed the sleeping baby. There was no reason for her to reject Brionney's offer, except her continuing reluctance to leave Stephanie in anyone else's care. "Go on," Malcolm said, as if reading her thoughts. "Stephanie will be fine with me."

She decided to go. The tests were over, and there should be no more pain for Steph—not today, anyway. And by leaving, she could put off Malcolm's searing questions.

They went to Brionney's house, where Karissa showered, ate a good meal, and talked quietly with the children, renewing their friendship. Not owning pants of a useful size to lend Karissa, Brionney washed and dried Karissa's clothes. Delinda arrived as the clothes were ready, carrying a rectangular package for Karissa. "June drew it from those pictures of Steph you gave us the last time we came visiting teaching," she explained.

Inside was another picture of Jesus, this time holding a baby that looked a lot like little Stephanie. There was a certain comfort in seeing her daughter with the Savior, but His eyes seemed to hold only reproach for Karissa.

"Thank you," Karissa said. She left it on the counter and promptly forgot its existence.

Simply being with Brionney and her children eased Karissa's sleep-deprived mind. It reminded her that in the face of all the trouble in the world, here at least was a slice of heaven on earth—albeit a noisy slice.

"The ward is planning a fast for Friday," Delinda said to her. "We are all praying for little Steph."

Karissa was touched more than she wanted to admit. Why would those people who barely knew her care so much about Stephanie? Had Malcolm made so much of an impression in the few months he'd been active?

"I need to get back," Karissa said, blinking away the moisture gathering in her eyes. "It's been an hour."

"Are you sure you don't want to eat any more?" Brionney asked.

Karissa smiled. "I'm already having trouble fitting into these pants, and they're two sizes bigger than I normally wear."

"I don't believe it," Brionney said. "They hang on you."

Karissa looked down at the Levis she had borrowed from Malcolm, noticing with surprise that Brionney was right. When had she lost the weight? "I've been too busy to eat," she admitted.

"I guess there's one blessing in all this," Brionney said lightly.

"Maybe," Karissa said, grabbing her coat from the sofa. "Come on; Steph might need me." She dreaded going back to face Malcolm, but knew she had no choice.

"Here," Delinda said. "I brought you something else to read. I've marked some really good parts." Glancing at the *Ensign* magazine Delinda shoved in her hand, Karissa saw that it was an old one, the November 1995 General Conference issue. Well, maybe reading it would keep her mind from Steph's problems.

"Thanks so much for everything," she said to Brionney as they got in her car. She threw her coat and purse into the empty backseat. "I really needed to get away. And it feels great to be in clean clothes for a change."

Brionney's blue eyes clouded, and she didn't start the engine. "There's something I've been trying to tell you," she began.

"What?"

I just wanted . . . well I thought I should warn you . . ."

"What is it?" Karissa demanded. Whatever Brionney had to say couldn't be worse than the nightmare she was going through with Stephanie, or the sense of impending doom she felt now that Malcolm knew her dark secret.

"Your dad's coming." Brionney's blurted it out quickly.

Karissa stared and Brionney looked away.

"I called them a few days ago," she added. "Your parents. I know I should have asked you, but I . . . I think you need them."

Karissa shook her head, wondering at her friend's audacity. "My father is the *last* person I need," she grated. "When I called to tell them about Steph's birth, all he wanted to know was when I was going to the temple. He as much as told me that I wasn't really married at all, and that my daughter was as good as born out of wed—"

"Maybe it'll be different during this crisis." Brionney's face pleaded for understanding. "Maybe he'll make things easier for you. I felt the impression to call him so strongly."

Karissa glared. "You just don't understand. There are three eternal facts in the universe: the earth revolves around the sun, the gospel is true, and my father is always right. Stephanie's illness isn't going to change anything. You shouldn't have interfered! Stephanie is sick because I aborted my first baby. She is having to suffer for my mistakes. I almost hate God for doing this to her! It's me who should suffer, not Steph!"

Karissa shoved open the car door and fled, leaving Brionney behind. "Wait!" her friend called, but Karissa kept on running.

Melting snow piled about the streets, dirty now from water the cars splashed onto the sidewalks. Dirty as Karissa's soul. Frustration, anger, and, yes, fear pulsed through her. Why? Why? Why? She wanted to shout it to the world. Why Steph? Poor, innocent Steph!

Tears stung her face, growing cold as soon as they left her eyes. As the flare of anger left her heart, she began to shiver in her ribbed turtleneck. Though it was long-sleeved, the green fabric was thin. Her Levis already felt stiff and frigid on her legs. She thought about returning to Brionney to retrieve her coat from the car, but she couldn't face her friend again. Why hadn't she minded her own business?

Karissa glanced up and down the street, completely lost. Houses flanked the road, but they were unfamiliar. Which way to go? She had to get to a phone to call a taxi. Steph might need her. This last thought brought a sense of panic. She waded through another slushy snowbank, grateful for the fur-lined leather boots on her feet. They kept out much of the cold, as her clothes did not.

Everywhere she looked there were houses and buildings, pavement and snow-filled lawns crowding in on her and making it difficult to breathe. She longed for her house on Kodiak set among the spruce and cottonwoods, with its backdrop of rolling hills and pristine mountains. The desire surprised her so much that she stumbled and nearly fell.

"Kar! Kar! Over here!"

She turned to see Damon calling her from his blue Mercedes. "Damon!"

"Hop in. I'll take you to the hospital."

"Brionney sent you," she said, and kept on walking.

"I let Jesse off just as she was pulling out to go after you. She said you'd had a disagreement and you took off. That's all I know. Come on, get in." He leaned across the passenger seat and pushed open the door. With one hand on the wheel and the other trying to keep the door from closing, he looked comical.

Karissa shook her head.

"For crying out loud, Kar! It's cold, and you're not dressed for it. I have your coat here and your purse—you can't go far without either. Now stop being difficult. You just had a baby three weeks ago. Do you want to get sick? How will you help Steph then?"

Her steps faltered and stopped. Damon braked the car and pushed the door wide open. Karissa slipped inside, relishing the heat of the interior. She rolled something in her hands and, glancing down, was surprised to see it was the *Ensign* Delinda had given her.

Damon put the car in motion. "What happened?" he asked after a while.

"It's nothing."

"You don't run away for nothing. What you mean is that it's none of my business."

"It's not that at all!"

He shrugged. "If you don't want me to know—"

"She called my parents. My father. He's coming to Alaska. I don't want him here."

"Why?"

"Because . . . because . . . I don't want to be judged by any more people. When my father sees what a mess I've made of my marriage . . . my life . . ."

Damon slowed and pulled to the curb. "I thought you and Malcolm were getting along great." He spoke as if choosing his words carefully.

Karissa stared at her hand, twisting the *Ensign*. "We were. And then this thing with Steph—" Her eyes flew to his. "Steph! I have to get back."

Damon handed her his cellular phone. "Call if you're worried."

The thought of talking to Malcolm frightened Karissa. "Could you just talk to Malcolm?" she asked hesitantly.

Damon studied her for a long moment without speaking. Then he picked up the phone and dialed.

"Don't—please don't tell him I'm here."

His yellow-brown eyes bore into her, full of questions.

"Room four-oh-three, please," he said into the phone. "Malcolm? Hi, Damon here. Is everything all right? How's Steph?" There was a long pause. "A web in her stomach? Oh." Another pause. "Well, that's good they can fix it. Can I do anything for you? Okay, let me know. You're welcome. 'Bye."

He clicked the phone shut and put it down. Silence. *Why doesn't he say something?* Karissa thought. "How's Steph?"

"Sleeping." The engine still purred, but Damon made no move to put the car into gear. "Why didn't you want to talk to your husband, Karissa?" he asked in that same careful voice.

"We had a fight—no, a problem."

Damon watched her. "I know it's none of my business, but is there anything I can do to help?"

"You could take away the past," Karissa said bitterly.

"Karissa, you're making no sense! This isn't like you."

"It's not?" She snorted. "You know so little of the real me! Just like Malcolm. You might as well know—everyone else does, or soon will." She glared at him defiantly, but inside she felt a wrenching sadness. Now Damon would also look at her with revulsion and disappointment. "I had an abortion before I married Malcolm," she continued before her courage failed. "I never told him."

Damon blinked twice, but that was all. "How old were you?" he asked.

"I was sixteen. But what does it matter? I knew I was wrong. I *knew* it was murder."

An odd expression filled Damon's face. "What about your parents?"

"They never knew. I went all alone."

"What about the father?"

Karissa pushed her hair back from her face. "He gave me the money."

Damon's face changed now, and it was an expression Karissa recognized. Anger! Disgust! She closed her eyes and waited for it to rip into her.

He grabbed her hand. "What a horrible thing to face alone! I'm so sorry you had to go through that!"

Her eyes snapped open. Her shock must have shown in her face because Damon continued earnestly. "Sixteen! Sixteen years old and alone! You can't condemn yourself forever."

"I did it, Damon. It was *my* choice."

"What if he had stayed by you?" he challenged.

Karissa's voice was hardly more than a whisper. "Then I would have run away with him. I would have had my baby."

She gripped Damon's hand as if his touch alone kept her alive. "I hate my father," she said. "Why couldn't he just love me? Why couldn't I have told him? I needed him." She began to sob.

Damon pulled her close and patted her back. "I can't answer for your father, Karissa. But I do know the Savior loves you."

"It's too late."

"No. It's not. I don't believe that. That's not what the gospel teaches. You were so young—can you honestly say that you understood the consequences?"

She waved his words aside. "Malcolm will never forgive me."

Damon's lips curled. "Then he's a fool! You're the best thing that ever happened to him, and if he's too blind to see it, well, I'm not. I don't blame you for what happened in the past. I know you. You're a good person."

"What do you know about it?" she said through her tears.

He took his arm away from her shoulders and grasped both her hands. "I know that if it had been you and me all those years ago, I would have married you and loved you and supported you," he said earnestly. "You wouldn't have had to make the choice you did. No, don't look away." He turned her face toward him. "I'm still willing to do that. I love you, Kar! I have for a long time."

"But—" Karissa's tears had ceased, almost as if an internal tap had been shut off. She blinked, feeling her mouth open slightly, unbelievingly.

His hand moved to stroke her temple. "You're so beautiful to me, Kar," he whispered huskily. "Did you know that your sweater exactly matches your eyes?"

The fading light from outside the car filtered in and reflected off Damon's blonde hair. She had never noticed how kind his face was, or how strong. He looked a lot like she imagined an angel would look. Her angel.

But this angel wasn't following the rules.

She pushed his hand away. "Damon," she protested, "you don't understand. All this is wrong—wrong! I'm married to Malcolm, and no matter what problems we're going through right now, my commitment to him is first, above all. You shouldn't be saying such things to me, and I shouldn't be listening." She remembered Jesse and Malcolm talking about how new members often had difficulty understanding how the missionaries were off limits for romantic relationships until someone explained it to them. Damon was a relatively new member, but surely he understood that his feelings for her were wrong and that voicing them was a greater sin. Even as an inactive member, she understood where this conversation could lead and what the consequences might be. She had been down a similar path before, and she wouldn't repeat it. "Think about how important covenants are in the Church—especially marriage covenants! I know you've only been a member a short time, Damon, but you must understand that we shouldn't be here together, talking like this!"

His face turned ashen. "I'm sorry," he said softly with such remorse that she almost regretted the vehemence with which she had spoken. "You're right. I am truly sorry. I'm completely out of line. The last thing I wanted to do was add to your problems. I simply wanted you to know that I love you just the way you are." He raised a hand. "No, Kar, just let me finish, and then I'll never bring it up again. I promise. Please, hear me out!"

She inclined her head slightly, and he continued. "You need to know that you are worthy of anyone's love! Satan would have you believe that you are lost, that there is no escape or relief. He wants you to be in despair and to give up. He wants you to think you're evil, even when you're not. Most of all, he wants you to believe that you're no longer loved. But it's a lie, Kar. A big lie! I believe in the Savior. I believe in His redemption. I believe He loves you. Like I do." Without waiting for a reply, he turned from her and flipped the car into gear.

They drove to the hospital in silence as Karissa pondered Damon's confession, marveling that the frantic anger possessing her had disappeared in the face of his love. Even after knowing about the abortion, he loved her! *And how do you feel about him?* a voice inside her asked, unbidden.

She thought hard, unmindful of the progress they made through the cold, wet streets. The many times she had worked with Damon filtered through her mind—the laughter, the friendship, the trust, the acceptance. Why couldn't Malcolm be like more like Damon? Thoughts of her husband steered her back to common sense. She liked Damon and enjoyed being with him, and perhaps she could even grow to love him. But what was happening right now was between her and Malcolm. He was her husband, and she wanted to be with him.

Relief flooded her being. It was almost a spiritual feeling, though Karissa dismissed such a notion. She felt too soiled at the knowledge of her own guilt to expect help from the Lord. And now her confused feelings for Damon only added to her burden. Yet at the same time, knowing that he cared for her gave her comfort.

"Thank you," she said to Damon when they arrived at the hospital.

"Remember what I said about the Lord forgiving you," he told her as she stepped from the car. "I meant every word."

Karissa nodded and turned away.

"Wait, your magazine!"

Karissa went to Steph's room, the rolled *Ensign* in her hands. Malcolm looked up. "She's awake," he said tonelessly. "Do you want to feed her?"

Karissa dropped the *Ensign* onto the table and took Stephanie in her arms. "Hi, sweetie, Mommy's back."

Malcolm stood. "I'm going to stretch my legs."

Damon still cares for me, Karissa wanted to say. *Why can't you?* Instead, she nodded and watched Malcolm leave the room without once having looked her in the eye.

Karissa held Steph tighter. "I've lost him," she said to her daughter. "Please don't let me lose you, too."

CHAPTER 23

He had lost Karissa, and it was all her fault! A mountain-size portion of hurt and anger made Malcolm stay away from Stephanie's room until late that night. Instead of finding Karissa and Stephanie asleep, he found his wife attempting to clean throw-up from the floor using her foot and a towel, while his daughter cried feebly in her arms.

"She doesn't keep anything down," Karissa said, her voice full of panic. "I don't know what to do!"

Malcolm felt pity and a certain measure of guilt for leaving Karissa to face this alone, but her betrayal blotted out most of those kinder feelings. He helped Karissa clean up the milk. It didn't smell sour, and he knew it hadn't spent much time in the baby's stomach.

"This is the fourth time since you left," Karissa said. "I keep changing her clothes." Malcolm saw that her own clothes were soaked, and the various wet parts were at different stages of drying. "It's my fault," she added dully.

Karissa's face crumpled, and Malcolm almost went to her, but before he could act, her mouth clenched tight and her expression became rigid. The pity in him died. She was right: it *was* her fault.

They spent an uncomfortable night, with neither getting much sleep. When Stephanie threw up, they cleaned it with towels the nurses gave them and rocked the baby back to sleep. They didn't talk. During the early morning hours, Malcolm heard Karissa moaning. "No! I didn't let you fall! Please, please don't die!"

Karissa shuddered and jolted to consciousness. Again Malcolm felt something in his heart other than the terrible anger, and if his wife had reached out to him, he would have held her close and stroked her long, silky hair. The desire to comfort her grew, but Karissa made no move toward him. *It's just as well,* he thought. *It will be easier this way.*

Easier to do what? his inner self mocked. Malcolm didn't know; he hadn't thought that far. He only knew that Karissa had destroyed their marriage by her secret sins.

There was no window in their room, but the increasing activity of the nurses told them Thursday morning had finally crept into sight. Karissa's eyes were red and swollen, and Malcolm wondered when she had cried; he hadn't heard her.

"Look at her arm," Karissa said, her voice gruff from disuse.

Stephanie's right arm had doubled in size where the IV needle pierced the skin. Karissa called a nurse. "It looks fine," the young woman said after examining the arm.

"Fine?" Karissa said. "It's swollen. Just about all the nourishment my daughter is getting is from this IV," she said. "And it's not normal to be this swollen."

"I see that it's swollen, but the needle seems to be in fine," the nurse said. But she was hesitant now, and Malcolm wondered if she was still in training.

"I want to see a doctor," Karissa asserted.

The doctor who came was one they didn't recognize. He examined Stephanie and told the nurse to change the IV to the left arm, as the solution was no longer going into the baby's vein. It took the nurse three tries with the needle, but Stephanie seemed to rest more easily with the saline and electrolytes once again pumping into her vein.

Without warning, Karissa spoke, "My father's coming soon. I don't know when. I'd—" She glanced up at him, and the sadness in her beautiful eyes made Malcolm want to weep. He wanted to hold and love her. He wanted all this to be far behind them. Why couldn't he let it go? "I'd appreciate it if you wouldn't tell him anything about . . . about us . . . and all."

"Our relationship is none of your father's business," he answered. He pictured Karissa's stern father and wondered why she had asked him to come. He thought she hated the man. "When did you call him?"

"I didn't. Brionney did." There was no anger or feeling in her voice at all.

Damon came into the room a short while later. He looked rested and eager. "Hi, Kar, Malcolm," he said. "I've brought you some breakfast. And I want to know if I can baby-sit while you two go for a break."

Karissa shook her head and looked at the crib, where she had laid Stephanie only moments before. "I'm not leaving her." She met Damon's gaze, and Malcolm saw something personal pass between them. Anger flared in his heart, but he couldn't pinpoint what emotion they shared. He felt excluded, like an outsider.

"Everything's going to be okay, Kar," Damon said softly. He touched her arm, and Karissa didn't pull away. Suspicions tumbled through Malcolm's mind. *Could they be more than friends?*

He scowled at Damon, who met his gaze without flinching. "You're a lucky man," Damon said. "Karissa is a wonderful woman and mother." There was an insinuation there that Malcolm couldn't ignore.

"If only you knew," he said bitterly. And he meant it. If Damon Wolfe knew what sins Karissa had committed and what agony she was causing her family, he wouldn't look at her with such longing and admiration.

"I know Karissa," Damon said lightly. "And that's enough. *I* trust her."

So had Malcolm—once, and look where that had led him. He opened his mouth to continue this subtle war with the man who had now become his overt enemy, but a sudden intake of breath drew his gaze back to his wife. Karissa stared at the door, the remaining color draining from her already pale face. Her jaw set and she lifted her head high. "Hello," she said.

"Karissa." Her mother crossed the room and pulled her daughter into a hug. Sharon Apple was a slender woman; and it was from her that Karissa had inherited her willowy figure and graceful movements. There were strands of gray in Sharon's brown hair, cut just above her shoulders, and her face was heavily lined from years of stress. "I've missed you. I'm so sorry you have to go through this. Why didn't you call sooner? I've missed you so much!"

"I missed you too, Mom," Karissa said in a small voice.

Warren Apple watched as his wife and daughter tried to condense the last few years into a single conversation. He was tall like Karissa and had the same green eyes. Malcolm had never noticed any other similarity between them, but today their faces wore the same hard expression. Malcolm saw with a strange satisfaction that Warren had gained weight since he'd last seen him, and it showed in his face and stomach. The man who had so opposed their civil wedding wasn't as intimidating as he had been years ago. Malcolm wondered what his father-in-law's face would show if he told them Karissa's secret.

"It's good to see you, Father." Karissa proffered her cheek with none of the warmth that had shown in her greeting with her mother. Malcolm noticed that she spoke to her father in the same cold, expressionless voice she had used to address Malcolm since her confession. The realization didn't sit well on his empty stomach.

Karissa introduced Damon to her parents. "Pleased to meet you," they said automatically.

Damon walked toward the door. "If you'll excuse me?" To Malcolm's mind, his voice held reluctance to leave, but Malcolm was grateful for the privacy. "Let me know if you need me for anything."

Karissa nodded. "We will. And thanks."

After his departure, Karissa's parents filled the ensuing silence with trivialities about Karissa's siblings and their lives. "We're going on a mission soon," Sharon said, "now that all the children have left and your dad's retired."

Malcolm saw a momentary surprise in Karissa's expression before she squelched the reaction. "How wonderful," she murmured.

When the small talk had dribbled to its inevitable conclusion, Malcolm walked them out to their rental car and gave them directions to the hotel. On his way back to the room, he ran into Damon.

"Is everything all right?" Damon asked.

Malcolm knew he did a poor job of stifling his irritation at the man's constant interference. "Yes," he replied tightly, reminding himself that it was Damon who had found the help they needed for Stephanie.

Damon studied him for a full minute before continuing. "I know you don't like me," he said, "so let's drop the pretense. I have to tell you that I hate the way you're treating Karissa."

"It's none of your business," Malcolm retorted. "You know nothing about our relationship. She's *my* wife."

"I know. She has made that very clear. But I feel it *is* my business how you treat her, because I care about her."

"You stay away from us," Malcolm warned.

Damon shook his head. "I'm only here if Karissa needs me. I'm her friend."

"Needs you?" Malcolm sneered. "She doesn't need anyone."

"Can one mistake be so serious?" Damon taunted. "Tell me, is it your sense of morality that Karissa wounded, or is it simply your ego?" He laughed without mirth. "You have a lot to learn about real love."

Has Karissa told Damon? When? Before Malcolm could speak, Damon turned on his heel and stalked away.

Malcolm thought about running after the man, but decided against it. Instead, he went for a long walk. He thought about the way Damon had looked at Karissa, and about how she had lied to him. *All this time, she has kept this secret,* he thought. *And not only had she slept with another man, she'd taken a helpless life!* How could he forgive her for that? Maybe it was just as well that Damon was around. She needed somebody, and at the moment Malcolm couldn't find any love for her in his heart.

He returned to the hospital when it began to rain. Karissa looked up as he entered the room, but she quickly buried her nose in the *Ensign* she had brought back the day before. Stephanie was in her crib and Malcolm picked her up, gently rocking her and wishing he could make her better with the strength of his love. *So tiny,* Malcolm thought. *It could have been yesterday that you were born.*

Malcolm wished the clock could turn back. He wished he had never heard Karissa's confession. But more than anything, he wished he could be someone who could look past his pain and forgive her.

CHAPTER 24

Before the surgery on Friday morning, Karissa and Malcolm went with Stephanie to the prep room. They talked briefly with Dr. Schmidt, Dr. Mizra, and the anesthesiologist. To Karissa's surprise, Malcolm began to cry. Tears leaked out of his eyes, seemingly of their own accord. She had never seen him cry before, not ever. Involuntarily, she reached out and clutched at his sleeve.

"I love her so much," he whispered, looking down at their daughter. "I don't want to lose her."

For the first time since her confession, they were drawn together by their love for Stephanie. In that moment the past was gone, and only right now mattered.

"We'll pray," Karissa murmured.

He looked at her. "You will? I thought you were mad at God."

She had been, but that didn't mean her faith was completely gone. "I know He can help the surgeons make her well," she said.

Malcolm had said the same thing in the blessing he and her father had given Stephanie early that morning. Funny how her father had seemed impressed with Malcolm and his new activation in the Church. Under other circumstances, Karissa would have laughed.

If only things could be different, thought Karissa. She longed for Malcolm to hold her in his arms and comfort her, but there was too much keeping them apart. More than anything she wanted to be back in her house taking Stephanie down the slide in the greenhouse.

"We need to get to it," Dr. Schmidt said.

Dr. Mizra smiled. "Don't worry. Your daughter's in good hands."

Karissa kissed Steph, knowing that she should see her very soon.

But there was an unspeakable dread in her heart. What if something went wrong? What if Steph died? She knew she would never forgive herself. If her baby died—again—Karissa didn't want to live either.

As Karissa and Malcolm left the prep room, the wall went up again between them, strong and immutable. Malcolm's tears were gone and his fists clenched. Karissa didn't know what to say to reach him.

She went to the waiting room to talk to her parents, but found it too much effort to carry on a conversation. She tried to read the *Ensign* Delinda had given her. The few articles the visiting teacher had marked talked about forgiveness, a theme Delinda apparently enjoyed discussing; her lessons for the past months had been full of nothing else. So far, none of the lessons or the reading affected Karissa; not one of those people had committed the heinous act that tortured her conscience. She deliberately avoided the talks Delinda had marked.

Damon had slipped quietly into the waiting room without alerting her to his presence. He smiled at her with a look so full of love that she was sure everyone must know how he felt. But seeing him made her heart lighter. Damon stayed well away from Malcolm, whose brooding eyes stared into nothingness. Had they talked about her the day before? Karissa found she didn't care. All that mattered was Stephanie.

She let the *Ensign* slip to the floor and began to say the longest prayer she had ever attempted. As she prayed, she imagined Delinda's Jesus pictures in her mind, particularly the one she had been given at Brionney's. The baby was Steph; perhaps that vision of her in the Savior's arms would mean her safe recovery.

Or could it mean her death.

Oh, please, dear Father. Please. I know I'm not worthy, but please!

Karissa didn't know what else to say. She said the same words over and over. She knew that the Lord could save her baby—if it was His will. If not, Stephanie would die.

All at once, she could feel a rapidly beating heart inside her ears. It was far too fast for an adult, and she knew it was Stephanie's tiny heart. For some unanswered reason, God had allowed her to feel the pulse of her daughter's physical life.

Karissa suddenly had trouble breathing, and she couldn't move. *I'm with you, Steph,* she said in her mind. For twenty minutes she couldn't stir, not even to open her eyes. It was as if every muscle of her body had simply stopped working. She heard worried voices talking to her, but there was no way she would sever the physical and spiritual connection she had with Stephanie by attempting a response. Not being able to move or breathe frightened her—or was it Steph who was afraid?—but through it all the steady thump, thump, thump of her daughter's heart comforted Karissa.

Gradually, the immobilizing effect wore off, and Karissa felt the connection with her daughter slip away, the baby's heart still beating strongly. Karissa opened her eyes. The first person she saw was her mother, sitting next to her and patting her hand. Malcolm and her father stood in front of her with worried expressions on their faces. Some remote part of her wondered if perhaps Malcolm still cared. Behind Malcolm she could see Damon standing with Brionney and Jesse, who must have come in during the surgery.

"It's over," she said. "And Steph's okay."

They gaped at her, but Karissa stood and waited by the operating room door. In five minutes Dr. Schmidt emerged, smiling. "Everything went well," he said, "but we did have some complications. Not only did Stephanie have a web, but her pancreas had also grown around her bowel. We had to cut a new hole in her bowel to bypass the pancreas, then sew the intestine to the new hole in the bowel. So essentially, what we thought was going to be a minor procedure was actually major surgery. But your daughter is a strong little girl, and her chances of full recovery are very high."

"When can I see her?" Karissa asked.

"She's in recovery now. When she begins to wake, we'll call you. But only you and your husband will be allowed in the intensive care unit. When she's stronger, she'll be able to have other visitors. I'll warn you, though: it's going to take a lot longer than we thought for her to recover. Any time you do surgery like that, you interfere with the way a person can assimilate food. So until the tests tell us she's ready, Stephanie will be able to eat nothing except the nourishment we can mix in her IV solution. It will probably take a week until she can eat normally."

Karissa looked at Malcolm to see how he had taken this news, but he turned away to talk with her father, avoiding her gaze. She felt like crying. Maybe she should leave Malcolm; obviously their life together could never be the same. But she didn't want to leave him. She loved him.

"You felt Steph during the surgery, didn't you?" her mother said.

Karissa nodded. "It was the strangest sensation." Why had the Lord allowed her, a sinner, to have such an experience? Karissa had no answer.

Damon studied her. "I think you and Stephanie must have a very strong connection—something extremely special."

Karissa sighed. "I'll spend my whole life making this up to her, if only . . ."

Nobody cared to finish her statement.

When Karissa was finally allowed to see Stephanie, she felt her heart breaking. This wasn't the same baby she had kissed before the surgery. A long, bloody patch stretched across her stomach, and she had a new IV coming out of a vein in her head. Wires dangling from her thin body were hooked to nearby monitors. Stephanie whined as if she was in agony, pushing her tiny stomach out with the force of her shallow breaths.

Tears blurred Karissa's vision as she and Malcolm tried to comfort their child. Stephanie's pain only increased as she came to full consciousness, and she began to scream—bloodcurdling screams that were the stuff of nightmares. *My fault. This is my fault.* The words echoed in Karissa's mind.

Finally, the nurse gave Stephanie a dose of morphine. Almost immediately, she stopped crying and went to sleep. Hours passed before Karissa was allowed to hold her daughter, and then carefully because of the wires and IV. She cradled Stephanie gently in her arms until deep into the night, when Malcolm relieved her. Then she went into the bathroom, expressed milk from her swollen breasts, and poured it down the drain.

* * * *

The next morning, Malcolm prepared to leave for his parents' house to shower and rest. "Call if she needs me," he said.

Karissa didn't miss the insinuation. If Steph needed him, he would come, but not if Karissa needed him. She had lost the right to need her husband. A sliver of resentment surfaced in Karissa's heart. He had turned to religion for his comfort, but his treatment of her surely didn't agree with gospel standards.

But you deserve it, she told herself, and she knew it was true.

"Malcolm," she began.

"What?" He paused, his face stern.

"About us. What—"

His face twisted into some emotion she couldn't place. Disgust? Anger? Hatred? Probably all three. "I don't know," he said steadily. "I just don't know."

When he was gone, the nurse came in to give Stephanie another dose of morphine, preventing Karissa from thinking about her husband any further.

"Your daughter will be moved out of intensive care tonight," the nurse said. "She's doing really well."

For the first time that day, Karissa smiled.

"And oh," the nurse added, "there's someone in the hall waiting to see you. He's been there quite some time. I told him to leave, that only family could visit, but it seems he has some pull with Dr. Schmidt."

"Damon Wolfe," Karissa said.

"Yes. He wants you to grab some lunch with him at the cafeteria."

Karissa glanced down at Stephanie.

"I've just given her the morphine," the nurse said. "She won't wake up. I'll stay with her until you return."

Karissa felt comfortable with the care Steph was receiving. She and Malcolm had never left Stephanie alone in the nurses' or doctors' care except during the surgery, but maybe now it would be all right for a short time. "Thank you," she said. "I won't be long."

Damon grinned as she came out of the room. She could see his gold filling glint briefly in the flourescent light. "Are you a sight for sore eyes," he said.

Karissa laughed. "You're nuts, you know that? Here I've been sleeping in hospital chairs for five nights, and I've bathed only once since we came here."

"You look good to me." The unusual dark amber eyes glinted with amusement.

They went to the cafeteria. Karissa ate quickly, as was her habit since coming to the hospital. "Slow down or you'll choke," Damon said, drawing his thick eyebrows together in mock disapproval. "Chew at least twice before you swallow."

Karissa tried to slow down, and to her surprise, the chicken tasted good. She smiled at Damon, feeling almost shy. The warmth in his eyes threatened to overwhelm her—especially after Malcolm's coldness. "I think Malcolm might leave me," she said.

Damon's feathery eyebrows drew together. "You sound sad. Is that how you feel?"

Karissa flipped back the ends of her hair, remembering how Malcolm had reacted when she had told him she was pregnant. Oh, how they'd loved each other then! Did all that now mean nothing?

She became aware of Damon's eyes on her, watching, waiting. "I have to go back," she said. "I don't like leaving Stephanie."

He walked with her to intensive care, but hesitated in the hall. "Why don't you come in and see Steph?" she asked. "They seem to let you do just about anything you want at this hospital."

"It comes with the job. I'm on the hospital board here, too."

"Job?" she teased. "You haven't been to work today."

"Of course not. It's Saturday."

When they reached the door to Steph's room, they found it open. Karissa was startled to see a doctor bending over the open side of the metal crib. The nurse stood poised with a large needle near the IV line, her face pale and frightened. By contrast, Stephanie's entire head was blue.

"Stephanie! Stephanie!" Karissa rushed to her daughter's side. She seemed never to reach the bed. *My baby!* she cried silently.

The doctor resuscitated Stephanie several times with a hand pump before the baby responded. As he worked, the nurse shot the drug into the IV.

When Stephanie was stable, the nurse said, "I'm sorry about the morphine. It was too much."

"What?" Karissa asked.

"That's what made her stop breathing," the doctor answered. "Too much morphine will put a part of your brain to sleep—in this case, the part that tells you to breathe. It's hard to judge the correct amount, especially on someone so small."

"But she's okay now?" Damon asked quickly.

"Yes. We put a drug in her IV that shocks the brain into waking up. She'll be all right, but in a while she'll be in pain again."

The nurse and doctor withdrew, leaving Karissa and Damon alone with Stephanie. The monitor showed that Steph was all right, but Karissa knew her baby had nearly died.

"It never ends!" Karissa cried hysterically. "Never! She's had to go through too much Too much! I will never have any more children, ever! What possessed me to think I could do it? I won't ever risk making another child going through so much pain because of my sins!"

Damon drew her into his arms and held her until her sobbing subsided. "Did you ever think that maybe Stephanie chose this path?" he asked gently.

She froze. "What are you saying–that Steph knew she would go through all this pain but agreed to do it anyway? That's ridiculous!"

"I'm not so sure. Having a body is a wonderful privilege."

"But she could have any body, not the poor one I gave her."

Damon shook her, but without anger. "Kar, you are special! Is it so difficult to believe that Stephanie chose to come to you because she loves you and wants to share your life? Well, I can believe it, because that's exactly how I feel. I would go through hell to make you happy."

"What is going on here?" Malcolm demanded, suddenly appearing in the doorway.

Karissa stiffened against Damon, and he released her. "I don't care a hill of beans about what Malcolm thinks," he said, "but I know you do." He turned to Malcolm. "There's nothing at all going on here," he retorted. "I'm only doing what you should be doing—taking care of *your* wife and baby. If you weren't so blind you'd see that you're throwing everything away." He stalked out of the room, and Malcolm glared after him.

Karissa looked up at her husband, her eyes full of unshed tears. "We can't let them give Steph any more morphine," she said. "Steph stopped breathing because of it. I almost lost her . . . as I've lost you."

"Dear Lord," Malcolm prayed. To her utter surprise, he put his arms around her. She clung to him, letting her fears rush out in heartrending sobs.

CHAPTER 25

Malcolm had never been so confused in his life. Not even when he and Karissa had clashed over his smoking. Yesterday, when he had held her in his arms, he had felt love for her. But something wouldn't allow him to forget that she had loved another man before him and had lied about it. Not only had she shattered his dream of the woman he thought she was, but she had affronted him by both the action and the lie.

A part of him didn't care, and that part wanted to protect her, to soothe away her pain. But could he trust her again? And where did Damon fit into the picture?

"There's someone in the waiting room to see you, Mr. Mathees," a nurse said, interrupting his thoughts.

Malcolm saw that Karissa was asleep in the easy chair next to the empty metal crib, with Stephanie lying face up on her chest. They had been moved from intensive care the night before, though Stephanie was still on oxygen. She also had a tube going into her nose and down to her stomach. This connected with a pump which extracted anything that might be in her stomach, allowing the intestines and bowels to heal. Stephanie had a new IV in her leg, and Malcolm wondered how long until this vein would blow as the others had. He felt disheartened at Stephanie's continuing pain, and wondered how Karissa could bear it.

His wife shifted in her sleep. She had dark circles under her eyes, and the hollows in her cheeks were deeper than he had ever seen them. "I wish things could be different," he whispered. Tears of remorse and pain escaped from the corners of his eyes.

In the waiting room, he found Jesse pacing the carpet. "Hi," Malcolm said, forcing a weary smile.

"How're you two holding up?"

"We're fine," Malcolm lied. "You don't have to keep coming by every day."

"Are you kidding? Brionney would kill me if I didn't. Besides, I want to see how things are for myself."

"Well, they are still getting too much fluid out of her stomach, which means her system might not be healing the way it should. The doctor warned us that she might need another surgery." Malcolm swallowed hard, finding it difficult to speak. "And her veins keep blowing. They're worried about her not having any good ones left to feed her. They've given us two choices, both minor surgeries to put in a permanent type of IV. We've agreed to take the one with the least risk. Other than that, Stephanie seems to be holding steady. She's in pain, though."

Jesse groaned sympathetically. "That's really tough, Malcolm. I'm sorry."

"It can't be helped," Malcolm murmured.

"What I came to ask you was that since you can't come to church, we wondered if we could come to you."

"What do you mean?"

"The doctors have agreed to let us use one of their staff rooms. We thought we'd get together and have a sacrament meeting. We have it approved by our bishop."

"And the room is no doubt Damon's gift," Malcolm said, tasting gall.

"Yeah. Nice guy." Jesse didn't appear to notice Malcolm's displeasure. "Your parents and Karissa's will be there. And Brionney. Damon, too. What do you say?"

Malcolm thought how good it would feel to take the sacrament. Maybe in the meeting he could find some solution to his problem. "It sounds good. Thank you for thinking of it."

Jesse slapped him on the back. "Don't mention it. But when your daughter is baptized, I expect to be an honored guest."

Could that be my face smiling? Malcolm wondered. "Jesse," he said, "when Stephanie is baptized, I'll personally fly you out to

Kodiak." His smile vanished. Even if his daughter survived, he didn't know if she and Karissa would be on Kodiak in eight years. He knew Karissa hated the island. If they were to separate, she would most likely leave.

"Uh, Jesse," he said as his friend turned to leave, "I wonder if you could tell me something."

"Sure, what is it?"

"It's pretty personal."

"Go ahead, shoot. I'll tell you if you've gone too far."

"About Brionney. She was married before. Doesn't that bother you?"

A shadow passed over Jesse's face. "Bother me? Heck, yes! I hate the way that jerk treated her. I almost wished I could kill him."

It wasn't quite what Malcolm wanted to know. "But doesn't it bother you that she was with another man?"

Jesse's eyes narrowed. "What are you saying, Malcolm? That it's Brionney's fault her husband left her? She did everything in her power to make it work, and when it didn't, I was grateful to be there to help her put the pieces back together." He paused, as if dissecting Malcolm's soul. "I'll tell you what really bothers me, though. It bothers me that I didn't accept the gospel when you first taught it to me. It bothers me that because of fear I wasn't at Brigham Young University when Brionney met Derek. *I* should have been there to fall in love with her, to protect her. Me. It's not her fault."

Malcolm tried again. "But her having had his child . . . doesn't that bug you?"

Jesse held up his hand. "Stop right there, Malcolm," he said angrily. "You just stop right there! Savannah is Derek's biological daughter, but that's all. I'm her father in every other sense. Now, I don't know why things happened the way they did, but neither Brionney or I would cut Derek out of our past, because he gave us Savannah. She is unique, and we couldn't have gotten her any other way. And Brionney is who she is—the woman I love—partly as a result of her experience with her first husband. I know she loves me, that she's mine for eternity. That's all that matters, not my ego."

He took a deep breath and plunged on. "I think what you're trying to ask is if you are justified in divorcing your wife because of

her past. Isn't it? Yes, Brionney told me all about it this week after
Karissa told her that you knew. She thought you might ask me about
it, and she wanted me to know Karissa's side."

"What, that she lied, that she aborted—"

"She was sixteen!" Jesse said passionately. "And for support, the
boy gave her the money to get an abortion. She had no one to turn
to—you know how her father treated her. Good grief, Malcolm!"

Malcolm's whole body tensed. "She knew it was wrong!" he
protested. "She failed me! How can I trust her again?"

"The way I see it, *you* failed *her*. Where were you when she
needed you?"

"But—"

"No, I'm not talking about when she was sixteen, I'm talking
about when you first met. You loved her, didn't you?" Fire blazed in
Jesse's eyes, and he didn't seem to care about the other people in the
waiting room who could hear his raised voice. "You could have found
out her problems and gotten everything straightened out then. You
could have taken her to the temple and done it right the first time.
You, Malcolm. But no, you took the coward's way out! You loved her,
you wanted her, but you cared more about your own immediate
desires than you cared about Karissa's future! Why didn't you find out
why a deeply spiritual woman like Karissa would let tobacco get in
the way of eternity? Did you really love her at all?"

"I'm the one who's been wronged here!" Malcolm hissed.

"Have you? What, and now you're waiting for her to crawl across
a bed of nails and beg for your precious forgiveness? She knows she
was wrong! She's going through hell because of it. Even I can see that.
Don't you think she's suffered enough? And anyway, who are you to
have to forgive her past? It had nothing to do with you!"

"There's such a thing as justice!"

"Whose?" Jesse countered with all the fierceness he had shown
when clubbing the bear on Pillar Mountain. "Yours or the Lord's?
Abortion is wrong, Malcolm! We all know that. But we can never be
the judge of someone else's load of sin. All I know is that under
certain circumstances, the Lord's atonement is expansive enough to
cover *all* things. Look at the Apostle Paul, who was responsible for the
deaths of so many Christians, or Alma the Younger, who caused the

spiritual deaths of countless people before he repented. Even the Savior, as He was nailed to the cross, asked His Father to forgive those who murdered him. Murdered, Malcolm. And you know what? We don't know the circumstances of the choices Karissa made—only the Lord does. And He alone will decide who is forgiven and when. You don't want the Lord to remember your sins, so why are you so intent on keeping Karissa's alive? Boy, do you have a lot to repent for!"

"Me?" Malcolm could hardly believe what his friend was saying.

"You. And if you don't start doing it soon, your relationship with Karissa will shatter, and I've no doubt Damon will help her pick up the pieces." Jesse stomped to the elevator. "Think about it. We'll be back at two with the sacrament. Will *you* be worthy to take it?"

Malcolm realized he was staring after Jesse, his mouth agape. He shut it with a snap. The other people in the waiting room pretended to mind their own business, but when his back was turned, he could feel their eyes following him.

Jesse's words churned inside his mind, especially the vivid picture of a bloodied Karissa crawling across a sharp bed of nails, pleading for his mercy. Is that really what he wanted? Would it make any difference?

He returned to Stephanie's room. Karissa was still asleep, and he noticed how fragile, tiny, and alone she looked. Moisture filled his eyes and he blinked it away. What was happening to him? Where was his anger? He felt more vulnerable than he ever remembered feeling. More than anything, he wanted to feel her in his arms. *I love her,* he thought. *I will always love her. But is it enough?*

* * * *

Karissa thought a long time before coming to the decision. Since her experience during Stephanie's operation and subsequent conversations with Damon, she had come to the amazing conclusion that somehow the Lord still cared for her, even though she no longer had a chance for salvation. This miraculous knowledge gave Karissa the strength to pray again, silently but fervently.

Dear Father, I love this little girl with all my heart, and if you let her live, I'll be the best mother anyone could be. I'll teach her about the gospel

*and how important it is. I'll do everything in my power to see that she
makes it back to You. I promise I'll be there for her when she makes her
mistakes, before it's too late.*

She paused, reaching past the terrible pain in her heart for what
she really needed to say. *But, dear Father, if You want her back, take her.
Spare her this pain. Spare her another surgery. I know she'll be much better
in Your care than in mine, and I love her too much to see her suffer this
way. She shouldn't have to endure such horrible pain. Please, if it be Thy
will, take my baby now. I will still spend the rest of my life trying to make
up for what I did. Please don't let her suffer anymore for my transgressions.*

A warm, comforting spirit filled Karissa's heart. She didn't know
whether or not that meant Steph would soon die, but she did know
that God would do what was best for her child. Whatever that was,
Karissa would accept His will.

* * * *

At two that afternoon, their friends and family gathered in a staff
room as promised. Malcolm sat on a chair near Karissa. Her mother
and a nurse had promised to stay with baby Stephanie, who was
much stronger today. Even so, Malcolm was sure she would have
refused if Damon hadn't said something to convince her to come.
Damon now sat on Karissa's other side, talking quietly with her. To
Malcolm's annoyance, the pain etched on his wife's pale face relaxed
every time Damon spoke. He felt a mixture of jealousy and disgust.

Brionney settled next to Damon, her round face soft and pretty.
On the front row sat Faith and Richard Mathees, and next to them
was Warren Apple, who occasionally glanced over his shoulder at
Karissa. The tender concern in his face went against everything
Malcolm knew of Karissa's stern father. The man seemed almost
human. Next to Warren, Delinda brightened up the room with a
dazzling red dress and glittering gold jewelry. Her attire made
Malcolm notice that all their visitors wore Sunday clothes. Only he
and Karissa wore Levis.

"Malcolm," said a voice beside him.

"Jud!" Malcolm grinned with genuine pleasure. "What are you
doing here?"

The muscle under the skin on Jud's cheek twitched. "Came to see how you were doing." He nodded his head at Delinda, who sat in the row of chairs in front of them. "Can't let the Relief Society sisters get all the credit."

"It's a long way for a home teaching visit."

"I wanted to make sure you couldn't use another hand."

"Well, I'm glad you're here," Malcolm said.

Jud leaned over him. "Hello, Karissa. How're you holding up?"

Her smile flickered briefly. "I'm doing okay. It's nice to see you."

Jud ducked his head, showing his balding spot. "We all fasted today, you know. The whole ward."

"Delinda told us," Karissa said. "I'm very grateful to you all."

"Of course we're here for you," Damon said. Malcolm felt his anger rise. "We'll do anything to make this easier."

Karissa shrugged. "I'm just taking one day at a time." Her gaze flashed to Malcolm, and he saw her lips tighten.

"Let's get going." Jesse stood in front of the two rows of chairs. He placed two of the chairs in front, facing the small audience. A short man came from the side of the room and sat in one of the chairs. "This is Bishop Gunther from my ward," Jesse announced. "He'll be presiding, and he's asked me to conduct. We thought a testimony meeting would be particularly appropriate, although we don't have much time. The doctors and nurses have allowed us an hour."

After the opening song, Delinda gave a prayer. Richard Mathees passed the sacrament. Malcolm accepted the tray, took a piece of bread, then passed it to Karissa, who served the tray to Damon without taking a piece. Damon motioned for her to take one, but she colored and shook her head. An odd look came over Damon's face, and Malcolm was startled to recognize it as compassion. Tears started down his wife's face, and Damon hurriedly passed the bread to Brionney.

Jesse opened the meeting for testimonies, beginning with his own. Faith, Richard, Delinda, and Jud filed up in turn, each bearing a brief testimony. Malcolm remembered from his mission what constituted a pure, basic testimony: the knowledge that God and Jesus Christ lived, that Jesus was the Savior who atoned for the sins of the world, that Joseph Smith was a prophet through whom the Lord had restored the only true church, that the Book of Mormon was the word of God, and lastly that living prophets spoke for God on earth. With these simple yet potent declarations, the Spirit came and entered Malcolm's heart.

When the others had finished, Damon stood and moved to the front. He also bore a pure testimony, but instead of sitting down, he remained standing, willing them to the utmost attention with his intense eyes. "I want all of you here to know of the great admiration I have for Karissa. She has proven so strong during this trial. Some might believe that little Steph's problems stem from past sins, but that's simply not true. I believe that Stephanie knew what she would face here on earth, and she chose to bear these trials because she loves her mom and wants to be with her and no other. I feel this very strongly, more strongly than I have ever felt anything, and I thought you should all know." He closed in the name of Jesus Christ and returned to his seat. Malcolm saw that Karissa didn't look his way, but sat listening, her eyes focused on her lap.

Brionney stood next. "I am so grateful to my Savior for all He has done for me," she began, "and I know that someday we are going to look back at this trial with different eyes. Years ago, when I lost twin babies, I couldn't imagine ever being happy again. But now that seems almost foolish. I recovered, and we went on with our lives, and we were happy. I know it's not Church doctrine that our miscarried babies come back to us, or that they will even be our babies at all—no one except God really knows when the spirit enters the body—but it is my personal feeling that the Lord gave me another chance with my babies. He hadn't forgotten my pain or my loss. I am so grateful that I was finally ready to be their mother. I believe we will look back upon Stephanie's trials with greater understanding in the years to come."

Jesse touched his wife's hand briefly as she passed him on her way to her seat. Malcolm could feel their love, and out of habit he reached out to Karissa. Before he could touch her, she stiffened and brought a hand to her mouth as she stared at her father, who was standing in front of the room.

Warren said nothing for a long time, but looked at Karissa. The room grew utterly silent as everyone sensed the importance of this moment. "I need to bear my testimony," he said. "The last time I felt the urge this strong was when my eighteen-year-old daughter asked me why I didn't go up and bear my testimony in sacrament meeting. I told her I would do it the next time. But that day was the last time I saw her in church. To my knowledge, she has never returned." The room had been reverent before, but the hush that now prevailed made Malcolm's very breathing seem loud.

"I think," Warren continued, "that if I had borne my testimony to her that day, perhaps she would have been strong enough on her own to make better choices. I failed then as a parent, and especially as my family's patriarch, and over the past years I have learned how serious that error was." He blinked rapidly, then wiped a finger over his right eye. "I want you to know, Karissa, how sorry I am. And I want you to know that I know God lives! I know He loves you. For many years I have blamed you for the life you have chosen, instead of seeing that I, too, am to blame." He stopped and raised his hands to Karissa in a pleading gesture. "I know I've been wrong, but I'm here now. And I love you, no matter what."

Karissa hurried to her father and hugged him. "Thank you, Dad," she whispered.

She faced the group, holding her father's hand. "I also have a testimony," she said. "I always have." She stared at the floor a full minute before continuing. "I had an experience during Steph's surgery. I felt my baby's heartbeat and had difficulty breathing. I couldn't move at all. It was as if I was there with her in spirit. I didn't understand this experience until today. Damon helped me. While we were waiting for the meeting to begin, he said perhaps this was God's way of showing me that it's time to come back to the gospel. I feel maybe that's right. It's time I started spending the rest of my life making things better—if it can be done. Thank you, Damon. Thank you all."

She hesitated, as if there was something more, something she was unsure if she should share. Her father put his arm around her, and she seemed to find the strength to continue. "This morning I did something I never thought I could do. I prayed that the Lord's will be done. If Stephanie isn't supposed to live, then I want her to go back to the Lord. I love her so much, but if loving her means giving her up so that she doesn't have to go through any more pain, then I can accept that. I must accept that." She looked up at the ceiling, as if searching for God, and Malcolm looked there too, almost expecting to see Him. "She's Yours, Father. Thy will be done. In Jesus' name, amen."

Karissa and her father returned to their chairs. Jesse looked over at Malcolm, who was the only person besides the bishop who had not borne his testimony. Malcolm shook his head slowly, feeling suddenly unworthy, and Jesse stood to close the meeting.

As the group sang, Malcolm silently stared at nothing. Karissa had experienced a spiritual connection to Stephanie during the operation. Why would the Lord allow such a thing? Could it be that His justice had actually been satisfied? Malcolm reviewed the steps of repentance in his mind. Had Karissa done all she could?

Malcolm had to admit that it seemed she had. But then why was he still so angry at her? Was it only his ego standing in the way of their happiness, as Jesse had inferred?

Oh, Lord, Malcolm prayed. *Help me understand.*

It was the first time since Karissa's confession that he had prayed for his marriage, the first time he had really considered any option but divorce. *What I need now is some revelation,* he thought.

And maybe some repentance. The thought didn't surprise him the way it had when Jesse had first suggested it.

He returned to Stephanie's room in silence, kissed the baby, and turned to Karissa. "I'm going out for a while," he said softly. "When I come back, we need to talk."

Fear leapt into Karissa's eyes, but she only nodded.

As he turned to leave, Malcolm spied the *Ensign* Karissa had been reading. Without knowing why, he stopped and scooped up the magazine. Confusion ate at his soul; perhaps in the words of the prophets he could find some solace.

CHAPTER 26

Karissa knew by the seriousness of Malcolm's tone that the little talk he had planned would change their lives. She was glad he had left her time to prepare her fight. For fight was what she intended to do.

Stephanie made a cooing sound from the crib, and Karissa stroked her daughter. "I'm so sorry, Steph, but it's almost over now." Karissa firmly believed that. One way or the other, the Lord was in charge.

The baby's skin still sagged, but for the last two days she had gained weight slowly on the IV solution. New hope blossomed in Karissa's heart. As soon as Steph could resume nursing, Karissa knew her weight would jump dramatically, and she now pumped her milk every few hours with a double electric pump the nurses let her use, donating her milk to the premature baby bank.

An intense love for her daughter dominated Karissa, and for a moment, it was as if she could see beyond the child's tiny physical shell and catch a glimpse of the beautiful woman she would one day become, in this life or the next—a tall and strong daughter of God.

A soft coughing sound drew her thoughts away from the baby. "Damon," she said. "You startled me."

"I came by to see little Steph." He glanced around the room. "I see your husband's not here."

"No."

Damon stepped closer, so close she could smell the clean scent of his shirt and the masculine aroma of his cologne. Her heart pounded as his hand closed over hers. She was all too aware that besides Stephanie and another sleeping baby, they were alone in the room.

"Have you and Malcolm talked?"

She knew Damon wanted to know if she and Malcolm would stay together, but that he wouldn't come right out and ask or announce his feelings—not after the way she had reacted the last time. "No," she replied.

"He's not treating you right."

"Maybe not. But I'm not treating him right eith—"

Damon's hair flew as he shook his head. "For crying out loud, Kar, you didn't damage him by what you did. Can't you leave it in the past?"

"I know the Church is true."

"Well, that's a start. So do I. But what does that have to do with Malcolm?"

"Everything." She chose her words carefully. "It was you who made me realize that the Lord loves me despite what I did. And knowing He expects me to make the best of my life means that I will fight for Malcolm." She stared into his tear-filled eyes, praying he would understand. "The easy thing to do now would be to run, to not have to see the accusation in his eyes—or the disgust. But if I did, I would be breaking my marriage covenants, and I can't do that, not when I know how strongly the Lord feels about marriage. I've been honest about that with you from the very start."

Damon's face crumpled with pain. "Kar," he whispered raggedly. And then, "What if he leaves you anyway?"

"I'll face that possibility if and when I come to it. But I won't let him go easily."

He nodded slowly, and a tear slid down his cheek. "I know you're right." He hit his chest. "But it hurts right here."

She laid a hand on his cheek, cupping it slightly to fit the strong curve. "You gave me something I desperately needed," she whispered. "I will always be grateful for that. I think your love saved me when I was about to give up."

He grabbed the hand on his cheek and held it to his face tightly. "What am I going to do now?" he asked in a voice rough with emotion.

She wondered if he had spent the last week allowing himself to hope, despite her earlier warning. Karissa was reminded vividly of how Damon had declared that he was willing to go through hell for her. It seemed that now he would. She wished she could ease his pain as he had once soothed hers. "Go home to your children," she said gently. "They need you."

"And you have Malcolm." The words bordered on bitterness.

"And I have Malcolm."

For a long while after Damon left, Karissa thought about his last statement. Did she have Malcolm? Or was he truly lost to her? One thing she did know was that the fight had only begun. Whatever craziness Malcolm might be prone to give in to, she was not going to let their relationship die so easily. They had come too far for that. As with Stephanie, she would spend the rest of her life making it up to him. And maybe by doing so, she could atone in even some small way for her sin. She might not make it to heaven, but she would make sure her daughter and husband did.

* * * *

After hours of pleading on his knees in a broom closet, in the men's rest room, and finally in a stopped elevator, Malcolm found the revelation he searched for. Each time someone interrupted his praying he had moved on, not thinking twice or even caring about what those he encountered might say about him.

In the broom closet, he had remembered the words Jesse had used when blessing him to abstain from smoking. "You must also love your wife and remember that she is a special daughter of God. Cleave unto her and no other." The words hadn't made much sense then, but they did now. Malcolm knew the Lord had been preparing him to learn about Karissa's past.

Knowing this still didn't make it any easier to accept what had happened, so Malcolm prayed on.

In the men's rest room, he began to understand that he didn't love Karissa with his whole heart as he had always assumed. He had set rules: he loved her only as long as she was the person he had believed her to be. Karissa had no such reservations. When he had refused to quit smoking, she had kept on loving him, though she believed it might prevent her from having the baby she longed for. Women were perhaps more complicated than men, but apparently it took a woman to love someone in spite of his faults.

In the stopped elevator, he realized that Jesse was right. It wasn't his place to forgive Karissa, but the Lord's. Malcolm could only help Karissa find her way back. But was it possible? He had always believed that abortion was murder; how could she be forgiven? How could they build an eternal life together when one of them was barred from entering the celestial kingdom?

"There has to be a way," Malcolm said aloud. He pictured Karissa as she had been that morning, thin and white, with black shadows under her eyes and deep hollows in her cheeks. Emotion for her filled his heart so completely that it almost hurt. How much he loved her! And how much he needed to protect her, to help her.

Malcolm determined to put his ego behind him—and his judgments. The Lord would be both Savior and judge, not Malcolm. But as the patriarch of their family, Malcolm would fight to answer to the Lord in her place. As her husband.

"Please, I love her," he begged. "Please let us find a way. I'll do anything. I know I haven't been much of a husband lately, but I know now that I was wrong! I will gladly take upon myself her sins, and spend the rest of my life trying to atone for them and make it up to her. Please, dear God in Heaven. She has suffered so much. Please!" As he said it, a pure, powerful love flooded his entire being, larger and more encompassing than he had ever felt. The feeling held no pain, only exquisite joy. Suddenly, in his mind, he saw his wife as the Savior saw her—and she was clean!

The pure, divine love filled Malcolm's soul, replacing all the anger and bitterness and betrayal he had previously felt. His life with Karissa wasn't over—far from it! They could yet build an eternal marriage! He wanted to laugh and shout and scream for joy, but his limbs were so weak with his emotions that he could only kneel on the floor of the stopped elevator and sob. The Savior's atonement could repair his life—and more importantly, Karissa's.

But how to convince her?

He had seen the devastation in her eyes and knew it wouldn't be easy. Especially after the atrocious way he had treated her, his precious wife. The woman he should have protected and supported. "I'll spend the rest of my life trying to make her happy," he vowed. But how to begin?

How could he make her see that she was still a beloved daughter of God who would be welcomed home with open arms?

Then he saw it, written in bold black and white on the floor in front of him, where the *Ensign* magazine lay open to a conference talk by Elder Boyd K. Packer.

Here was the answer!

CHAPTER 27

Malcolm didn't return until long after Karissa and the other mothers in the room had turned down the lights in order to catch a few moments of rest while their babies slept. Ominous shadows taunted Karissa. What if Malcolm wouldn't forgive her?

He'll come for Steph, she thought. *And then I'll make my case.*

Some hours earlier, her lower stomach had begun to ache, but the dull pain was nothing compared to the anxiety in her heart. Oh, how she wished she could change the past!

When Malcolm finally arrived, he wasn't alone. His mother was with him, her ebony hair swept up into a pile on her head. It was dark enough in the room to hide all the new gray streaks and the age in her face, revealing a younger, prettier woman. Karissa wished she could ask her how she could regain Malcolm's love and trust.

Malcolm's gray eyes were black in the dark, his chiseled features softened by the shadows. "Karissa," he said, his voice low. He took Steph from her arms, kissed her, and handed her carefully to Faith. "Mother will watch over her. Come with me." Malcolm took both her hands in his, pulling her to her feet. Then he put an arm around her and led her to the door. *Why was he being so nice? Was this how divorce began?*

The ache in Karissa's stomach began to resemble the pain in her heart. To make it worse, her pulse throbbed in her temples, making her head feel as though it were on fire.

The waiting room was empty, and they settled themselves on a dark green couch with a ruffled skirt at the bottom. Its pillowed back felt comfortable after the stiff easy chair in Steph's room, but Karissa couldn't relax. She was unable to read her husband's expression as she normally could, and it unnerved her.

"I'm sorry," she began before he could speak. "I know I wasn't what you expected, and I'm sorry for everything. And I know you may not forgive me or love me like you did. That's okay. I just want you to stay. I'll do anything you want. You'll see, I'll make you happy. I'll be a good mother to Stephanie. I'll—"

Malcolm was shaking his head. *Oh, dear Father,* she thought. *What if all she could do wasn't enough? What if he still left her?*

"We can make it work, Malcolm!" she exclaimed desperately. "I'll make it up to you! You can't throw ten years away without giving me a chance! Six months! Then you can leave if you're not happy." She touched his arm frantically, her voice rising to a higher pitch. "You can finish your movie. I'll help you. I'll do *anything!*"

"Stop," Malcolm said, his voice firm but gentle. "Stop for a moment and listen to me." He held her hands again in his. They felt cool to her touch. "I don't want you to prove yourself to me; I want you to be my partner."

She stared, wondering if she had heard him right. She decided she hadn't. "Steph needs both a mother and father," she continued. "You have to at least—"

"This has nothing to do with Stephanie," Malcolm said, scrunching his eyebrows together. "This has to do with us. I love you, Karissa. I always have, and I always will."

She had opened her mouth to begin another round of convincing arguments, but now it snapped shut. She swallowed twice. "You do?" she asked, amazed.

He put his cold hands on either side of her face and looked deeply into her eyes. She noticed that there was more gray in the short hair near his temples. "Oh, yes, Karissa. I love you! So much! I always have. And I'm sorry for how I've been acting. There's no excuse. Not a single one, except that I'm a man." Tears coursed down his cheeks. "I'm so very, very sorry."

"You forgive me?" she asked, not quite believing how easy it was. "But what about the . . . about what I did? What about what I put Steph through?"

"What you put Stephanie through?" Malcolm made a noise in his throat, letting his hands drop. "You can't believe that! Stephanie didn't go through all these troubles because of *your* sin. Don't you remember? 'We believe that men will be punished for their *own* sins, and not for Adam's transgression.' Sure, we've learned a lot, and maybe the Lord even allowed this to happen because you and I needed to learn these lessons. But I believe what Damon said. I believe Steph chose you as a mother, despite the trials she would have to go through, and you will be the best!"

Happiness seeped into Karissa's heart at the power in Malcolm's voice. "But what about after?" she asked.

"After what?"

"This life. I'm not going to make it to—"

"Don't be so hard on yourself," he interrupted in a voice full of compassion. "You've already suffered so much. And you aren't the judge of where you are going after this life. Don't you think a man murdering in cold blood is different from a scared little girl doing what she sees as her only option?"

"Not really," Karissa said dully. "The result is the same."

"But take that experience you had during Stephanie's operation. Doesn't that show you the Lord's forgiveness? Why would He allow an unworthy person to have such a revelation? He wouldn't! And that means you're on the right track."

Oh, how she longed to believe him. If only it were true! The happiness she glimpsed just beyond her grasp made her want to collapse on the floor and weep with grief.

"Here, look at this."

To her surprise, Malcolm reached around to his back pocket and pulled out the *Ensign* Delinda had given her. It was bent now at the bottom where he had rolled it to fit into his Levis, and the tattered pages were worn and used. He opened the magazine to the article he wanted.

"It says here in this talk that He will forgive. Listen! 'Save for those few who defect to perdition after having known a fulness, there is no habit, no addiction, no rebellion, no transgression, no offense exempted from the promise of complete forgiveness.' *Complete forgiveness,* Karissa. The Lord knows you and your heart, and He knows how much you've suffered. I believe he has forgiven you—even for the abortion."

Blood rushed to Karissa's head. "No, it can't be," she heard herself murmuring. She grabbed at the *Ensign*. Sure enough, the words Malcolm had read were there, staring her in the face. She had not defected to perdition after knowing a fulness—no! That she had not done. And now the Lord was telling her through an apostle of God that everything else could be forgiven. *Everything!* Her world seemed to suddenly burst with possibility as she allowed a small portion of her soul to believe. Even though abortion was wrong and horribly evil, perhaps with enough repentance—perhaps with enough suffering and remorse—it was possible to obtain forgiveness!

"But how?" she asked.

"You've spent years atoning for this, haven't you?" Malcolm slid off the couch and onto his knees in front of her, taking her hands in his. "I'm so sorry I added to your pain. I'm so sorry I wasn't there for you. But I will be there now—forever. Will you let me?"

Karissa couldn't believe what he was saying. "But I always believed you had to restore what was taken. How can I restore that life?"

"Only where possible," clarified Malcolm, tightening his grip on her hands. "But I think that in your case, the life has been restored."

"Are you saying—Steph!"

He nodded. "It came to me a while ago, while I was reading this article. I remembered what Brionney had said about her twins."

"She got them back!"

"She *feels* that she did. And do you know what the odds are of a woman having identical twins twice in her life, when it doesn't run in either her family or her husband's?"

"Not good?" Her voice wavered.

"Exactly. And just maybe she got her babies back, so why couldn't we get Stephanie?" The intensity of his voice deepened. "I know there's no Church doctrine to support or deny this feeling I have, but I feel it all the same. Other parents who've lost babies so young may feel differently—that it wasn't a baby yet at all, or that they'll be given that child to raise in the Millennium. And maybe each case is different. Who really knows? It's what we feel that makes a difference. It's our belief in a loving and all-powerful Father in Heaven that makes a difference."

Tears blurred Karissa's vision. "My baby was a girl. And I was going to name her Stephanie."

"I wondered where you got the name."

She took a deep breath. "But if that first body was meant for Steph, why would she want to come back to me after what I did?"

Tears now wet Malcolm's entire face, and his jaw trembled slightly. "I believe she chose you because she knew you would need her," he said with quiet conviction. "Because she forgives, and because this way she could heal us both and bring us back to the truth. Isn't that what she's done? Haven't we returned to the Lord because of all this?" His voice broke and his eyes delved into hers, as though begging her to believe. "But most of all, I think she came to us because she loves you. You and she have a special bond. Damon felt it. I felt it. In fact, I've felt it so strongly that I was afraid that if I lost Stephanie, I might lose you, too."

"But—"

"No buts, Karissa. None at all." Malcolm was still on his knees in front her, holding her hands and crying silent tears. "Of course we'll have to go the bishop, and it'll still be painful. But we will see it through together—with the Lord. He can do *anything,* don't you believe that? He made me see how wrong I was—what an idiot I've been. That's an even bigger miracle. Please believe, Karissa."

Karissa did. Intense hope flooded her heart, obliterating the searing pain. Like an illness cured by medicine, her sin had been cured through sincere repentance. For the first time in her life, she felt with certainty her Father's love and acceptance. *I won't let You down!* she vowed. *I will live each day as though it were my last.*

Malcolm stood and pulled her to her feet. He wrapped his arms around her, drawing her close and kissing her. She nearly shook with the force of their love. She slipped her hand around his head to the longer strands of hair in the back, enjoying the coarse feel of it against her flesh. His two-day-old beard scraped against her cheeks.

The kiss deepened, and Karissa felt dizzy. For some reason, the ache in her head and stomach hadn't left with the pain in her heart. Fire seemed to consume her.

"Karissa, you're burning up!" She heard Malcolm's voice from a distance, and felt his arms tighten around her.

"Steph," she muttered. Then blackness swallowed her world.

She and Steph picked lingan berries on Pillar Mountain. Steph's face was stained with bright red as she stuffed more of the sweet berries into her mouth than into the little silver pail. The little girl ran behind a bush.

"Don't go too far away," Karissa called.

Steph emerged from the bush and came toward her, riding on a huge brown bear. She smiled and laughed at Karissa's surprise.

"Stephanie, get down!" Karissa said in a panic.

The little girl grinned, waving in triumph, her other hand buried in the bear's fur.

Karissa knew it was a dream and that it would end as all the others—with Steph dying because of her mother's neglect. She glanced down desperately to find something to save her child, but all she saw were her hands, stained blood-red with berries.

"It's okay, Mommy," Stephanie said, coming up to her. She slid off the bear's back and came to stand behind her mother. The bear gazed at Karissa with his sad eyes, then licked the berry juice from her fingers before disappearing once more into the bushes.

Steph hugged her. "I'm okay, Mommy."

Karissa looked at her hands and saw that they were no longer stained red, but washed clean and white. She had been forgiven! And in that instant, she knew that by being willing to give up her daughter to the Lord, she had somehow saved her. Stephanie would live!

"She's coming around," a voice said.

Karissa opened her eyes to see Malcolm approaching the bed. He leaned over and held her hands, bringing his face close. "You scared me," he said gruffly.

"What happened?"

"I'm kissing you, and the next thing I know, you faint in my arms."

"What an effect you have on women!" She grinned weakly up at him, wishing her head would stop pounding.

He gave a short laugh. "A dangerous talent."

"Thanks for catching me."

"Any time," he said seriously. "I'm always going to be here for you."

Karissa knew he meant it. Malcolm hadn't been the perfect husband, nor she the perfect wife, and they might not make it to that level for many years—if ever. But things would never be the same as they had been before. With the gospel and Stephanie in their lives, everything could only be much better. Hand in hand with each other and the Lord, they would carve out their happiness, every step of the way.

"How's Steph?" she asked, though because of the dream, she felt she already knew.

"She's doing great. Mom's still with her, but they might agree to move her in here with you in the morning if she keeps recovering so well. The doctor wants you to stay for a day or two. He thinks you might have an infection in your uterus, but they seem to have it under control now."

"I guess I overdid things."

"Well, no more. I'll be taking the night shift from now on, and we're going to let your parents and mine help. That's what they're here for."

"I feel kind of woozy," she murmured.

"That's the drugs. Do you want me to call a nurse?"

"No, I just want you to hold me."

Malcolm took her in his arms. "I love you," he whispered. Then he laughed softly. "You know, I think I'm finally worthy to say that. I guess I'm beginning to understand what love really is."

Karissa touched the stubble on his cheek. "Me too."

* * * *

Since Karissa's brief two-day stay in the hospital, she had been sleeping nights at Brionney's, leaving Malcolm to the night shift with Stephanie. The Hergarters' apartment in Anchorage was situated closer to the hospital than Malcolm's parents, and Karissa felt comfortable with the family. Because Jesse and Damon worked so closely together in their new partnership, she worried at first about running into Damon, but he carefully avoided her.

"So when does Stephanie go home?" Brionney asked shortly before bedtime on Friday night, a week after the surgery.

"I'm not sure. They keep testing her to see when she'll be able to drink milk. Hopefully tomorrow. Then it'll probably be another week, maybe less if she continues to get better at the same rate."

Seven-month-old Forest sat in the middle of the room, toys surrounding him. As usual his mouth was open, screaming, as he tried to steal the only toy his brother was interested in.

"Forest, do you ever quit?" Brionney said with a sigh. She picked him up as the phone rang.

"Mom, it's for you!" Savannah called from the kitchen, where she was busy with her third-grade science project.

"If that's your daddy telling me he's going to be even later—"

"It's not Daddy. It's Grandma. From Utah."

"Would you mind?" Brionney handed Forest to Karissa.

"Now, boys," Karissa said, "you two have to learn to share."

"It's not Gabriel's fault," little Rosalie protested. "It's Forest's."

"He's ambitious, that's what Daddy says," added Camille, tearing her face away from her picture book about plants.

Karissa tickled Forest, and soon he forgot about Gabriel's toy. She had him giggling wildly when Brionney entered the room. One look at her face showed that all was not right.

"What's happened?" Karissa asked.

Brionney shook her head in disbelief. "It's my sister, Mickelle," she said. "Her husband's dead."

Karissa's jaw dropped. "Oh, no!"

Brionney looked at her, but her eyes glazed as if seeing something else. "Just last Sunday I talked to her. We were planning to have a big dinner at our parents' when we got back. They're all anxious to see the twins. One minute he was there, and then this morning . . ." She started to cry, then lowered her voice so the children couldn't hear. "It's just horrible! Oh, poor Mickelle!"

"Do they have children?" asked Karissa. Still holding Forest, she awkwardly rubbed Brionney's back with her free hand.

"Two boys."

Camille and Savannah began asking tearful questions, and Rosalie too, though more from sympathy than from any remembrance she had of her uncle. Brionney's face calmed as she began comforting her children.

After the initial shock, the girls went back to their individual projects and Brionney met Karissa's eyes. "It's time for me to go home to Utah. I've been feeling the urge before, but now I know it's really time. You'll forgive me for leaving before Stephanie's out of the hospital?"

"Of course. She'll be fine, I think."

"My sister needs me."

Karissa felt her mouth droop. "I'm going to miss you." She put Forest down on the floor with his brother.

"Me too."

"Keep in touch?"

"Of course," Brionney said.

The women hugged. "Thank you," Karissa murmured. "I never did thank you for calling my parents. You did the right thing—I know that now. I don't know what I'd have done without you."

Brionney smiled. "Or I you. I guess we're spirit sisters."

"That's it exactly."

They turned when the front door opened. Jesse, with Damon in tow, came into the front room. Karissa flipped back the ends of her hair nervously as Brionney ran to her husband to explain quietly about her brother-in-law's death. He held her tightly.

"I guess it's time to go back to Utah," Jesse said.

Damon hadn't taken his eyes off Karissa. "I've already sold my house," he said quietly, "so what's stopping us?"

"You're going too?" Karissa asked.

He nodded. "There's nothing keeping me here." Karissa could hear the deep sadness in his voice. "And besides, Jesse and I are on the path to becoming very rich."

"Or in your case, richer," Jesse added.

Damon's mouth formed a tight smile, but his eyes remained sorrowful. "I may not be lucky in love, but I sure know how to make money." He tore his glance away from Karissa and focused on Brionney. "Did you talk to that girl in France yet?"

Brionney nodded. "Yes, I did. And she's excited to come. She's flying in tomorrow night." When she saw Karissa's puzzled look, she explained. "The French family my brother married into has some close friends who have a daughter named Rebekka. We became friends while I stayed in France one summer when she was just a kid. We've kept in touch. She's twenty-four now. She's served a mission, completed a double major in French and English, and works at the

American Embassy, but she's feeling a little trapped in France. She asked if she could come and visit to sort things out. When Damon mentioned that he would be losing his nanny when we go to Provo, I thought Rebekka might be willing to fill in for a while. It would help them both until she decides what to do with her life."

"You see, she's still hung up on Marc Perrault, Brionney's sister-in-law's twin brother," Jesse added. "She's been in love with him since she was five. He's thirty-four and not married yet, but he still doesn't notice her; never has. He thinks of her as a little sister. But who knows? Maybe when she leaves France, he'll realize what he's lost."

"I don't know," Brionney said. "Marc's stuck in a rut. I wonder if he's ever going to change. But Rebekka seems ready to move on with her life. It shouldn't be too hard for her once she's out of France. Heaven knows she's had no end of men wanting to go out with her. She's really beautiful, and nice besides. She looks just like her mother."

Karissa glanced at Damon. He was in his late thirties, probably only a couple of years older than Marc. Perhaps something would grow between Damon and this Rebekka, despite the age difference. By the light in Brionney's eyes, Karissa knew that was what her friend hoped, and Karissa cared for Damon enough to hope for it, too. He was certainly ready for a relationship—one that Karissa couldn't give him.

"Good, I'm glad that's settled." Damon's smile didn't reach his eyes. "I'll talk to my connections about some plane tickets."

"And my father has found some houses for us to look at," Brionney said. "He knows what we want." Since Brionney's father ran a real estate business, Damon and the Hergarters would get the pick of the best homes Utah had to offer.

There was a commotion in the kitchen, and Jesse and Brionney ran to see what their daughters were fighting about. Karissa shifted nervously when Damon's eyes riveted on her again.

"You'll like Utah," Karissa said.

"I hope so, because I can't stay here."

"Why?" She was almost afraid to ask.

"Because you and Malcolm need a chance," he said, shaking his head slowly. "And I don't know if I could leave you alone if I stayed."

With two steps he crossed the space separating them, plowing through the array of baby toys. He took her arms and pulled her close in a brief hug. Karissa gently but firmly disengaged herself, glad there was not even a hint of the passion she felt each time Malcolm was so near. She noticed that Damon had started a new moustache, and again she was glad. That seemed to signal his healing and acceptance of her relationship with Malcolm.

Damon sighed. "Have a good life, Karissa. And if you ever need me, call. I'll send you the number." With those last words, he went out into the night. Karissa wondered if she would ever see him again.

"Where'd Damon go?" Brionney asked, coming from the kitchen.

Karissa shrugged. "Home to his children, I guess."

Brionney eyed her strangely. "Are you okay, Karissa?"

"I was just worrying about Damon."

Brionney put an arm around her. "He'll be fine. We'll make sure of that. He'll get over it in time."

"I didn't know you knew," Karissa said.

"Of course I did. And it worried me. I was afraid his feelings for you would get in the way of doing what was right."

"For me or for him?"

"For both of you. But don't worry. You're on the right path now."

Karissa knew it was true.

CHAPTER 28

The next Monday, when Stephanie was thirty-five days old, the doctors allowed her to nurse for the first time since her surgery. The baby remembered how with very little prompting, and Karissa's patient, tedious pumping suddenly became worth all the effort. Subsequent tests showed that Stephanie's newly arranged intestines worked as well as any new baby's.

Two days later, they took Stephanie home. She had already gained a pound on her mother's milk. For baby Steph, that meant completely regaining her birth weight. It didn't seem like much when compared to how small Stephanie was, but to Karissa it was a miracle.

As Stephanie slept peacefully and painlessly in her own crib that evening, Karissa and Malcolm watched the sunset from their front porch. In the fading light, the fluffy white clouds turned pink like cotton candy.

"It seems too cold for May," Karissa said, rubbing her arms.

"It does this sometimes," Malcolm replied, his breath billowing in the cool air. "We can move, if you want."

"What?" His suggestion took her by surprise.

"I realize you're not happy here."

"But you are."

"I want to be with you."

She smiled, recalling how confined she'd felt in Anchorage, and how she had longed for the isolation of her home on Kodiak. "Finish your movie," she said, "and we'll see what happens."

"Damon sent me a check."

"What on earth for?"

"He says he wants to invest in the film."

Karissa laughed, feeling gratitude toward her friend. Apparently, he did want her life to work out with Malcolm. "Then it's a success for sure. Everything he touches turns to gold."

"You think I should accept it?"

"Yes. I do. He's been a good friend."

"Okay. I'll send him a receipt."

A comfortable silence fell over them. Then Malcolm took her in his arms. "Will you marry me, Karissa? I mean, in the temple."

Until he said it, Karissa didn't know that was what she had been waiting for. "Yes, I will," she said simply.

The wind blew darker clouds overhead, and it began to rain. Karissa found she didn't mind. The constant rain seemed to wash her clean like a continuing baptism.

Later, they had hot chocolate in the living room, where the picture of Jesus with the crown of thorns looked down on the room. His expression wasn't at all the way she had remembered it when Delinda had first given her the picture. His dark eyes weren't sad and full of recrimination, but hopeful and confident that she would find her way.

At that moment, she could not imagine being happier.

* * * *

In November, when Stephanie turned eight months old, Karissa and Malcolm traveled to Washington, where they were sealed in the same temple in which her parents had been married. Her whole family was there, along with most of Malcolm's, as they celebrated the event everyone had prayed for. Jesse and Brionney also attended the session.

Stephanie giggled as she was sealed to her parents, as if knowing she had helped bring it all about. She showed no signs of her ordeal, other than the fading scar on her stomach. The scar would always be there as a reminder, but a good one—one that proved how much the Lord loved her and her family.

When they arrived back on Kodiak Island, the land was blanketed in a lush, six-inch carpet of pure white snow, reminding Karissa of her temple experience. The brilliance of the snow hurt her eyes, and was broken only by the blue ocean going on forever until it curved out of sight.

Even after years on the island, this beauty was unlike any Karissa had experienced. The surrounding snow-capped mountains reminded her of ice cream cones dipped in a hard, pure white vanilla coating, waiting for her to take a bite, cracking the shell and tasting the hidden treat below. They were pristine, untouched, glorious.

"I'm about finished with the film," Malcolm said, hefting their luggage at the airport. "Do you want to move?"

"No. I want to stay." She laughed, knowing it was true. Somehow, in an unguarded moment, Kodiak Island had captured her soul. How could she ever have felt confined here? She had grown to love this land more than she had ever thought possible. No wonder Malcolm had wanted to return! He had been so right to insist. Only on this incredible island could she have been healed. Here they would raise Stephanie, as well as any other children they might be allowed to have.

She kissed Malcolm, loving the way he looked at her. There was nothing keeping them apart now, no differing values or deep, dark secrets. The truth had set them free.

"Come on," she said, leading the way to her Nissan. "Let's go home."

ABOUT THE AUTHOR

Rachel Ann Nunes (pronounced *noon-esh*) knew she was going to be a writer when she was 13 years old. She now writes five days a week in a home office with constant interruptions from her five young children. One of her favorite things to do is to take a break form the computer and build a block tower with her three-year-old. Several of her children have begun their own novels and they have fun writing and plotting together.

Rachel enjoys traveling, camping, spending time with her family and reading. She served an LDS mission to Portugal. She and her husband, TJ, and their children live in Utah Valley, where she is a popular speaker for religious and writing groups. *Tomorrow and Always* is her ninth novel to be published by Covenant. Her *Ariana* series is a best-seller in the LDS market.

Rachel enjoys hearing from her readers. You can write to her at P.O. Box 353, American Fork, UT 84003-0353, send e-mail to rachel@ranunes.com, or visit her website at http://www.ranunes.com.